FLESH AND BLOOD

The Sixth and Final in the
Cycle of the Aphotic World

FLESH AND BLOOD

Tobin Elliott

*"Life isn't about finding yourself.
Life is about creating yourself." – Unknown*

*This one is about determining the answer to that question: Who
am I? It's about discovering, and uncovering, that person you
were meant to be.*

*For more than half my life, there's been one constant force in my
life. A force of good. A force of love. An undeniable force that has
pushed me forward, even when I didn't want to move.*

*She saw something in me when I saw nothing in myself. She's
loved me in a way no one else ever has. She's remained by my
side when almost everyone else has left. She's suffered for me.
She's fought with me, yet has always fought for me.*

*She's cried with me and she's laughed with me. Thankfully,
there's always been more tears of laughter than sorrow.*

*She found me when I was lost. And she allowed me the space and
time to create who I am. She allowed me to dream of a better life,
and she helped bring that life into being.*

When I reach out a hand, hers is always the one I want to hold.

Anything that's good in me is because of her.

*My friend, my joy, my love, my constant companion, my life.
This one is for my wife, Karen.*

ACKNOWLEDGEMENTS

Just as it takes a village to raise a child, as the saying goes, it also takes a solid group of friends and family to allow one to build a story. And when that story ends up running over six books, you'd better hope they're a patient lot. Thankfully, mine are.

A final shout-out to Dale and his family, to Ryan and Lisa and their family, and to all writer and non-writer friends and family, some of who love my stuff, some of who support me while stating, "Yeah, I'll never read that." My thanks to all of you.

One last time, a huge thanks to Jennifer Dinsmore. I don't know how else to sing her praises other than to say that these books would be a lot less readable without her. If they read well, it's because of her. If you still see a mistake…well, that's because of me.

I also need to thank Camille Codling, both a brilliant artist and my daughter-in-law. She took my vague ideas and brought them to life, creating six of the most stunning cover images I've ever seen.

I'd be remiss if I didn't thank the local Indigo bookstore where I both work and shop far too much. My co-workers are also good friends, and incredibly supportive. The company as a whole has been wonderfully helpful and encouraging in allowing these weird stories, which once only existed in my head, to find a wider audience.

Again, thank you, COVID-19 lockdowns, for giving the time
to sit down and write this book in 111 days—lightning-fast
for a guy who typically takes years to get his shit down.

Last but not least, I want to acknowledge the store Good
Books and Magazines. Now long gone, it's the place I
haunted in the early seventies. The store you'll meet in this
book is inspired by that one, and this series is inspired by all
the magical stories I found there—including, of all things, the
fifty-year old bookmark which inspired the tale you're about
to read.

Inspiration's a funny, fickle thing, and you never know where
it's going to be found.

"It is not in the stars to hold our destiny but in ourselves."
– William Shakespeare

FIRST INTERLUDE
CLARINGTON HIGH SCHOOL, 1981

HIS NAKED BODY broke out in gooseflesh and his balls shrivelled up tight to his body. His breath fogged out with each exhalation.

◆ ◆ ◆

NYARLATHOTEP GAZES THROUGH the ether at the stupid boy kneeling in the bathroom of the school, grimaces as the boy practices the words, then readies himself for what he likely believes will be his salvation.

Peter Wilson. Stinky Pete.

Pathetic, doomed fool, just another thing for the Book to use and discard.

The demon watches the boy's bumbling attempts to summon one of its kind, one of the Outer Gods. The unmitigated hubris! To think this…whelp of so few years, this being so far beneath the Outer Gods' notice that he might as well be a protozoan, seeks to summon a god.

Still, the simpleton has his uses.

He thought to use the Book to end his father's cruelty.

He has no idea that Nyarlathotep is using the Book, just as the Book is using Stinky Pete.

But enough of this. The Outer God can no longer bear to hear the child fracture the language of the Elder Races. It can't make the opening in the ether, but it can work through the Book to influence the idiot child's incantation enough that it will work.

With its interference and some luck, Nyarlathotep might just be able to break through.

◆ ◆ ◆

THE QUALITY OF the light in the room changed. Like the air before a big rain, the atmosphere appeared darker, yet at the same time, it took on a glow.

Then, the wall behind the toilet split and opened. There was no cracking of tiles or breaking of concrete. One second, the room was normal, the next, Pete faced a hole with swirling, out-of-focus edges.

◆ ◆ ◆

THE CHILD SEEKS the help of one of Nyarlathotep's children. That treacherous Book has guided the fool toward all'Gueroth, and the trusting whelp has not the intelligence to question the selection.

all'Gueroth. To silence one stupid, drunken, violent human. It was the rough equivalent of throwing a planet to squash a bug.

Still, this is the opening — literally, the opening — Nyarlathotep has been waiting for.

The child moves on to the next part. Nyarlathotep's offspring is a creature with only one goal, and that is reproduction, so the Book suggested an appropriate offering.

Nyarlathotep takes a prurient pleasure in watching the child masturbate.

This is something it can assist with as well. Nyarlathotep speaks.

~Just close your eyes.~

♦ ♦ ♦

"OH GOD." PETE'S breath puffed out in surprise and pleasure. The feel of his working hand had *changed*. Pete was a virgin, so it wasn't like he had a lot of experience in the area, but damn! This felt better than any pussy he had ever imagined.

Then the voice of the Book was in his head again.

~*...jusssst cloooose yoooour eyyyyessss...*~

Pete began to thrust himself enthusiastically.

♦ ♦ ♦

AND THEN THE offering. The pathetically minuscule volume of liquid shoots from the whelp and becomes the key that unlocks the door between the two realms.

It is a very specific key, fashioned only to allow all'Gueroth—which means both the main body of the giant, hulking beast, and also the small satellite creatures that act as its senses—through that unlocked door. No other creature can breach it, not the Outer Gods, the Elder Gods, not even the Great Ones.

But...

If Nyarlathotep could just work the child a little more, get him to utter some other significant phrases...

The demon Nyarlathotep would then be able to follow its offspring through that all'Gueroth-shaped opening.

♦ ♦ ♦

PETE'S KNEES BUCKLED, and he dropped back down to the piss-stained floor, breathing in gasps like he'd just run a marathon. His hand was still on his cock, but it was just his hand again, and he quickly lost his erection, his dick bobbing in time to his pulse. All thoughts of demons, school, his dad, and revenge were gone, replaced by the buzz only a truly spectacular orgasm could create.

The buzz didn't last long. Pete opened his eyes at the sound of ripping. What he saw made him forget all thoughts of…anything. His mind turned white. He crab-walked backward fast enough to break the stall door off its hinges.

The quiet of the washroom blasted away in a frenzy of sound and motion as dozens and dozens of small black creatures pattered out onto the tile floor…

◆ ◆ ◆

NO, NO, NO!

The demon's anger soars. How did such fragile creatures attain any sort of dominance on this planet when their brains and bodies shut down at the first threat of danger?

Nyarlathotep needs only a few moments of the whelp's clarity. It is mere moments — a few words and gestures — from being able to come through.

But its offspring's sense-creatures first overwhelm the child, then the offspring itself crosses through the opening. Nyarlathotep, despite being the reason for all'Gueroth's existence, holds no sway over the younger creature.

And all'Gueroth proceeds to wipe Stinky Pete's mind clean.

◆ ◆ ◆

THE DEMON TOOK in its new surroundings, sniffing at the air, its thick, fleshy tongue lumbering over its teeth, twisting this way and that, all without seeming to notice Pete. There was no sign of urgency in its manner. It seemed to have all the time in the world, like appearing in a third-floor high school washroom was a normal thing for it to do. After it finished scanning the entire tiled wasteland, only then did the demon all'Gueroth acknowledge the figure slumped in the corner.

Its nostrils flared and it advanced toward Pete with an unexpected grace. The demon bent lower on its haunches and extended one clawed digit to Pete's still-dripping penis. Delicately, it lifted the shrivelled member and sniffed the air. It nodded once, almost as a confirmation that, yes, this was the human who had called it to this world.

The demon ran a claw as long as a forearm up Pete's quivering belly to his hairless chest. Almost a caress, it left no trace. Then, with a clawed finger over Pete's pounding heart, it pushed, almost imperceptibly.

The demon slid its huge three-fingered hand behind Pete's head and neck, and gently eased him forward until their foreheads touched. The demon's granite-like skin surprised Pete with its slight stickiness, like it was coated with a thin layer of snot. Underneath, its skull was hard and rough, like a concrete sidewalk. Its breath was heavy, moist, and pungently unpleasant, like the smell of a skunk — okay for just a whiff, but overpowering when he sucked a lot of it in.

As their heads met, Pete got that same warm buzz the Book had given him. He felt himself relax, all the tension leaving him. *Yes*, he thought, *this is it. This big son of a bitch is going to kick my father's ass. I'm gonna be the boss. I'm gonna do what I want to do. Maybe I'll even ask Steph out on a date. Everything is going to be al —*

The screaming snarling tearing wall of pain ripped through Pete's head like a rabid animal, shredding his thoughts, chewing his memories, cracking his skull and sucking the marrow of his brain dry. He didn't have time to make a sound. It swallowed his mind.

The demon pulled Pete's head back with a wet *pop*, the mucus layer between them stretching like caramel. Pete's mind ran on base, primitive instinct now. All knowledge now in the demon's mind, but still Pete's body lived. There was no visible damage—only a wet spot on his forehead and a pool of piss expanding outward from where he sat. He slumped against the wall, a wrung-out sponge. His mind was white and blank, but his body could still function. It could still experience pain.

Slamming its claws through Pete's chest, the demon lifted him off the tiles. With its free hand, it ripped into Pete. Its reward would be to live. But not without knowing what mad well he had been foolish enough to dip into. Not without knowing what power he had tapped. Not without understanding what that power could do.

Pete's eyes snapped open. Though he had lost virtually all reason and intelligence for the moment, some primal instinct kicked in. He looked down to see gobs of himself splashed about the washroom. Neurons connected and allowed his mouth to open.

And he screamed.

♦ ♦ ♦

ALL'GUEROTH WIPES STINKY Pete's mind clean…but the summoned demon does not take his life, despite the ravaging of the child's physical form. The child will not die. Not yet.

There may be one more slim chance…

PART ONE
OPENING WORDS

"What feels like the end is often the beginning."

AUTHOR UNKNOWN

CHAPTER ONE

*"*H*AVE YOU DONE this before?"*

He stares at me.

"Have you killed others?"

"You don't – "

"Have you killed others, Duane?"

He drops his head. "Yes."

"Dear god."

He says nothing.

"How many?"

"I don't know."

"Guess."

"I don't fucking know, Monica!"

"Ten? A hundred? A thousand?"

"I don't know…"

"Duane…"

He looks up at me.

I grab the Staff out of Lex's hands and drive It into his chest.

He falls back, pulling the Staff from me as he rolls back to the pavement.

One of his hands falls open, and I see my wedding ring.

And then Duane is dead.

I've just killed my husband.

♦ ♦ ♦

IT'S THE SHOCK of remembrance and the sound of the bottle hitting the floor that makes me jerk awake.

"Shit," I say, and my tongue is dry and too big for my mouth. I flail my numb arms to push myself to a more upright position in the easy chair.

I'm still struggling to get to a place where I can actually vacate the chair when Lex pads down the hall. It's dark, so I hear her more than see her. She stops at the far end of our living room, crosses her arms, and leans against the wall. She's not wearing anything.

She was in bed. I woke her.

She's probably angry with me.

"You ever coming to bed, Monica?"

Yeah, she's angry with me. There's a too-sharp edge to her voice that I've learned I have to be careful around.

"Yeah," I say, and try and stand. It doesn't quite work. I wobble a bit, then fall back to my ass in the chair. "Yeah," I say again weakly.

Lex doesn't move. I can't really see her face, but I can imagine the disgust I'd see there.

We remain where we are for long moments. Lex, not moving, not speaking. Me, scared of a repeat performance of my Olympic-level ass-plant.

"You need help?" she finally says. The words come out clipped by that sharp tone.

"No," I say. "I got it." I plant my hands on the armrests again. "I got it, Lex. Be right in." My brain is encased in fog.

She stays where she is, presumably allowing me to prove that I do indeed have it. I don't have it, and we both know it.

"Fucksake," she finally says. Her arms uncross, fall to her sides, and she turns and pads back down the hall to our bedroom. I can barely make out the muttered words as she enters the bedroom. She says, "Can't keep doing this."

I'm not sure if she means her, or me.

Goddamn, I think. *Six months ago, I would have followed her naked form down that hallway, wet with anticipation.*

I don't follow her. I'm incapable of following her right now.

Six months ago, we were a happy couple.

Now, we're not happy.

We're barely a couple.

Goddamn.

♦ ♦ ♦

SIX MONTHS AGO, Lex and I fell together, somehow finding each other again, the partners we didn't realize each one needed. And when we fell together, we fell hard. But it was a good feeling. A warm feeling.

Along the way, both Lex and I came to understand that this world was a lot…stranger, a lot darker than either of us had ever given it credit for. Hamlet once said something about there being more things in heaven and earth than are dreamt of in your philosophy.

That line's been rattling around in my head for most of the past six months.

Because we live in a world with beings that shouldn't exist, but do. People with powers that can only be described as magic. Demons. Vampires.

And werewolves.

I found out my long-lost husband Duane wasn't quite so lost. But he was barely Duane anymore. One of those beings that shouldn't exist, but did, changed Duane. Remade him from a man into a beast. A werewolf.

And then, I killed him.

We're gonna have to eliminate the problem.

I killed my husband, Duane.

And now, I'm having a hell of a time living with that.

Because he comes into my dreams every night. Makes me relive it. Makes me kill him again. Every single time I close my eyes.

Lex knows. She's tried to help. She's even suggested I go see Talia, the one with powers that can only be described as magic. Lex thinks she might be able to pull that memory out of my head, like removing a tumour.

And maybe she can.

But is that the right thing to do?

I killed him.

I killed him.

I *killed* him.

Shouldn't I suffer for that? Isn't that part of the penance of the living? To burn for those whose potential has been snuffed out? To grieve for those who no longer live?

We're gonna have to eliminate the problem.

I live. Duane is dead. Because of me. Should I not suffer for what I've done?

♦ ♦ ♦

OBVIOUSLY I'M NOT going to bed. Only judgment awaits me there. Justified, for sure, but I can't face it right now.

Seems I can't face much of anything right now.

Instead, I put some coffee on to sober up and, while it brews, I have a very quick, very cold shower. When I get out, I want to put fresh clothes on, but my guess is Lex will be awake and, while I love the woman, right now, I don't even know the right words to say.

Though, I remember a time, not so long ago, when I didn't even have to think of the right words. Every word was right, and every right word just came naturally.

Instead, I climb back into my day-old clothes, head back into the kitchen, warm with the smell of fresh coffee, and quietly pull a travel mug down.

Lex got me hooked on chocolate milk in my coffee, so I pour a good amount in the bottom of the mug and fill it with coffee.

I move to the foyer, slip my shoes and jacket on, gingerly pick up the keys to mute their jingling, and ease out the door.

It occurs to me that, because the words that used to flow between us have dried up, I can't deal with anything. It occurs to me that, because I'm a hollow shell now, just a single event looping through my mind — the Staff driving into his chest, his hand falling open, my wedding ring released from his grip — I cannot face the woman who loves me.

It occurs to me that I'm running away from the one I should be running to.

If I can't be with the love of my life, then I'll be with my old friends.

♦ ♦ ♦

IT'S NOT EVEN four thirty in the morning when I park my car and walk toward the bookstore. There's not a single car on the streets, the sky is dark behind the streetlights, all is quiet, and nothing is stirring.

Nothing except the slightly intoxicated, PTSD-suffering, depressed store owner unlocking the front door to the place she uses to hide from her lover.

I juggle travel mug and purse in one hand while I unlock the front door with the other. Slipping inside, I leave the lights off and enter the code in the alarm keypad, disengaging it. Then I cross the floor, only a little unsteady, and I think, *Yeah, probably shouldn't have been driving.* I set down keys, purse, and mug, then turn and lean against the comforting dark wood of the cash counter.

There's something to be said about just being in my bookstore by myself. The lights off, the music off, just the glow from the streetlights creeping through the windows to illuminate the dark panelling of the shelves.

I like the quiet. The smell of the books.

My oldest friends.

Lex took over her old family home after the death of her father. She spent a lot of time with the renovations while living with me. Those months were… I close my eyes and smile for a moment, letting that time wash over me.

Those months were very likely some of the best times of my life.

And they were the start of some of the worst.

I push that thought away. *Not going there again tonight.*

After the renos were completed, it was time for me to put in my notice, pack all my stuff, and move into our new home.

In the process of the packing, however, at the back of a storage closet, I found a couple of very old boxes with handwriting that I'd only seen, though never really knew the person who'd done the writing.

My dad. Dan Holt.

All the boxes had written on them was *Books*.

My mother told me, before she died, that they'd emptied out the spare room in preparation for their daughter, who was on the way. Dad had taken down the shelves and replaced them with a change table, a crib, baby stuff. The books were relocated, but there were a couple of boxes that just didn't get a new home.

Mom told me she could never bring herself to open those two boxes. There was too much Dad in there. After she died, I understood. I could never bring myself to open them either.

Now, sitting in the dark of my store, where it's quiet enough that I hear the building making the odd settling noise, its bones easing into the foundation, with my silent, unconditional friends and coffee for company, I decide now might be the right time to dig into them.

Maybe the thoughts I couldn't articulate to Lex could be offered up to a father I never got to know. Maybe, if there were not answers there, perhaps there might be some solace.

I move behind the front counter. I'd stashed the boxes under there three weeks ago. I pull the first one out, bring it around to the floor in front of the counter, then go back and do the same with the second one. My last trip around the counter is to grab a box cutter and my travel mug.

I take a sip, then sit on the floor, my back to the comforting dark wood. I set my mug out of the way, then slide the first box toward me. The surface of the cardboard is silky with old dust.

This box has been sealed up for almost thirty years. He died back in April of '84. In his own bookstore.

He died just a month before I was born. I never knew him, except through photos and stories.

Most people have built up their ideas of mythical creatures from the stories they heard in their childhoods. Unicorns. Dragons. Hansel and Gretel.

My mythical creature was my father. The man who died under mysterious circumstances in the store his father had started, and he was set to inherit. The Last Word.

The good thing to focus on—drawing on all that therapy I'd spent so much money on—was that I built my own bookstore in the same location, on the family-owned property. The daughter's phoenix rising from the father's ashes. I was tempted to call it The Last Word. Just stick with the original name. If it was good enough for Gramps and Dad, then The Last Word was good enough for me, too, right?

But calling it The Second-Last Word…was more…I don't know…evocative. The most frequent question I got was, "Why The *Second*-Last Word?" Like the best stories, it set up a question, right at the outset.

Jesus, Monica, I think. Your mind's going in a million different directions tonight. Husbands and fathers and girlfriends, oh my!

Anyway. The boxes. *Yes. Dad's boxes.*

I run my hand over his too-neat-for-a-guy handwriting one last time, then slide the blade into the crease and break the three-decade seal on this time capsule.

◆ ◆ ◆

Twenty minutes and both boxes later, I have everything sorted into "keep" and "discard." The keep stuff is old paperbacks that I can put on the Gently Read and Greatly Loved shelf.

Aside from the keep stuff and the toss stuff, I have four other items sitting on the floor. Three books—*Lucifer's Hammer* by Larry Niven and Jerry Pournelle, *Doc Savage: The Man of Bronze* by Kenneth Robeson, and the novelization of the 1977 original *Star Wars*, back before it picked up the "Episode IV" tag. The first two I wouldn't have had any interest in, but both have my dad's name on the inside cover. The first is some end-of-the-world thing, and the second? Doc Savage? Looks like a whole lotta overripe cheese to me. I'm also not much of a *Star Wars* fan, but I'm pleasantly surprised to find it's a first edition in surprisingly good condition. My dad, lover and caretaker of books. He even managed to resist putting his name in this one. A clean copy. That's worth something.

But better than those three things, I found something I never thought I'd see again.

A bookmark from my father's store. It was still Gramps' store, but Dad—from what Mom told me—was always hounding his own father to make the place a little more "hip." He pressed Gramps to start carrying stuff like the Conan the Barbarian series, more science fiction and horror…and presumably even those cheesy Doc Savage books. Gramps apparently hated it all, but it sold.

Emboldened, Dad then apparently went rogue and got some bookmarks made. Like the one I now hold in my trembling hand.

It's a cream-coloured bookmark, bigger than most, with a weird image of a person, hard to tell if it's man or woman, with their hands together over face, the tip of each middle finger touching, and thumbs pointed up. The image isn't close to sharp, and it's all toned in black and white, no greys. It looks like it should mean something. It says *The Last Word* across the top, then *good books and magazines* at the bottom, with the address and phone number in smaller print below it.

The weird thing is the word that's printed almost as part of the image, angled at ninety degrees. Four letters.

Zyxt.

Never heard of it before, so I Google it. Turns out it's an obsolete term, the second-person singular past tense for "to see"…as in "you zyxt him yesterday."

And at one point, it was the last word in the *Oxford English Dictionary.*

Dad's private little in-joke. Zyxt. The Last Word.

I'm guessing Gramps hated the bookmarks, too.

I slip the bookmark between the pages of the *Star Wars* novel.

♦ ♦ ♦

TIME PASSES, AND I go slow, letting the coffee bleed in, and the alcohol bleed out.

I take another hour to answer emails and enter orders. I pack a couple of boxes of returns. I update the social media pages. I keep busy, but not too busy.

Also, there's something to be said about just being in my bookstore by myself. The lights off, the music off, just the light from the windows to illuminate the dark panelling of the shelves.

I like the quiet. The smell of the books.

I know the shop better than anywhere. I can walk blindfolded through the store, and likely lay my hand near, if not directly on, any book that we carry. It's times like these, when it's quiet, and I'm alone, that I often do walk through the various shelves, trailing a hand over the spines of the books. Each book a world unto itself. All a reader has to do is open it up to be transported to a different place, a different time, a different point of view. Stephen King is right. Books *are* a uniquely portable magic.

I drain the last of my coffee and set the thermos on the counter, then drop the screen on the laptop to put it to sleep, wishing I could put myself to sleep just as easily.

I look out the front window of my shop and see the long shadows of the rising sun. We don't open for another four hours. I should call Lex.

It's too early to call Lex.

A pang of guilty relief washes over me. I should call her. I need to talk to her.

But what do I say?

Hey, I'm having a bit of an issue about having driven a magical Staff through my ex-husband's werewolf heart.

I drop my head to the counter with a thud.

I don't know how to get out of this. I know the booze is making things worse. I know not talking to Lex is making things worse. I know avoiding everything is making things worse.

But Duane is dead. And I killed him. So really, how much worse can it get?

I raise my head and rest my chin on my crossed arms. Eventually, my gaze settles on the three novels from my father's boxes. I see the edge of that weird bookmark sticking out from the *Star Wars* novel on the top of the stack. I pull it out, look at it again.

Zyxt.

You zyxt this bookmark, didn't you, Dad?

It's like it's his last word to me, in some weird way.

I look at the address. The same as it is to this day, my store built on the rubble of his.

Then I look at the phone number. I don't recognize it.

I should call it, I think, then immediately dismiss the thought as stupid.

Sighing, I reach for the thinnest of the three novels in the box. *Doc Savage.* I move back around to sit on the floor and lean against the counter, open the book, and begin reading.

♦ ♦ ♦

THREE HOURS LATER, I close the cover. It was every bit as cheesy as I expected it to be. Absolutely ridiculous and completely improbable. And I think I understood why Dad liked it. It was fun.

If nothing else, I feel a little closer to the parent I never got to know, and I actually smiled a couple of times through the read. I felt briefly happy, a somewhat alien feeling lately. But I was lost in the world of 1930s New York, with Doc and his team of adventurers travelling the world to kick ass and right wrongs. For three hours, I wasn't Monica Holt.

That was a small blessing.

But now, with the novel finished, I'm Monica Holt again.

The woman with no parents. The woman who killed her husband. The woman who runs from her lover and her problems, rather than deal with them.

The bookmark is on the floor beside me. Again, I think, *I should call that number.*

Why call a number I know likely connects to some crotchety old guy who's sick of getting spam calls for duct cleaning? And besides, it's just after nine in the morning. The store opens soon.

I wonder who does own that number now? Do they know it used to be the bookstore's?

I imagine them getting the number almost thirty years ago—around the time I was born—after the original bookstore was destroyed. Did they get calls for The Last Word?

I glance at my watch. 9:12 A.M. If I *do* call it and someone *does* answer, I could apologize and claim wrong number.

Not that you're gonna call, are you, Monica?

Of course not. Store opens soon.

And yet, I watch my right hand reach for my phone.

No. Not gonna do it.

I check the number.

My treacherous hand enters the digits.

No, Monica. Don't do it.

Hits Send.

Then the phone is against my ear.

Hang up. Hang up hang up hang up.

Ringing.

◆ ◆ ◆

"HELLO?"

"Hi, um…"

"Oh, crap. Sorry. Should have said, 'Hello, thanks for calling The Last Word. How can I help you?'"

Wait, what? I can't even formulate a response.

"Hello? You still there?"

"Yes, sorry, you said I'd reached The Last Word?"

"Yes, you did!"

"Sorry, can I ask…" — I swallow hard, not even sure how to process what I've heard — "…can I ask who I'm speaking to?"

"Sure. It's Dan. Dan Holt."

I know I make a sound, but it's more of a strangled noise than anything. I can't speak.

"Hello?"

"Dan Holt?"

"Yep, that's my name, don't wear it —" Then he takes a breath. Then his tone is far less light. Much more serious. "Wait a minute. Is this Monica? My daughter Monica?"

"Dad?" I say, but my voice is so tiny, I'm not sure he hears me.

He hears me.

"Monica," he says, and his voice is not that of a barely-in-his-twenties kid anymore. It's rich with compassion and concern. "Monica," he says again. "Honey, what happened to you?"

"What do you mean?" My voice is still a small, quiet thing.

"I was starting to think you weren't going to call me anymore."

And just like that, everything I knew fell away.

CHAPTER TWO

"Now, I'll be darned if I can remember the name of it. It came out just a little bit ago, and I know it's got a red-and-green cover. Oh, why can't I remember the name of it?"

"Do you remember the author? Anything about the title?" *God, maybe I shoulda went to college.*

"Isn't that the darndest thing?"

Silence. He could wait. *Coulda got a degree*, he thought.

She said, "Is it Jackie Collins, maybe?" Like he'd know.

Dan takes a guess. "Is it *Hollywood Wives*?"

"No, no. I read that one."

Didn't matter. Cover was mostly white.

"You say the book came out a little bit ago," he said. "Like, a month or two? In the past six months?" *Coulda got a real job. Wouldn't have to deal with crap like this.*

"Sometime in the past…oh, I don't know…year or two?"

Narrows it down. To thousands.

Red-and-green cover. Fairly recent. Probably not Jackie Collins, but maybe in that ballpark.

"Give me a second, Missus McKenzie." Dan set the phone down and scooted out from behind the desk. *Like this is what I came into work for today. To read the shockingly blank canvas of Mrs. McKenzie's mind.* He scanned the shelves. The S authors. Red-and-green cover. Recent.

He found the paperback he was looking for, scanning the back copy as he came back around the desk, picked up the phone.

"It isn't *Changes*, is it? Danielle Steel? TV anchorwoman meets heart surgeon heartthrob?"

"Oh my goodness, Daniel! That's it!"

"Okay," he said, staring down at the sky blue-and-yellow cover. "I've got it behind the counter here for you with your name on it."

"Honestly, you astound me! However did you figure it out?"

"It's what I do," he said, and it was likely the most honest statement he would utter all day.

"See you soon, Missus McKenzie. Have a great day." Dan sent this insincere wish down through the telephone line with his bestest fake smile, just like his father had taught him. *Definitely in person, and even if you're on the phone, you talk to the customers with your biggest, bestest, hot-damn-am-I-glad-to-help-you smile, Dan. They can hear the difference, even if they're on the phone.*

Mrs. McKenzie tittered graciously, obviously hearing that bestest smile in his voice, and as she was setting her phone back in its cradle, Dan heard her say something about how sweet a boy he was. Presumably to Mr. McKenzie.

Dan wrote Mrs. McKenzie's name on a scrap of paper, wrapped an elastic band around the book with the paper, and set it in the box under the counter for customer holds. Then he dropped his head to the counter with an audible thud.

A real job would be wonderful right now.

Still though. *You astound me.* He had to admit to a little satisfaction.

Still, he thought. *College.*

◆ ◆ ◆

DAN HAD BRIEFLY considered college. Even university. His grades had been there.

Two things held him back.

The first was his father. He'd obviously been treading water from about the time Dan hit high school, running the bookstore pretty much by himself. Dan's mom had died a month after he'd started Grade 9, so from October of '75 onward, it'd just been the two of them. Well, the two of them and The Last Word bookstore his father had started in the late '60s.

Dan had kicked around the store most of his life, but started getting paid when he hit the tender age of ten. That was around the same time Stan Holt started charging his son for the books he devoured. A deeply discounted rate, but he still charged.

You're gonna find out soon enough, Dan, nothing comes for free. That includes all these books you read. You want to read? You gotta work for it.

Just after he entered high school, his dad stopped paying him under the table and put him on the payroll. And he waited for June of 1981, when his son was finished school and could become the only other full-time employee.

It had been an expectation from his conception that he would follow in the steps of his father.

Dan hadn't always been so sure.

But then that second factor came along. Well, second and third.

The second was Lila Pirsig.

He'd first caught sight of her on the first day of Grade 10 as he was putting his combination lock on his new locker for the year. Robert Bostash—Stash to his friends—had pointed out some of the new minor niners. Dan's eyes had found one girl— it took him two more days to find out her name was Lila—and never moved past her. He'd never admitted it to anyone, not even her, but he'd been…well, his father would use the term "smitten" and despite sounding so damn old-timey and kinda creepy, it fit. He saw her, and he was smitten.

It took until one of Crouch's infamous Halloween parties before he finally got the nerve to talk to her. He asked her out that night, when he wrangled her into allowing him to give her a drive home. They went out the following week.

And had been together ever since.

Everything was going smoothly, despite the low-grade fear of one or both of them considering a move to a different city to attend post-secondary. Then came the events of their graduating year, with so many of their friends and teachers dead, had thrown everyone off, left them questioning their future plans.

In the end, Dan was expected to stay and help run The Last Word, but Lila had been undecided. Stan stepped in and offered Lila a job too, with one condition.

They couldn't break up. *Makes it awkward*, he'd said.

They promised to not break up.

In fact, a couple of years after graduating, they did the opposite. Dan and Lila found out they were going to be parents. A hasty wedding was arranged.

And it looked like The Last Word would be the last word on post-secondary education for either of them.

◆ ◆ ◆

DAN'S FATHER CAME out from the backroom with a puzzled look on his face. He had a book in his hand.

"Rough day?"

"Mrs. McKenzie."

"Ugh," his father said, squinching his eyes closed in mock pain. "Got it sorted?"

Dan reached under the desk and pulled out the paperback. "Yup," he said. "Got her book with the red-and-green cover right here." Dan's father stared at the blue-and-yellow cover, then snorted.

"See?" he said. "You're a natural."

Dan angled his chin to the book in his father's hand. "What's that?"

His father waggled the book. "You bring this in?"

Dan held his hand out and his father passed it over. "Whoa," Dan said.

"Heavier than expected?"

"Yeah."

"Yeah," Stan agreed. "That's what I think too. Every time I pick it up."

Dan stared at the book. No cover image. Just a generic face of a man, a small curl of blood on his lower lip, the only colour on the black cover, aside from the title and author, in dark grey.

Callahan's Lot. Stephen King.

Callahan's *Lot?* Dan thought. *Sequel to 'Salem's Lot?* He didn't know King even did sequels. He hadn't done any in the dozen or so books he'd put out up to now.

But of course his dad would have thought he'd brought it in. Stan Holt didn't read "that horror crap."

"No," he said, hefting the book in his hand, as though weighing it. It was a thick paperback, not quite *The Stand*, but definitely thicker than *The Shining*. And though it felt normal now, it had really felt a lot heavier initially. "Where'd you find it?"

"Laying on the floor between the stacks. Must have fallen off one of the shelves, but I'll be damned if I could figure out from where."

"Horror section?"

His father looked at him a little strangely. "No…general fiction."

"Okay," Dan said. They agreed on where most books went. But some books, such as what Dan considered a classic, his father vehemently disagreed with. Or something like the *Alien* novelization. Dan considered it horror first, science fiction second. His father said it had space ships, so it was science fiction. Period.

Mork & Mindy had a freaking space ship in it too, but is that science freaking fiction?

Whatever.

"Anyway, I was just wondering where it came from. I didn't order it. You didn't order it."

"Maybe we got it second-hand from a customer?"

His father nodded slightly. "Maybe. We did take in a lot of stuff from that estate sale for the…"

"Yeah." Dan knew his father didn't like to talk about what had happened at the high school a couple of years back. Dan and Lila were both on set decoration that Friday, but Dan's father had been sick as hell, so they'd both skipped it to get to the store so his father could go home and collapse into bed.

It had probably saved their lives.

Because of all that, because of a damn bout of flu, Dan and Lila were still alive when many of their classmates and teachers weren't.

"Okay, well, regardless," he said, nodding to the book. "You mind putting it back on the shelf?"

"Sure, Dad." *I'll put it in the horror section with all the other King books.* He looked at the cover one more time. *Callahan's Lot.* He decided he'd put it back once he'd read it himself.

His father gave the book one more unreadable look before he headed back into the backroom. The store phone rang. His father said, "Get that, willya?"

Shit, Dan thought. *Better not be Mrs. McKenzie again.*

♦ ♦ ♦

"HELLO, THANKS FOR calling The Last Word. How can I help you?"

"Dad?"

"Yes," he said, though it sounded like she'd said "dad." *Weird.* "This is Dan. What can I do for you?"

"It's me. Monica."

"Hello, Monica." Dan didn't know what else to say, so, perhaps more awkwardly than he wanted, he said, "So, um...what can I do for you?"

"Dad," she said again. *Nope, definitely saying dad, not Dan.* "It's *me*. Your daughter. Monica."

He couldn't help it. He guffawed. "Good one. Who is this? Michelle? Cindy?"

"It's Monica," she said. She wasn't breaking character, and she actually, legitimately sounded a little freaked. "I don't have a lot of time, Dad. Have you started the summoning yet? Please tell me you haven't."

"I'm sorry," he said, "I don't know what you're talking about, and I really don't have time —"

"*Dad!*" she said, her tone sharp. "Dan Holt. Son of Stan Holt. Your mother died around October of 1975, when her car left the road. Your wife is Lila Pirsig."

"Okay, you're creeping me out, whoever you are."

"Have we never talked before?"

"Gonna have to say no to that," Dan said, running a hand through his hair.

"Okay," she said. "Dammit. Okay." He heard her inhale and exhale. "Okay. Then, somewhere down the line, we're going to talk again. A few times. But what you need to know right now is, we're coming. All of us. We're going to help you."

"Well, um, that's...great?"

She sighed. "I know this makes no sense right now. Just remember two things for me, okay?"

"Sure?" he said, but it came out more like a question. He was humouring her.

"It's important. Believe me." Another sigh. "First, there's a Book. A bad Book. You need to stay away from It."

"Sure," he said. "Not a problem. Life's too short for bad b—"

"*You're not taking me seriously,*" she said. "This Book was behind the destruction and death at the high school. This. Is. Serious."

"Okay," he said. He was even more creeped out.

"Next," she said. "Just remember we're coming. We'll help you. We're gonna save you."

Ah, he thought, *now I've got it.*

"Okay," he said. "I'll remember. Bad book, gonna be saved. Got it."

She sounded a bit more relieved. "Okay, we're coming very soon. All of us."

"Fantastic," he said. "Can't wait."

"Bye, Dad," Monica said. "I love you."

"Love you too," he said, then hung up the phone, rolling his eyes.

Damned Jehovah's Witnesses.

CHAPTER THREE

E SAID MY name.

The phone rattles against the desk as I set it down with a shaking hand.

He said my name.

I pause then. I need to just…just take a moment. I set both hands, palm down, on the desk, feeling the solidity of the wood underneath. I close my eyes and take a deep breath, the smell of the books helping to calm me. I do my best to allow the shop's absolute stillness, the quiet, to enter my mind. To slow my trip-hammering heart.

I give it a count of twenty, then open my eyes and move my gaze slowly from the desk, to the shelves of books along the walls, to the shelves in front of me. I let my eyes roam until they find the front windows that look out on the street, just now beginning to show signs of life.

"This is real, Monica," I say. "You didn't dream this."

I don't really dream the other, either. Duane. No, that's a memory that's metastasized into a nightmare. But it's not a dream.

And neither is this.

Holy mother of god, I just talked to my father.

And he said my name.

He'd been gone before I was born. I'd never met him, knew him only through the anecdotes of my mother, also gone over twenty years. I only knew him through other people's eyes.

I'd never heard Dan Holt's voice. My *father's* voice.

And now, I'd heard him, heard his voice as he said my name.

And then I think, *But how?*

♦ ♦ ♦

I SIT HERE in my quiet bookstore for a long time, hand to my mouth as though stopping any words from exiting prematurely. I stare out at nothing. I see nothing. I hear nothing.

I replay the call in my head again and again.

And I truly have no idea what to do next.

The biggest part of me wants to call the number again, to repeat the experience. But what if it doesn't work?

What if there's still too little blood in my alcohol stream? What if I imagined it all?

And then, a thought that scares me even more…

What if I didn't? What if it was real?

I need to tell somebody, but there's only one person to tell. And, after last night, I don't know if Lex is even in the mood to hear my voice.

You gotta try, Monica.

Do I call her? Tell her to come here?

Do I go to her?

How in the hell do I tell her this?

I pull a pad of paper to me, grab a pen that doesn't work, a second pen that doesn't work, then find a third that does, and scrawl a note for the Muracks, telling them I'm taking the morning, possibly the day off, to call if I'm needed. I reread it once, scrawl a heartfelt apology and a thank you, then lay it on the register where they can't miss it.

Then I gather my stuff and lock the store behind me.

It's not until I'm halfway home that I think of how stupid I am. *How in the hell do I tell her this? Duh.* My girlfriend and I, barely six months ago, dealt with her demon of a father, several vampires, an unaging woman who can do magic and implant knowledge in other people's heads, and Lex also became the proud owner of a Staff older than our planet.

Put in that light, this wasn't that big a deal.

◆ ◆ ◆

LEX IS STILL in bed when I get back home. She's not—by any stretch of the imagination—a morning person.

So, instead of just going in and dumping this on her, I decide to get my head straight on how, exactly, I will dump this on her. And I think we'll both need coffee for that, so I wash out the pot and get some fresh brew going.

I guess I space out while the coffee maker burbles away because I don't hear Lex until she speaks.

"So you don't talk to me anymore, you skip out on sleeping with me, and now you're not even going to work today?"

Dammit. This isn't how I want this to go down.

My first instinct is to snap something back. To rip her like she just did me.

But no. Instead, I bite back the snark, take a deep breath, let it out slowly, then turn to face the woman who is the love of my life.

"Sorry, Lex," I say. "I have something to talk to you about, so I was just making some coffee for us."

Lex crosses her arms and leans on the counter opposite me.

"I wanted to wake you up bearing gifts."

"What do you want to talk to me about?"

Okay, straight to the point. That's my Lex.

"It's gonna be a little strange, hon, so—"

Lex holds up a hand. "Please don't."

I give her a questioning look.

"Don't use pet names," she says. "I'm pissed with you, Monica. I've been pissed with you for a while. So, right now, I'm not 'hon' or 'babe' or whatever else you might come up with. Right now, I'm the person who's trying to figure out exactly how bad this trainwreck is."

Ouch. I drop my head, unable to face her. She's right, of course.

"And I haven't talked to you much about what's going on, either. I understand that."

Lex snorts out a derisive noise. "Ya *think*?"

"Lex," I say, and can feel the tremor in my voice as much as I hear it, "I'm trying here." I stab a finger at the ground. "Right now. I'm here. I'm trying."

I'm still not looking at her, so I don't know her expression, but she's quiet for a long moment. Then I watch her legs as she pushes off the counter and moves across the kitchen. She pulls down two mugs.

"I'll pour," she says. "You get the milk."

Okay, I think. *Okay, this is something.* I pour a measure into each mug. Watch the darkness lighten in each in turn.

Maybe our minds can lighten up a touch, too.

Lex hooks a finger through each handle and walks them over to the dining room table. We both sit.

…and I don't know how to start.

"If we're gonna talk, Monica, you need to start," she says. "The last time this happened to me, I started, and I ended it."

She's talking about her last girlfriend, Kelly.

"Do you want to end it this time, too?" I say, and that tremor is back in my voice.

"I don't," she says. "But I gotta be honest with you, Monica. I can't keep on like it is right now."

I nod as a tear slips down my cheek. I swipe it away angrily. I don't want to cry right now.

"So…" Lex says, and rolls her hand, "…talk."

Easier said than done, Lex, I think. Still…I start.

◆ ◆ ◆

"BEAR WITH ME for a bit, Lex. Before I can talk about what I want to say about this morning, I need to go back a bit."

"Okay." She takes a sip of the coffee, then sets it down carefully and folds her hands in front of her. She meets my gaze but says nothing more, telling me she's going to listen.

I still don't know where to start, so I say his name. "Jeff Ambrose."

That makes her sit up straighter. She blinks. "Tim Ambrose's brother?"

I nod.

"Tim's the one—"

"—whose father blew his head off in an accidental gun cleaning incident, yeah." I make finger quotes. "Accidental."

"So what about Jeff, then?"

"I've never told you about what happened right after Mom died."

"You went to the Muracks'…" Hedges says.

"Eventually, yes," I say. "But there was a short period where I was…with the Ambrose's."

"You never mentioned it."

"I've never talked about it." I can't look at Hedges, can't meet her eyes. "I've never told anyone about it, except Gabe and Val."

"You don't have to tell me, Mon," she says.

"I do," I say. "I do…because it's part of…of…"—I look around the room—"…all this shit."

"Okay." Hedges stands from her spot at the far end of the table, moves to the chair next to me. She sits, then slides her mug over. She places one hand on mine. "Tell me," she says. But gently.

♦ ♦ ♦

MOM'S GONE NOW. My dad's been gone for eight years. All my life. He died just a month before I was born. All my life, I've heard people say, low enough that they thought I couldn't hear, but I always could, they said, "Such a shame" or "Such a tragedy" or "That poor little girl."

It never made a lot of sense to me, because I always had Mom. She was wonderful. The best mom anyone could want. She knew my favourite stories before bed. She knew how to make me the perfect grilled cheese sandwiches. We snuggled perfectly when we watched *Who's the Boss?* and *The Wonder Years*.

She was the best mom. But then, two weeks ago, when I got home from school, Mom was laying down. She said she had the worst headache ever. She kept one eye half-closed when she talked to me, and said the pain was *right there*, right above that eye.

I was going to make us grilled cheese sandwiches for dinner, but Mom said, "No, no, it's okay, I got it."

She lifted the blanket from her, sat up, then stood up.

And then she fell back on the couch.

I couldn't wake her up.

I wanted her to wake up. But I couldn't wake her up.

I...

Couldn't...

♦ ♦ ♦

MOM WAS GONE.

My world was gone.

◆ ◆ ◆

TWO WEEKS LATER, I was sent to live with my new foster family, the Ambroses. Angie, my foster mom, was nice, but really quiet. She didn't look at me much, but she was always kind.

Jeff was loud and funny. He was the first one to get me to smile after Mom passed. The first morning with the Ambroses was quiet. I got up, got ready, and went back to school. It was weird. Everyone stared at me. I didn't like it.

But when I got home, at first, it was better. The Ambroses never seemed to use their front door. I walked around the side of the house, the hedges, maybe ten feet tall, forming a wall on either side of their yard, as well as the back, like a big green box. I thought it funny that the backyard was so isolated, because the Ambroses' closest neighbours were a good distance away at to either side. I knocked on the back door, and Angie opened it and smiled. "Oh, honey," she said. "You live here now. You don't have to knock."

I came in and took my school stuff to my room.

When I came back down, Jeff was home too. He said he'd got off work early to bring me a surprise. A co-worker's dog had had puppies, and he picked out the best two as a "welcome to the Ambroses'" gift.

They were so tiny, they couldn't even bark yet, they just squeaked and yipped. They were adorable. One was a soft brown colour, with a white diamond on his chest. The other was more of a golden brown, with white socks on three of her paws, like one had slipped off.

"For me?" I said. I don't think I'd ever received such a wonderful gift in all my life. I couldn't believe it.

"For you," Jeff said. "Whatcha gonna name them?"

That was easy. I pointed to the darker of the two. "He's Dan." Then I pointed to the other one. "She's Lila."

Angie smiled, but there was a strange look on her face. I

can't say it any better than her eyebrows weren't smiling along with the rest of her face. Jeff's face just seemed to freeze.

Everything was silent for a few seconds. Then Jeff said, "Okay," but really slowly.

That was the Friday.

By Sunday, I was deeply, madly, wholly in love with my two dogs. I spent most of Friday evening, and all of Saturday, in the backyard with them. We played together. We rolled around in the grass together. We even napped together under the warm mid-afternoon sun. They captivated me and entranced me with their every move.

I'd never owned a pet, so these hours were filled with a magic I'd never experienced before.

On Sunday morning, I woke up to Jeff standing at the side of my bed, arms crossed. I sat up quickly, thinking something was wrong. Were Dan and Lila okay? Was Angie okay? I remember thinking, *Oh, please god, please don't let anyone else be dead.*

Jeff said, "Get up." Then he left the room.

A few minutes later, I came down the stairs, Dan and Lila bumbling after me, my constant companions. The back door leading to the yard was open, and Jeff stood on the patio. It was only then that I realized it was still dark out.

The pups immediately ran outside. I followed after, stifling a yawn. I'd calmed somewhat, because it was obvious there was no emergency. Nothing was wrong.

I stepped out to the patio, the light from the kitchen bathing us in warm light. The air was cool, but pleasantly so.

"What's up?" I said.

"Okay," Jeff said. "That's the first thing that's gonna change. It's either 'sir' or 'Mr. Ambrose' from now on."

I blinked a couple of times. "Pardon?"

"You will address me as 'sir' or 'Mr. Ambrose' from now on. And you'll refer to my wife as 'ma'am' or 'Mrs. Ambrose.'

And the next thing is, don't you dare make me repeat myself ever again."

"Okay," I said, bewildered.

"Okay what?"

"Okay, sir," I said. *What the heck is going on?*

He nodded, satisfied. "Next, don't think staying here is some damn joyride, missy, because it isn't. There's furniture to be dusted, floors to be swept and mopped, carpets to be vacuumed, beds to be made, laundry to be done. I'm guessing your mother was one of those who haven't teached you anything about cooking and ironing and such."

"Taught."

"Excuse me?"

"Sorry," I said quickly, "taught, sir."

He took a step forward. The look on his face told me he wasn't understanding, and he was scaring me.

"You said, 'teached,' sir. It's taught."

"All that talking, and the only thing you got out of it is me using teached instead of taught?" He stalked closer.

"Well, no, I—"

"No, what?" Standing too close.

"No, sir." He'd come up so fast, and was throwing his words at me so quickly, I was off-balance. I felt like I was falling, despite standing on the hard concrete patio steps.

He grabbed my shoulder and my whole body shook with the motion. He squeezed and I felt his thumb sinking into my muscles, the pain bright and sharp.

"No, sir, what?" he said, but it made no sense to me.

"I...I..."

He screwed up his face as he drew it close to my own, nose to nose. His voice was high and whiny as he mimicked me. "I...I..." He pushed hard with the hand digging into my shoulder, knocking me sideways. He let me go and I tumbled to the ground, my tailbone impacting hard on the concrete.

"We are not getting near enough money every month to keep you under our roof, missy. So you're going to have to make up the difference. And trust me, there's a *lot* of difference to be made up."

"Okay, sir," I said, without really knowing what I was agreeing to.

"You *understand*, now?" he said, his eyes wild. "You *get it*, now?"

"Yes, sir," I said. I felt the tears coming. I'd cried too much the past two weeks, I was getting too good at doing it.

"I don't think I believe you, missy," Jeff said. "And there's one problem we can rectify immediately anyway. Solves a problem, teaches you a lesson. I call that a win-win."

I was so off-balance mentally that I could only sit where I'd fallen, staring stupidly at this man I'd thought was loud and funny just yesterday. Now, he was loud and terrifying.

He stalked away from me, deeper into the backyard. I saw him stop, stoop down, then stand and march back to me.

He had Dan in one hand.

No.

He stood over me, one leg on either side of mine, so he was right above me. "This dog," he said, "is an expense we don't need and can't afford."

No, I thought. *Please don't make me give up one of my pups.*

"You have any idea how much a damn dog costs? The food? The shots? Plus all the time wasted just dealing with it?"

"N-n-no, sir," I stammered.

"Well, it's a lot. And you'll be too busy doing chores with to spend with a dog. So…" — then, still cradling the dog in one arm, he reached over with his other and wrapped his hand around Dan's head — "…we're gonna have to eliminate the problem."

His hand twisted sharply. Dan had time for one soft peep and then he was limp and still in Jeff's arm, his head cocked at to an awful angle.

The dog's bowels loosed, and Jeff must have felt the sudden warmth because he looked down, said, "shit," and threw the dog's corpse into my lap.

And I screamed. I screamed at the horror of what I'd just seen. I screamed at the loss of my pet. I screamed because another loved one had been taken from me. I screamed because it was the only thing I could do.

I wanted to touch my dog, to put a comforting hand on him. I wanted to take the last minute away from him, to take away the pain. The death.

I wanted so much and I couldn't articulate any of it beyond a scream.

I heard a sound behind me, but didn't look. Couldn't look. I could only stare at the pup in my lap. The pup that was awfully silent and horribly still.

In my anguish, I hadn't noticed Jeff's absence until he was over me again, with Lila now in his arm.

"No," I pleaded. "Please, Mr. Ambrose, no. Please. I'll do anything. Please. Don't."

A small voice behind me, at the door. "Jeff?" she whispered.

Jeff's eyes blazed as he shot a look at Angie, unseen behind me. I heard an intake of breath, then heard nothing else from her.

"I'm not paying for this one either," Jeff said, addressing me again.

"…please…"

"I'm not gonna kill her," he said, and it was enough for me to raise my burning eyes to him.

"You are," he said.

What?

"Stand up."

What? I couldn't stand.

"Stand up, right the hell now, missy," he said, his voice a low growl. "Don't make me pull your ass up."

Somehow, I got my hands moving. I had to move Dan, and my fingers trembled as I slid them between his still-warm body and my lap to gently lift him.

Jeff's foot shot out and kicked the body from my hands. The pup landed in a boneless sprawl beside me and I felt like I was going to throw up. I gagged.

"You puke, I'll make you lick it straight off the ground, so you better swallow it down and get your ass up."

I looked away from Dan as I got my hands and feet under me and stood unsteadily to face Jeff.

"Put your hand on her head. Firm like."

I reached out slowly, hand shaking, tears streaming. Jeff stood, resolute, waiting. I put my hand on Lila's soft fur, and I felt her tongue lick my wrist in greeting.

And somehow, of the entire night so far, that one little motion of love was the worst. I sobbed.

"Now, you grab her head, and you twist hard."

"I can't."

"You're gonna."

"I can't."

"You'd damn well better—"

"Can't."

"—because if you don't—"

"Can't."

"—I'll break your neck," he said. "Missy."

I stared up at him.

"You believe me?"

I nodded.

"You, or the dog."

I stared up at him.

"Because, I swear to god, no one will miss you. You'll just be one more little lost girl who ran away from home."

I shook my head. I honestly didn't know what I was disagreeing to.

He hefted the dog slightly. "Do it."

I felt the tears hot on my face as I stared at him.

"Goddamnit," Jeff said, then his hand was on mine and he squeezed and I felt Lila's soft fur under my hand, the small skull underneath, and Jeff's hand was over mine and he twisted his wrist and I tried, I really tried to not follow with his motion but I couldn't he was too strong, too strong, and under my fingers I felt a small snap and heard a soft exhalation of breath, felt the warm air from Lila's lungs drift across my forearm, and then Jeff's hand was off mine and he dropped her before she could void herself on him.

I was on my knees.

The two pups lay before me.

I could not think. I could not see. I could not hear. I could not breathe.

I could only be still.

Faintly, faintly, I heard Jeff say something about cleaning up my mess.

I heard another voice, a different voice.

I heard yelling.

I was on my knees. I could only see the two pups.

I heard the crash of a lawn chair breaking.

I heard Jeff's voice, first in rage, then pain, then fear.

I might have thrown up then. I'm not sure.

But the last thing I remember is two strong, gentle arms lifting me and cradling me, and a kind voice, a man's voice, saying, "I'm so sorry, honey, I'm so sorry. You're safe now."

♦ ♦ ♦

"GABE MURACK LIVED down the street. It was around five-thirty in the morning, and he'd been coming out to his truck to head to his job at the lumber mill. He heard me scream, I guess.

He came over, but by then, both dogs were dead. He got hold of Ambrose, threw him into his own lawn furniture, then beat him enough to subdue him."

Hedges sits very still. Her eyes are red from crying.

"Then he took me home, and they formally adopted me."

"And Jeff?"

"I saw him in town, but he would never meet my gaze. I don't know where he is now, nor do I care."

"His wife?"

"No idea, but I hope she got away from him."

"Probably not."

"Probably not," I say in agreement.

"Monica," Lex says.

"Please don't say you're sorry, Lex," I say. "Please don't. You didn't know. Nobody knew but the Ambroses, the Muracks, and me."

"Still…"

"Still," I say, " I saw the worst of humanity and the best of humanity in the span of minutes. Cruelty and compassion. Cowardice and bravery."

"But what he did to you," Lex says as fresh tears fall. "After what you'd just been through."

"There's a reason I tell you this, Lex," I say, "and, not to sound harsh, but it's not for your sympathy."

She's swiping away tears with the back of her hand. "Okay," she says. "Tell me."

Chapter Four

DAN COULDN'T READ *Callahan's Lot.*

It wasn't from lack of trying. He'd tried his damnedest.

But the book…it felt like the book fought him. He'd read two or three words, then it's like his brain would shut off. He'd tried to start it that night. Around ten, Lila had kissed him good night—she was going to bed earlier and earlier with this pregnancy—and rolled over so his bedside light wouldn't bother her.

Dan got his pillows settled, then pulled the book from the bedside table. He opened the cover, flipped past the opening pages, found the start of the story.

He read, *The man staggered…*

And the next thing he knew, Lila was poking his arm. "Dan!"

He blinked, shook his head, turned to Lila.

She had strange look on her face. Half-amused, half-worried. "You okay?"

"Yeah," he said, still trying to find his bearings. He looked down at the book. "Must have drifted off."

"Well," she said, angling away from him as she left the bed, "if you did, it was creepy. Your eyes were wide open, and your lips were moving, like you were reciting what you were reading, or something."

"I don't move my lips when I read."

"You normally don't sleep with your eyes open, either," she said. Then she winced and cupped her palm on the swell of her belly. "Gotta pee." She went down the hall to the bathroom.

He glanced at his alarm clock. The LEDs told him it was 2:07 A.M. *What?* He'd lost four hours.

Dan looked down at the book. He was still on the first page. *What the hell?*

He read the first line again.

The man staggered —

"What the hell's the matter with you?"

"Huh? What?" He looked up. Lila was right beside him. *How'd she sneak up like that?*

"I have a pee, get a drink, maybe eat a cookie or five, I'm gone no more than fifteen minutes, and you turn into zombie Dan again?"

"What the hell are you —" He flicked a glance at the clock again. 2:21 A.M. *What the hell?*

"Babe," Lila said, worry the only expression on her face now, "what's going on?"

"Sorry," he said. "Guess I'm a lot more tired than I thought." He made a show of closing the book, putting it on his nightstand, and shutting out his light.

She stayed there another long moment. "You sure that's all it is?"

He leaned up, tugged on her forearm to bring her down, and kissed her. "I'm sure. Didn't mean to scare you, hon."

She kissed him again, then kept her face close, searching his eyes. "I need you, you know." She rubbed her belly. "We both do."

"I know," he said. "I need the two of you, too."

They kissed once more, then she went around to her side and clambered into bed.

It took them a bit to get settled in, Dan snuggled in tight behind her, one arm protectively over her belly.

"Love you," she said.

"Love you too," he said back.

"Now, move your ass over to the other side of the bed. I'm sweating like a pig here," she said. Dan smiled as he rolled over. He saw the book parked on the bedside table.

The smile didn't last long.

◆ ◆ ◆

HE WAS ON the precipice of sleep when he heard a voice in his head. A sharp voice.

There's a Book. A bad Book. You need to stay away from it.

The words echoed behind him, all the way down into sleep.

◆ ◆ ◆

"WHAT'S THE DEAL with that book, Dad?"

"Which book?" his father said, tapping his cigarette into the ashtray. He only smoked in the office, never in the main store, though he never minded if the customers smoked. He kept ashtrays strewn strategically throughout the store.

"*Callahan's Lot*," Dan said, holding the book up. "The one you asked me to put away the other day."

"I have no idea what you're talking about."

Dan waggled the book again. "This. *Callahan's Lot*." His father looked at him blankly. "Stephen King?"

Stan Holt snorted. "That hack?

"Dad…"

His father squinted as he dragged on his cigarette, put up a hand. "Okay, okay, we run a bookstore, we shouldn't judge readers' tastes," he said. He pulled the butt out between two fingers and pointed at Dan. "Still…judging you. You watch, Dan. King's gonna spit out another book or two, then put out a stinker, then another one, and you'll never hear from the guy again."

Dan rolled his eyes with as much drama as he could. "*Ohhhh*-kay…"

"I'm tellin' ya. Horror authors don't last."

"Right. Lovecraft, Poe, Mary Shelley…"

"And what have they done lately?"

"Dad," Dan said, both of them cracking up. It was an old argument. "*Anyway…*"

"Yes," his father said. "Anyway."

"Seriously, what's up with this book?"

"In what way?"

"I've tried to read it seven different times, and I can't get more than three words into it."

"That bad?" He waggled the cigarette at him. "Told you. His first stinker."

"No, Dad. I'm serious. You know me. I'll read anything. I read the damn ingredients on a box of cereal." His father smiled. They both did it.

"So?"

"So, I can't read this to save my life." He put the book in front of his father. "You try."

"What's this got to do with King?"

"Just try."

Stan sighed, opened the book, flipped to the first page. Dan watched him. His eyes flicked. He stopped, took another drag, tapped the ash. Looked back down at the book.

Then he just…stopped. Dan watched as his father went very still, his cigarette trapped between two fingers, a twist of smoke curling to the ceiling. And he moved nothing but his lips. As though he was puzzling out the words.

"Dad."

His father didn't react.

Dan put a hand on his shoulder. Shook him. Then shook him more violently.

Finally, he yelled, "Dad!" and cuffed him on the shoulder. *It's like banging the TV to get the signal back.*

His father's eyes widened, gained focus. Then he squinted. Grimaced. Took another drag. Slapped the book closed.

"Yeah, not sure," he said. "I can't get past the first few words." *Like he didn't just haze out for a solid minute.*

"Right. 'The man staggered' and no further?"

"No," his father said, a little confused. "I couldn't get past, '"Her husband," she answered.'"

"What?" Dan said. "I never read that." *Weird.*

"And I didn't read anything about a staggering man."

"Either way, you can't get more than a few words in, right?"

"Yeah."

"I mean, I know there's printing and binding errors and stuff," Dan said, "but have you ever come across a defective book? One that can't be read?"

"Doesn't even make sense."

They both stared at the book.

"Okay," Dan said. "I'm gonna try an experiment."

His father raised an eyebrow.

"Gonna put it out on the shelves. If it sells, it sells. But if someone brings it back because they can't read it, then we'll try and track this."

"Okay," his father said slowly. "I guess."

"Okay," Dan said. He scooped up the book and took it with him. "Thanks."

"Still don't know what this has to do with that hack," Stan muttered.

◆ ◆ ◆

STAN HOLT REMAINED seated at his small desk. The wooden surface was pockmarked with scratches and dents and stains and — thanks to him — more than a few cigarette burns.

Off to the left and right corners of the desk stood an In tray and an Out tray that years ago he'd optimistically placed as a key to organizational freedom. The stack of various papers and invoices in the In tray never seemed to be less than a foot high. The Out tray? Yeah, nothing ever really seemed to escape, to actually go out.

And, aside from a small foot-square area in the middle where his coffee cup and ashtray crouched, and a small area at the back with a banker's lamp and an old photo in a frame, the rest of the desk was littered, inches deep, with new books, old books, ripped books, papers, invoices, notes…

It was chaos, but somehow he managed to navigate it.

But today, it all had faded away for just a moment, a brief second, while he tried to concentrate on that weird book of Dan's.

But what the hell was all this talk of Stephen King?

Stan had asked his son to shelve a book a couple of days back. He remembered it because it had been a book he didn't think had existed. *The Decembrists* by Leo Tolstoy. He'd have to look it up, but Stan had it in his head that Tolstoy died before finishing that one.

It was tweaking something in his memory. Quite a few years back. Hadn't there been a book like that in his bookstore? Early '70s? Marcia Mayer, who he normally would never have remembered, but when they found her murdered the day after the whole high school thing…

Stan was sure that, a few years before, she'd bought a book for that weird kid she'd been babysitting. When she was purchasing it, she kept saying how the kid loved Dr. Seuss, and Stan saw, very clearly, that it had not been a Seuss book at all.

But, hey, she'd been happy with it, and she'd never returned it.

Now, though, Stan's brain was ticking over a young Marcia talking about a Seuss book that wasn't Seuss, and then in comes Dan yapping about some book by King that clearly wasn't a King book.

No, the book he'd asked Stan to try reading had been *The Original of Laura* by Nabokov, yet another book that, like the Tolstoy one, he absolutely should have known about, but didn't. And, since when did his son start stepping away from all the guys with swords, like Conan and Elric, and start reading stuff like Nabokov? And again, why all the shit about King?

Ah, darling, he thought, reaching for the photo of himself and his wife Monica at Niagara Falls, their first trip together as a married couple. *I'm sure you think I'm too hard on the kid. I'm doing my best. But if he's going to be a good business owner after I'm gone, and a good dad in a few months, he's gotta smarten up and toughen up a bit.*

He touched a single finger to Monica's cheek. *God, I miss you, baby.* Then he chuckled a bit, carefully set the photo back in its spot, and took a final drag of his cigarette.

Listen to me, getting all misty over you. Guess I gotta toughen up some myself, huh?

He stubbed out his butt in the ashtray, pulled a fresh one from the pack, lit it, then, sighing, pulled a thick stack of papers toward him.

CHAPTER FIVE

I SAY, "DUANE."

Lex says, "Mon…"

"Hear me out," I say, but softly. Lex's face still tightens up a bit. My ex isn't a sore subject because he's my ex, but more because of what talking about him does to me. Lex sees it's hard on me, and it bugs her. I get that. There's landmine topics in her past, too.

"I need to get this out, I say."

And I almost start crying again because I see Lex's expression soften. Because, tough as Lex is, she gets it.

"When I…" — I feel my throat close up, so I swallow past it and muscle through — "…when I did what I did." *Say the words, Monica.* "When I murdered him. I knew it had to be me to do it. For a bunch of reasons."

We're gonna have to eliminate the problem.

I take a moment because there's stuff that needs articulating, and I need to do it right.

"First, if *you* had done it, all this rage, all this anger, all this…*sadness* that is roiling around in me would have been directed at you."

She nods. Keeps her silence.

"But there's more than that," I say. "There's Jeff Ambrose. And those two poor pups." I close my eyes for a moment and breathe. The memory is old, but still very sharp. "Ambrose was a wolf in sheep's clothing, Lex. I actually *liked* that guy even more than I did his wife for the first day or so." Hedges nods. "But what he did. To two dogs who never did a damn thing but give me unconditional love."

"And what he made you do," Lex says.

Still, my throat goes dry as I say, "Yeah."

"So…Duane…" she says gently.

"Duane was a wolf in my husband's clothing," I say. "And he was giving you no choice but to put him down."

Eliminate the problem.

Hedges's mouth tightens. "So, if I'm getting this right, for you, Duane was both Jeff Ambrose and that last pup. He was Jeff because he was putting my hand on something you loved and telling me to kill. But he was also the one to be killed."

"Yes," I say, the word coming out in a push of breath.

"And you'd played out that scene. And the hell it put you through…"

"Yes," I say, as I slash away the tears sliding down my face. "I'm sorry," I say. "I couldn't let you go through that, too," I say. I'll say anything to get this across.

"Jesus, babe," she says. "You should have told me all this before."

"I couldn't, Lex. How do I just take all that and toss out a few words and hope that you get it?"

"Because I've seen some shit, too, Monica," she says, "and you know that."

"Yeah," I say.

"Yeah," she says.

"Sorry," I say.

"Shut up," she says, but kindly.

We both shut up for a few moments. Both swiping at the tears. Then I think, *Finish it, Monica. You're not done yet. Help her understand the last part.*

"Anyway," I say. "There's all of that. And I accept all of that. And Duane? It was him or us. I understand it. But…" I crab my hands, grasping at something I can't quite catch. "But, for all of that, despite all I've just told you, the reality comes down to this: I *killed* him, Lex. When all is said and done, I killed the man who, not that much earlier, I'd pledged to bind my life to."

"May I say one thing," Lex says. I nod. "The thing you killed was only barely Duane. Like you said, he was a wolf in Duane's clothing. It looked like him and sounded like him, but fundamentally, Duane's mind was killed by a…I don't know, call it a cancer…long before you killed the body. You more pulled the plug on life support than you did kill someone."

I nod again, not necessarily in agreement, but more to let her know I hear her. I run a finger over the mug's handle, thinking it over.

"I'm not saying that's not right, Lex," I start, not quite sure where I'm heading, "but…just like we are together, you and me, we were also together, him and me. We had experiences. We had memories. We shared a life."

Lex nods.

"I can still call up those memories, you know? Changing a flat tire in the pouring rain. Getting in a huge fight in the grocery store. Laughing over forgetting the barbeque and burning two forty-dollar steaks into shoe leather and ordering pizza afterward. A collection of memories," I say, tapping my forehead, "both good and bad, heartwarming and sad, that I shared with someone. I had half, and he had half. And now one half is gone."

She nods, a tear slipping down her own cheek. "You know what I mean," I say.

She does. Her ex, Kelly, was murdered a few months back. Lex was indirectly responsible, and I know she blames herself every day for it.

"All his knowledge, all his memories, all his thoughts…they're just gone." I snap my fingers. "Gone. And I did that. I erased them."

Lex opens her mouth, preparing to say something, so I hold up a palm. "I know what you're gonna say."

She quirks an eyebrow.

"You're gonna say something along the lines of, 'I'm sorry you feel that way, Monica, it sucks, but you need to remember that life is ultimately one hundred percent fatal.' Am I right?"

She reaches for her cup and says, "as you were," as she brings it to her lips.

I can't help it. Even at our worst, the woman can make me smile.

I luxuriate in that for a moment, then dive back in. Because I've got to get this out.

"What's rolled around in my head since that night—and it started slowly, Lex, but it's built up bigger and bigger, and uglier and uglier, like a…like a breeze that's now a hurricane— this *hurricane* of thoughts in my head that I can't make sense of."

One of Lex's hands unfolds from the other, reaches out, touches my fingers.

"The only thing that I keep coming back to, Lex, is…" I hesitate.

Her voice is warm. Soft. "Say it, hon. Just say it."

"We talked about this before," I say. "When we're young, we're told we can do anything, be anything."

Lex nods.

"And, depending on circumstances, the possibilities ebb and flow. We choose a certain path, and those possibilities are narrowed. We zig or zag in a different direction, and the world opens up to us."

Another nod.

"Like, when I met you again after all those years, Lex, when I walked up to that table and we looked into each other's eyes for the first time in forever, I felt my possibilities opening up again. Blossoming."

She squeezes my hand. "Me too."

"And, as we went along, that expanse just kept widening. We could go anywhere, do anything, be anyone."

"As long as I was with you. As long as we were together."

"Yes," I say. "So, while that's happened for us, what's…tornadoed around in my head is that, not only did I erase Duane from the world…Lex, I also erased all that possibility. Whatever he had done is only remembered by those who remember him. But whatever he could have done, whatever worlds might have opened up for him…that's all just gone."

"Okay. I get what you're saying, and…" — she takes up both of my hands in both of hers — "…and thank you for letting me in. I understand a lot more of what's driven you in the past few months." She looks down at our hands. Joined. Filled with possibility. "I just don't know where you're going with it."

"I know," I say. "Sorry."

Another nod. Lex is a lot more comfortable with silences than I will ever be.

"This morning, after leaving here, I went to the store. And I ran across an old bookmark that Dad made for the store."

"Really?"

I get up, grab my purse, pull it out, and set it in front of her. She picks it up, examines it.

"It's a cool find," I say.

"It's more than that." She holds it up. "Your dad designed this?"

"Yeah."

"Then it's much more significant than just cool." I watch her squint a bit, then say, "What's that? Zyxt?"

"Yeah." I explain it.

"Wow. Damn. Your father was planting easter eggs before that was a thing."

I nod, tears welling again. *Dammit.*

I swipe at them again, drying my hands on my jeans. "*Any*way, I saw the number at the bottom, and, honestly Lex, I have no idea where my head was at, but…"

"You called this number?" She raises the bookmark again.

"…yeah."

"And?"

"And…" I try to get the rest out, I truly do. But my throat locks up, and the tears come yet again. I suck in a breath, try again. "And…um…"

"Monica," Lex says. She sees my distress and comes around to crouch beside me, a hand on my back. "Hon, what happened? Tell me it wasn't the number for this Ambrose guy, now."

I shake my head. But then I lock up.

I sit at the table and sob for what feels like hours, Lex's worried eyes showing me she cares, but she doesn't know what to do. Hell, *I* don't know what to do.

Lex breaks the spell by getting up, disappearing, coming back with a box of tissues. I pull a couple, dry my eyes, blow my nose, mumble, "I know, I know, I've never been sexier than I am right now," and we both laugh just a little and I feel a little better.

I crumple the tissues, then try again. This time, I get it out.

"Lex, I called the number and…"—my throat threatens to tighten again, but I push past it—"…and I talked to him, Lex."

Lex's eyes narrow as she tried to understand. "Wait, what? Who, Ambrose?"

"No," I say. "I talked to Dad."

♦ ♦ ♦

WELL, THAT BRINGS the conversation to a grinding, screeching halt. Lex gives my back another rub, then ambles back to her seat.

She sits, then stares at me, her expression unreadable. Several times over the next couple of minutes, she looks at me, looks down, opens her mouth to say something, closes it again with a shake of her head. She sips her coffee. Tries again. Fails again.

I'd like to say something, break her from her I'm-gonna-say-something-no-I'm-not cycle, but I don't even know what to say.

Finally, Lex swallows her mouthful of coffee, pushes the chair back, stands, then wanders into the living room. The house is open-concept, so I can see her clearly as she paces over to the woodstove, then back across to the overstuffed chair she's laid claim to. Back to the woodstove. Back to the chair. Then she approaches the dining room table again, and she grips the back of her chair so hard I see her knuckles whiten. Then, she finally boils it all down to one word.

"How…?"

Because, really, that's the biggest question right now, isn't it.

And my answer?

"Honestly, Lex, I have no fucking clue."

But what sits with me—very comfortably, thank you very much—is that she asks *how* and not *are you sure?* Which tells me a lot.

I look up at my girlfriend, and I say, "You believe me?"

"Babe," she says, "you've obviously been going through a lot—more than I knew, and I'm really sad about that, and we'll deal with that later—and Monica, you are a lot of things. Chief among those things is that you are someone I don't think could lie if your life depended on it. And after this past year, as wondrous and strange as this is, I think we've both learned there's more things in heaven and earth, Horatio, than are dreamt of in your philosophy."

"Did you really just throw me some *Hamlet*?"

"Figured you were probably sick of Heart lyrics."

"No, Lex, no, it's not that." More tears. *God, why am I crying so damn much?* "It's just, that damn phrase has been stuck in my head for months." *You get me.*

I stand and wrap my hands around her waist. I love the way we fit together, and I think somewhere along the way I forgot that fact. "Thank you for believing me," I say.

"De nada," she says.

"You even know what that means?"

She gives me that smirk that melts me and says, "Maybe not, but I think it fits."

I laugh. "It does. We do, too," I say, pulling her closer, and we kiss then. It's been far too long since we kissed like this.

It takes a while before we stop. When we do, she looks hard at me, eyes narrowed again. "Remember what you said to me," she says. "About kissing?"

"I think I once told you to never 'just kiss me' or something like that? To not ever take any kiss for granted?"

Lex's voice drops an octave as her face turns stern. "'Don't you ever kiss me quick again, Lex. Don't take your kisses, or mine, for granted.'"

"Did I really sound that mean when I said it?"

"You did," Lex says, her eyes brightening. "Scared the crap outta me. But I remembered." I feel her pull me tighter. "And I want you to know that I never have."

"Okay." I have, though. I've taken them for granted.

"I missed this, Monica."

"I did too," I say. "I just…got lost in the weeds. And I'm still there."

"I understand," she says. "Now I do." She leans back and views me from arms' length. "But if we can talk, we can get through anything."

"You believe that?"

"I *know* that."

I pull her back in, and kiss her again. Long enough and slow enough that I feel parts of me that have felt long dead are coming back to life. "Thank you for not giving up on me."

"De...nada?" she says, a little unsure.

"Close enough, Hedges," I say and kiss her one last time before I catch one of her hands and pull her through the living room and down the hall to our bed.

We still have a lot of talking to do, but it can wait an hour or so.

◆ ◆ ◆

OKAY, MORE LIKE two hours. We took our time. Sue us.

"Damn," Lex says, one forearm across her eyes. "Just...damn."

"Yeah," I agree. "I missed you too."

"Kinda glad you called in sex today."

"What?"

"Well, it's not like you called in sick. So, you called in sex. You had a really intense fuck that you had to get rid of."

"Oh dear," I say, pushing myself away from her slightly. "You think I'm contagious?"

"Definitely," Lex says, then in her clear, powerful voice, she sings, "I got the fuckin' pneumonia and the do-it-to-me flu!"

"Whaaat?"

"Come on, Monica!" she says, laughing. "Don't disappoint me. You've been with me long enough to get familiar with my playlists."

"It sounds familiar, but..."

She sits up, giving me an eyeful of those wonderful breasts of hers. "Johnny Rivers," she says. "1973. 'Rockin' Pneumonia and the Boogie Woogie Flu'?"

"Okay," I say. I mean, I love music. But *nobody* loves music like Hedges.

"'Okay,' she says. 'Okay.'" She flops back down to the pillow, forearm now draped far more dramatically across her eyes. "The love of your life spontaneously rewrites a rock classic with, if I may be so bold, *brilliant* new lyrics, and all she can get is an 'okay'? I may have to reconsider our relationship."

I throw the covers off us both and climb on top of her, straddling her. "You will, huh?"

She eyes me up and down, and there's a hunger there that makes me crazy. "Maybe not," she says quietly.

Our fingers, then our mouths, do scandalous, wondrous things to each other, and before we know it, another hour is gone.

♦ ♦ ♦

"HOLY CRAP, LADY," Lex says. "I gotta rehydrate."

"Get me some water too, Hedges," I say, watching her ass as she heads out of the bedroom to the kitchen. She gives me a wave.

I reposition the pillows up against the headboard and sit up, waiting for her to return. In the meantime, I just close my eyes and luxuriate in the feeling of our comingled, cooling sweat drying.

I feel better. We're talking again. Communicating like we used to, with words and looks and touches. But I know there's still the dark clouds on the horizon. They're not going to go away easily. They may never go away, but if I can keep them pushed back to that horizon, I think I can deal with that.

But this thing with my father? I don't know what the hell I'm supposed to do with that.

Lex comes back in, a tall, sweating glass of water in each hand. She must see my expression because her smile dims a bit. She hands me one of the glasses and says, "What's on your mind, beautiful?"

"Dad."

"Ah," she says. "Right." She slides into bed, snuggles in, leaning against me, her head between my breasts. "Tell me what happened again."

I tell her, trying to remember every single detail. Every slight change in the tone of his voice. His lack of surprise.

"Damn, Monica," Lex says. "That really happened, didn't it?"

"It really did."

"So..." she says, then takes a moment. "What happens now?"

"I don't even know."

"Why do you think your dad thought he'd talked to you before?"

"Don't know."

"You haven't, have you? Talked to him before?"

"No," I say. *God, I wish.*

"You gonna try it again?"

Yes.

No.

"Not sure. Probably."

Lex leans over, giving me another view of that ass, then rolls back, cell phone in hand. "Should we try now?"

"God, Lex," I say, all the spit suddenly gone from my mouth. "I don't...I mean...is that a good idea...?"

She holds my gaze for a moment. Then, after searching my face, she says, "Is it a bad idea?"

"No, it's just..."

She snuggles back into me, places the phone in the space between her breasts. "Forget the phone for a minute. Instead, let me ask you..." She awkwardly twists her face up to mine. Again, that searching look. "If you could talk to your dad right now, what would you want to talk about?"

"I don't—"

"No," she says, turning away, cutting me off. "'I don't know' is not an allowable answer. Take second, think about it. You can talk to the father you never got to meet. What do you want to say to him? What do you want to ask him? What do you need to know? What do you need him to know?"

The thoughts spin and swirl and drift like sparks from a fire, coalescing, then blowing away. She puts a hand on my thigh. "Don't overthink it, Monica. I don't think there's a wrong answer."

"Except 'I don't know.'"

"Right. Except that."

"What if it's all I've got?"

We sit silent for a minute or two. Her fingernails trace lazy spirals on my leg. When she speaks again, her voice is low, gentle. "I don't really have any good memories of my family. I know it was just you and your mom for the first little bit, then the Muracks. But, with your mom, she told you stories about your dad, right?"

"Yeah, she did."

"So, when you think of your father, what do you feel? How do you see him?"

"Funny, bright, nerdy. Loved my mom. Was very excited about me coming along."

"So, good thoughts? Love?"

"Yeah," I say, smiling. "Love."

Her hand is warm on my leg. "Then that's your starting point, hon."

She's right, of course.

Lex lifts the phone. "Should we try?"

She can't see me, but she can feel the tentative nod I make. I give her the number and she enters it, and puts the phone on speaker.

I feel my heart rate rocket up with each chirp of the ringtone. Then I feel it leap as the call is answered.

"Hello! You've reached The La—"

Three things happen simultaneously.

Lex sits up violently, yelling, "Shit!"

She drops the phone to the sheets.

And, finally, there's a click, then a colder, female voice. "The number you have dialed is not in service. Please hang up, and try your call again. This is a recording." Then the call goes to a discordant, hyperactive beeping that Lex quickly kills.

But she does it by gingerly poking the End key with a nail.

I feel the hammering of my heart as it pounds against my chest, against Lex's back as she leans back into me. I feel it in my neck, I feel it pulsing in my temples, at my wrists, behind my eyes.

But worse, I feel its echoes in the emptiness that suddenly fills me. I am nothing. A black hole surrounded by skin.

Then I'm pushing Lex off me. She makes a questioning noise, but I say, "I'm going to be sick," and I roll off the bed, land on all fours, then scrabble to the toilet off the main bedroom.

I vomit brackish, brown coffee and Crown Royal and bile. I vomit until my muscles lock and my stomach is somewhere in my throat. I'm dimly aware of Lex behind me, making soothing noises, holding my hair back.

Her hand gently rubbing my back is perhaps the only thing that keeps me from being swallowed up into that black hole at my centre. It's the tenuous, gossamer lifeline that I claw at to scrabble back to sanity.

◆ ◆ ◆

TWENTY MINUTES LATER, teeth brushed, some clothes pulled on, back at the dining room table.

The ruined phone sits on the table, between us.

"It just got so goddamn hot," Lex says. "I thought it was going to explode."

We both stare at the phone. Its screen is spiderwebbed and heaving outward, as though something tried to punch its way out from inside the phone. Which was, of course, impossible.

Isn't it?

The phone's plastic casing has reformed. It has softened, and there are visible marks where Lex's fingers had held it. I can see the whorls of her fingerprints, burned into the body of the phone.

Lex had had to run her hand under cold water after she'd finished with me throwing up. Still, her fingers and palm carry vicious red burns.

She hasn't touched the phone since. I'd been the one to peel it from the scorched sheets and set it on the table.

"But you heard, right?" I say. "Before it went to the recording, you heard him?"

Lex put her unburned hand over mine. "I did."

"So, why'd this happen?" I say, nodding toward her cell phone.

"Nothing like this happened at the store?"

"No," I say. "I used the landline at the store, not my cell, but still…"

"Didn't notice any heat or anything?"

"I was a little distracted by talking to the father I never knew, Hedges, but no. No heat."

"So, maybe it's cell phones?"

"Maybe," I say. "There's so many differences."

"Cell instead of landline."

"Both of us, instead of just me."

"Time of day."

"Location, store versus home."

We both fall silent then, pondering. Staring at the broken phone.

"Yeaaah," Lex says, drawing the word out. "Weird."

"Kinda defines our life together."

Lex smirks, squeezes my hand. "It does." She lets go, pokes her phone with a single finger, moving it only a fraction of an inch. "You still want to try to make contact again?"

"I'm not sure."

I hear her huff out a breath. "I know you better than that, Monica Holt. Yeah, you are."

"Yeah, I am," I say. "I do. But I don't want the next phone to die from the heat of a thousand suns."

"Well, if another phone's gotta suffer heat-death," Lex says, "can we make it yours next time? Blackberrys ain't cheap."

"I own a Blackberry too, Lex."

"Cheaper for me if yours dies."

"Thanks for that."

"Welcome."

One last time, we regard her burned phone. I give it a tentative poke of my own. "So," I say, "what now?"

"I think we need to call in some reinforcements."

I cock my head to the side, not understanding.

Then I do.

"Talia?"

"Yeah."

"Think she can help?"

"I can try," Talia says.

Chapter Six

DAN WALKED THE book over to the horror section—which was far too small, as far as he was concerned—and made a space between King's second and third novels, *'Salem's Lot* and *The Shining*. Normally, the goal was to place the books chronologically from their release dates, but Dan and his father did take a little artistic licence when it came to direct sequels or series. Customers could be shockingly blind when it came to self-discovering in a bookstore. Sometimes, a trail of very obvious bread crumbs was the only solution.

Book in place, he turned just as the bell rang, signalling a customer. He headed to the front counter.

As he walked away from *Callahan's Lot*, the words from that weird phone call came back to him, unbidden.

There's a Book. A bad Book. You need to stay away from it.

◆ ◆ ◆

THE CUSTOMER TURNED out to be a like-minded reader to Dan. He'd blown through all of the stuff by King, McCammon, Masterton, Farris, De Felitta, and even Charles L. Grant, who Dan considered one of his secret weapons for recommendations.

After a lot of back and forth, Dan finally hit on Shirley Jackson's *The Haunting of Hill House*. The customer hadn't read it.

"Okay," Dan said, pulling the book from the shelf, "then you have to remedy that quick."

"That good?" the customer said, swiping the shoulder-length hippy hair from his face. Totally seventies look, completely out of style, but it sure as hell was better than all those moussed and gelled freestanding hair structures he was seeing more and more.

Shit, man, he thought. *Sounding more and more like my old man every day.*

"Yeah," Dan said, "it's that good. Don't expect the Masterton gore. King and Grant take a lot of cues from her. It's quieter horror, but the creeping dread will get you."

The man nodded his shaggy head. "Righteous." He handed it to Dan. "Sold. Wrap it up."

Dan took the book and, as he turned to head back to the counter, just a few books over from where the Jackson had sat, he saw something that caught his eye.

In the King books, tucked neatly between *'Salem's Lot* and *The Shining*, was another King book.

But it wasn't the *Callahan's Lot* book he'd put there not ten minutes ago. He plucked the book out on his way by, and headed to the counter.

♦ ♦ ♦

The shaggy dude trotted out of The Last Word, his new book already tucked into his back pocket. *Another satisfied customer,* Dan thought, and found himself a little jealous that the guy was about to experience Shirley Jackson's best story for the first time.

He watched the guy as he headed down the street until he was out of sight.

"Righteous," he said, and smiled.

Then he looked down to the book he'd snagged on his way to the counter. Another Stephen King novel. Something called *The Doors*.

Another one I've never heard of? What the hell?

But this time, it was something other than the fact he'd never heard of it that stuck out to him.

This time, it was the cover.

Dan picked up the book, getting a better look at the illustration. Under the author's name and book title, Dan was looking at a desert scene, but with craggy peaks. Like Nevada or something close to it. The sky was fading from blood red to the indigo of night, and painting the desert in similar tones.

The silhouette of a man stood in the foreground, facing away from the viewer. Facing four doors, floating side by side. Each door was open and each one looked in on a different scene.

The first showed the inside of a car. Through the shattered window, the hood of the car was buckled from hitting what looked like a rock wall. But the vehicle itself was empty. Nothing but a couple of coffee cups, their contents splashed around the interior.

The second showed an empty jail cell. A pad of paper and a pen were on the floor, looking like they'd been casually tossed, or maybe dropped there.

The third showed a bed. Under the covers, the forms of two people were visible. But where the heads and shoulders should be emerging from the top of the blankets, there was nothing but two pillows, indented with the shapes of non-existent heads.

The final door looked in on a school hallway. Lockers lined both sides of the hall, broken only by classroom entrances. But the lockers were dented and bent, as though a great weight had been thrown against them. In the foreground, on the right side, a bloody palm print was imprinted on a locker door. Down the middle of the hallway, the floor was streaked with blood. It looked like a body had been dragged the length of the passage.

Dan looked at the title again.

The Doors.

This one was scaring the shit out of him because those four scenes were ringing some bells in his head.

He set the book down, very gently and very quietly, on the counter again.

"What the hell?" he whispered.

CHAPTER SEVEN

I PRETTY MUCH jump out of my skin. After the day I've had, the last thing I need is a goddamn jump scare.

I spin around. "Talia," I say, my tone far too strident for my own liking, "you *gotta* start using doors."

Talia sits on our plush sectional couch, her arms draped across the tops of the cushions, looking ridiculously gorgeous, as always. If I'd met her before me and Lex got back together…

Then again, no. This whole appearing out of thin air thing would get to me.

"It would," she says. "But I thank you for the compliment."

Get out of my head, Talia.

"What?" Lex says, looking between the two of us. "What'd I miss?"

I give Talia the side-eye and lean forward, cupping Lex's face in my hands and kissing her nose. "Nothing, babe."

Lex looks at me dubiously. "Nothing," she says. "Right."

She knows as well as I do. It's *never* nothing with Talia.

"If you two are finished with all your non-verbal communication?" Talia says. Then she laughs.

Talia frigging *laughs*.

That's a sight so rare that it should be noted on calendars.

"Talia," Lex says. "There's something weird going on."

The smile fades. She drops her hands to her lap as she leans forward. "Okay," she says. "I'm listening."

For the next few minutes, Lex and I go back and forth,

telling the story, dropping in details the other missed. Through it all, Talia sits quietly, at one point easing back into the cushions. After that, it was all eye movements. Narrowing. Looking down in thought. Looking up to reference a memory. Eye contact with whichever of us were speaking.

When we finish, Lex and I look at each other, and our hands meet over the table.

Talia sits there for a long time, silently concatenating all the information. Eventually, she says, "Interesting."

I say, "Seriously? 'Interesting'? That's all you've got?"

"No, there's a lot more, I'm just determining how to say it."

"Just say it," Lex prompts. I nod.

"To be fair," Talia says, "I'm truly out of my depth on this one. You have to remember, I'm just running on the fumes of the access I used to have with the Book."

We nod.

"So, take what I say in the spirit in which it's given. A somewhat experienced amateur, working on decades-old knowledge."

"You're guessing," I say. "Got it. Moving on." I roll my hand.

"The fact that I can hear you mention my name, and appear here instantaneously, regardless of wherever I am," she says, "relates to the fact that I know you, I've interacted with you both, and I've been inside both your minds."

"Creepy, by the way," Lex says. Again, I nod.

"Yet helpful," she says. "It's the same reason I was able to…do what I did back when I was a kid." Which was thirty-five years ago, though no one could ever tell from her unaging face. She looks younger than Lex and I, despite being a couple of decades older.

And seriously, the less said about what she did back when she was a kid, the better. That path leads only to pain and sorrow.

"Your point?" Lex says.

"My point is, Monica has made contact, more than once, if only briefly, with someone that, yes, she's blood-related to, but she's never met. He was literally dead before you were born."

"But, technically, we did have some overlap."

Talia points a finger at me. "Good point. You were in the womb while he was still around." Her hand drops, and her eyes lose focus. "I just question whether that's enough of a connection. It seems tenuous."

"What else could it be?" Lex asks.

"I...have a couple of ideas, but they're very much outlandish conjecture at this point, Lex," Talia says. "And though I know you're curious, Monica, it would be inconsiderate of me to throw them out until we know a bit more. I'd prefer to give you a more studied theory, if that's okay."

I can respect that. I nod.

Then Lex asks the question I was about to toss out there.

"So how do we learn more?" She reaches out, picks up her phone. "Without necessarily killing any more expensive technology?"

◆ ◆ ◆

THE THREE OF us enter The Second-Last Word about five minutes before the store is due to close.

Talia peels off to lose herself amongst the stacks until we're ready for her. She's got a thing for urban fantasy books—says she finds them hilarious—and also kids' books. Dr. Seuss, especially. She's very serious about her Seuss.

I've learned—very much the hard way—to not use any humour or sarcasm, or project any sort of negativity toward the Seuss books. I can crack jokes all day long about Kelley

Armstrong, Laurell K. Hamilton, Kim Harrison, or Charlaine Harris—most of whom I've read and enjoyed—but go near Seuss and the claws come out.

Lex and I angle the other way, toward the counter. Both Muracks are there, Val collating the day's receipts, and Gabe counting the cash. I've asked him time and time again to do that in the backroom, but he insists that, should any customer come in, he'll immediately hide what he's doing.

So, until we get robbed, I've pretty much given up on trying to school the man. Besides, I think it's his not-so-subtle protest at me not listening to his advice about living in sin with my female partner.

Gabe and Val accept it, but they don't dig it. But we've settled into an unspoken détente that seems to work well enough.

I wait until Gabe's done his current count—because it's also amusingly easy to get him to lose count, hell, just ask him the time or date—and then say, "How'd it go today?"

"Good," Gabe says, and Val nods.

"You okay, honey?" Val says.

"Yeah," I say, and I'm terrible at hiding the fact that I am in no way, under any stretch of the imagination, doing okay.

"Monica just kind of needed a mental health day," Lex says, jumping in.

"Don't we all," Val says.

"Don't we all what?" Colum says, coming out from the back with some new releases for tomorrow. "Heeeeyyyyy, Monica," he says, then his voice changes, gets artificially smoother. "Heeeeyyyyy, Lex, how *you* doin'?"

"Doin' great, Colum," Lex says.

"Still gay?"

"Still gay, Colum."

"You know I could change your mind."

"You and I both know you couldn't, kiddo," she says, then laughs. This is pretty much their standard routine. "And the age difference doesn't do you any favours. I prefer my partners more seasoned."

"And female," I say.

"Right," she says. "That too."

"Ah-*may*-zing!" Colum says, undeterred. "Me too!"

Both Hedges and I question whether the kid has even had a partner yet, but we weren't going to burst his bubble.

"Y'know, Colum," Lex says, "gotta say, what you lack in finesse, you do make up for in youthful exuberance."

"Oh, Lexi," he says and I wince. Lex isn't a fan of that twist of her name, but at least the kid has stopped calling her Sexy Lexi…under threat of job loss, but still. "You and I both know that my youthful exuberance just means I'd love you long time."

I glance over at the puckered faces of both Muracks. Both quite devout in their religion, both senior citizens, they're not a fan of Colum's youthful exuberance. But it does get Gabe to gather up the cash drawer and the money and head back to the office to finish counting.

Score one for Colum.

Val finishes up the receipts and pulls the keys from the drawer. "I'll lock up," she says.

Colum is, of course, blissfully ignorant of the carnage. Instead, he hears a noise at the far end of the store, sets the new releases down, peeks around the stacks, and whispers, "Holy *shit*! Talia's here!"

I cover my nose and mouth to bury my amusement as he stands a little straighter, rakes his hands through his unruly mop of red hair, then his even more unruly beard, then heads through the stacks. "Talia…"

Lex watches him go, then turns to me, hands out, palms up. "And suddenly, I'm a cigarette he smokes and casts aside?"

I shrug. "The Siren song of the magical being is a seduction that can't be denied," I say. I'm still trying not to laugh.

"Siren song, hell," Lex says in mock outrage. "I'm the

keeper of a damn magical Staff!"

"Yeah, but Talia's got a phenomenal set." I point to my chest to illustrate.

"Yeah," Lex says. "Okay. Fair point."

Val crosses back to the counter and puts the keys away. "You sticking around?" she says.

"Yeah, Val. Just some business to take care of."

I can almost watch the thought as it forms in her mind. *What sort of business can there be that involves Lex and Spooky Talia?* But she doesn't ask it. Just nods and heads back to hurry her husband up.

Around the same time, Colum rounds one of the stacks and heads to the office. Seconds later, he's back out front with his jacket and keys and heading out the door. "Uh…bye, Colum," I say. He doesn't look back as the door swings shut behind him.

"That child is insufferable," Talia says, leaning against one of the bookshelves.

"What did you do to him?" Lex says.

"Just put a burning desire in him to be at home, in his bedroom, for exactly two hours. Probably feels like the need to pee really bad, but in his head. Once he gets there, he'll be fine. And in two hours, he'll be able to leave his room."

"You know he'll likely spend that two hours…" And here Lex makes the curled hand motion that universally indicates the act of a male pleasuring himself.

"He may," Talia says, but then grins wickedly, "but he'll eventually figure out he just can't finish."

"Wow," Lex says.

"I'll not have that cretin ejaculating to thoughts of me."

"You're a mean one, Mr. Grinch."

Thankfully, the Muracks come out and said their goodbyes, breaking the ungodly image I have of Colum whacking away, denied his O-face.

Blech.

◆ ◆ ◆

I LOCK THE doors and then head into the office and kill all the lights. There's still enough light that comes in through the windows so we're fine. It won't be dark for another hour or two.

Lex and Talia are standing in front of the counter, like two customers waiting for service.

"What do we do now?" I ask.

"I think you need to try one more time to contact your father," Talia says.

"You think it makes a difference here?"

"I do."

"Why?"

"Time and space are strange things," Talia says. "I'm not going to pretend I understand any of it, but I've looked into a lot of research to try any understand both what I'm capable of doing, and what I did when I was a kid."

"Okay," I say. "I get that. You flip around from place to place, so that's the space aspect, but where does time kick in?"

"Two ways," she says. The first, she says, is that flipping around from place to place, thing. "For example," she says, "earlier today. I imagine for you, you mentioned something about calling me and then, to your mind, I *appeared* on your couch almost immediately."

"That's about right," Lex says.

"And it's friggin' *creepy*, Talia," I add.

"My point is, that's how it appears for you," Talia says. She leans against the counter and pokes a finger on the surface. "I'm here." She leans over, a span of four feet or so, and pokes a second finger down. "And you two are here." Lex and I nod. "You mention me. I get the feeling I'm needed."

"And boom, you go from there to here," Lex says, indicating both spots.

"Exactly wrong," Talia says. "I get the feeling, but I don't know how long I'm going to be, so I have a shower, then eat something, and then I head over."

"You…what…teleport?"

"Like *Star Trek*, or that blue guy from *X-Men*?" I say.

Talia's turn to scrunch her face. "What's an X-Man?"

"Not the point, Tal," I say. I point to the two locations she mapped out. "You disappear from there, and reappear here?"

"No," she says. "I walk."

"That makes no sense," I say.

"And still…" she says, shrugging.

Lex pumps her hands, palm out, toward Talia. "Hold on hold on hold on," she says. "Back the bus up. We were in the middle of freaking nowhere, Canada, a few months ago, and—"

"You needed me," Talia finishes. "So I came."

"You expect us to believe you walked across two provinces?"

"Yes," Talia says, and the calmness in her voice is strangely irritating. "I've gone much further."

"What if we'd been in Spain, or something?" Lex says, quite reasonably, I think.

"Trickier," Talia states calmly. "But doable."

"Trickier?" Lex says. "*Trickier*? The fuck does that even *mean*?"

"I thought you once said something about moving under the skin of the world," I say.

"Also true."

"Are you fucking with us, Talia?" Lex says.

"I think we're drifting off point," I say. "Talia, your point?"

Talia inclines her head toward me in thanks. "My point is, to you, I appear instantaneously, or close enough. For me, it's hours or days between initial thought and connection."

"Trickier…" Lex says under her breath. Her eyes widen, and she spears a quick look at Talia, then away again.

"I know what you're thinking, Lex." Talia raises her hands and waggles her fingers. "Spooky Talia."

"Not gonna lie," Lex says. "Goddamn right."

"It's my thing, I guess." She turns back to me. "My point is, space is different for me, but time more so."

"Fair enough," I say. "I have questions, but they'll have to wait. You said there was two things…"

"I did," she says. Talia mentions her lack of aging. She tells us that, after doing a lot of reading on the subject, that she doesn't think the Book slowed down her aging biologically. Instead, she's come to believe that she's moving slower through time. "Imagine it like a highway. All the cars are zipping along, but there's this one car that's just crawling along, well under the speed limit. I'm that car."

"That just brings up a ton more questions," Lex say. Her face scrunches as she considers them all. "Like, for example, how —"

Talia holds up a hand. "Trust me, Lex, when I tell you it's very easy to fall down these ratholes and get lost. If I have a point to all of this, it's that time is not a constant thing. It's mutable. Time is often compared to a river, but I've found, like a river, some parts flow faster than others. There are eddies and strange currents. And, depending on who's navigating, it can also be traversed against the current."

"Okay," Lex says. "Like Monica, I have questions, but they'll wait." She looks to me, back to Talia, to the phone, to the two imaginary points Talia had indicated on the counter. "You started this whole thing by saying you thought it makes a difference being here. Why?"

Talia nods. "I think it makes a difference because of where Monica's father is."

"1984?"

"No." Talia pops her index finger, points to the ground. "Here." I angle my head toward one shoulder, not getting it.

"Where was your father's bookstore, Monica?"

"Here."

"And," Talia says, "you kept the same layout, didn't you?"

"It's the exact layout," I say. I was rather proud of myself when I found enough photos and notes to pay someone to essentially recreate my father's store. I've even, as much as I could, kept the genre areas in the same spots.

"So, if you're standing *there* making the call, your father—"

"—would be standing in pretty much the exact same spot." Talia smiles. "Exactly."

"So, you're thinking there's some sort of proximity effect that helps things along."

"I do."

Lex and I both nod. I mean, this is all in the realm of woo-woo science, with an unhealthy dose of uninformed conjecture to spackle up the cracks, but damned if it doesn't sound somewhat feasible.

"So, what do we do now?" I ask.

"Like I said," Talia says. "I think you need to try one more time to contact your father."

Chapter Eight

HE KNEW WHAT was going through his mind, but he needed to try it with someone else with similar experiences. His father wasn't the right guy. There was only one thing he could think of to do. One person to try it with.

He would take the book home to Lila.

◆ ◆ ◆

HE ENTERED THEIR apartment, and the smell of dinner made his mouth water. Lila was a crazy good cook, and pregnancy had somehow seemed to up her game.

I'm gonna end up with a pregnancy belly, too, if she keeps cooking like this, he thought. *Woman's gonna kill me.*

Still, it'd be a hell of a way to die. Death by extreme satisfaction. He could think of worse ways.

Lila was in the living room with a book propped on her belly. She was barely showing, only about five months in at this point, but she was starting to get a touch sensitive about it. Which was kind of weird, because a month ago, they'd been shopping for a crib and change table, and she'd been complaining that she wasn't showing yet.

"The cashier's gonna think I'm weird, shopping for baby stuff, not looking pregnant."

"Yes," Dan had said. "*You're* gonna be seen as weird. Just you. Not the guy with you."

"You know what I mean."

Though he'd laughed, he had to admit, he kind of didn't know what she meant. She was pregnant. Baby was coming in a few months. So they bought stuff for the baby. Who cared whether Lila had a baby bump or not?

Dan's father always said he wasn't one for giving a lot of advice. But when Dan had related that shopping story, Stan had said, "Just gonna tell you one thing, son. Unless it's insulting to her, you agree. You don't have to necessarily agree with her here" —Stan tapped his temple with a finger— "and you absolutely don't have to understand it. But you agree. And, if necessary, you add a 'don't worry about it,' or a 'it's gonna be fine' after it."

"Okay."

"Trust me," his father said. "Makes life simpler."

"I guess."

"You guess?" His father blew out a breath. "What do you say if she says she's not showing enough."

"Um…I…agree?"

"You agree and say, don't worry about it. What if she says she looks like a hippo?"

"I…I agree?"

"No, Dan," he said. "Weren't you listening? That's insulting. You *don't* agree to that. You tell her she's beautiful."

"Right. Beautiful. Got it."

His father had leaned in then, almost nose to nose with his son. "She's. Beautiful."

"I understand," Dan said. And Lila was beautiful. Always had been. Always would be. "She is. Even one of our teachers used to say that. 'Women are the only true works of art.' I get it."

"That's a smart teacher."

Was, Dan thought. *Was a smart teacher. Hassy. Wish he'd made it through that high school thing.*

"One last one. She says she wants broccoli and ice cream for dinner."

"What? That's…"

"…a distinct possibility. Broccoli and ice cream."

"I really don't like broc—"

His father gave him a look.

"I agree."

"You agree wholeheartedly. 'Why yes, Lila, my love, broccoli and ice cream sounds delicious!'" His dad clasped his hands together. "I'll head straight out and get some. Is there a particular flavour or brand of ice cream?"

Dan laughed. "I don't think it'll come to—"

"Son, that woman is carrying your child. She says jump, you say how high. She says shit, you hold out your hand. Got it?"

They were both smiling now, but Dan also knew when his dad was serious. This was valuable information, and he filed it away with the important knowledge. "Got it, Dad. Thanks."

He kicked off his shoes as Lila marked her place in the book and closed it. "Dinner smells awesome, Lee," he said. "As usual."

"Cannelloni," she said.

"I love you," he said.

"You just love my cannelloni, Dan my man." She saw the paper bag under his arm. "New book?"

He was always bringing home a new book. He had a ridiculous stack of books waiting to be read, yet somehow, he always found a new one that he had to read first. She was used to it. It had kind of killed him to have to pack away some of his books to get the baby room ready. He'd managed to shoehorn a decent-sized bookshelf into their living room, but he'd had to make some hard decisions on some of the books. Two full boxes had been packed and stored. A well, one day, when they were rich and famous and living in the biggest house in New Hope…

But the one under his arm was a whole different matter. "It's a book," he said. "But…"

"But…?"

"Do me a favour, will you?"

She raised an eyebrow in question.

"Just…" He handed over the paper bag with the book inside. "Just pull it out and tell me what you see?"

The raised eyebrow dropped, then both scrunched up as she set the bagged book on her lap. "Okay…" she said uncertainly.

"Just humour me for a minute." Dan indicated the bag. "Just pull it out and tell me what you notice."

Lila reached into the bag slowly, like there was something in there that was going to bite her. She pulled it out just as slowly, but when she confirmed it was just a book, she pulled it out all the way and set it on her lap, discarding the bag on the coffee table.

"Heavier than I expected," she started.

"Okay," Dan said. "What else?" He expected the usual distaste at Stephen King — try as he might, Lila wasn't a fan.

Instead, she looked intrigued. "This looks interesting," she said. "Did you get this for me?"

Dan was too shocked to formulate an answer, so he stayed silent.

She held the book up to him. *Yes, yes,* he thought. *Stephen King.* The Doors. *Four doors on the cover.*

"I love true crime."

What?

She waggled the book. "And about New Hope? Even cooler." His face must have shown his confusion. "Babe," she said. "Do you not see the title?"

"Just…tell me what it is."

She gave him another furrowed-brow look. "It's called *New Hope, Old Disappearances*, by Danika Hilliers." Then she stopped. Stared at the cover. "Danika? Like *our* Danika? That we went to school with? That's wild."

Dan's heart was beating against the wall of his chest like it was trying to break out. "What..." His voice came out thin, reedy. He cleared his throat and tried again. "What do you see on the cover?"

Another look from the book to him. The kind that said, "You're kinda freaking me out here because you can see the book as plainly as I can."

"Please, Lee," he said, throat dry. "It's important."

"Okay," she said. "I see the title, the author, and then the desk, maybe a cop's desk? With four photos on it. Like they're evidence photos or something."

"And the photos?"

"One's the inside of a car, all smashed up. Looks like a cup of coffee or something fell." He watched her eyes flick to the next one. And he knew what she was going to say. "The next is a jail cell with paper and pen on the floor?"

"The next is a bed with no one in it, right?"

She looked at the book, looked at him. "Yeaaah," she said, drawing the word out to show the obviousness of the observation.

"And the last is a shot down the hallway of our old school? Bloody handprint?"

"Dan," she said. "Geez! You know all this. You brought it to me." She held the book up.

The Doors. Stephen King. That's what he saw. *The Doors.* Not *New Hope, Old Disappearances.*

"Yeah."

"What?" she said. "You act like you can't see it."

"I...can't."

"What?"

"I can't," Dan said. "I don't see what you see."

"What do you mean?"

"I mean, Lee," he said. "I see you holding up a book. I understand that you see a book called *New Hope, Old…*"

"*Old Disappearances*, by Danika Hillier, who we went to school with."

"Yeah…" he said. He drew a breath, then continued. "But what I *see* is a Stephen King novel that doesn't actually exist. I can find no record of it anywhere. It's not on any booklist that we purchase from at the store. Not even that specialty publisher that did that *Dark Tower* book you weren't happy about me buying."

"It was friggin' expensive, Dan."

"Okay, not the point. The point is, you see a true crime book. I see a Stephen King book that doesn't freaking exist. But that's still what I *see*. It's called *The Doors* and the cover shows four doors out in a desert, floating above the sand. But inside those doors is basically the same for images you see on your cover."

"I don't…get…" — Lila sighed — "…what?" She put out a hand to his. "Are you okay? You're not having a stroke? An aneurysm or something?"

"I'm not ruling it out," he said. *Because what I'm saying sounds goddamn crazy, even to me.* "But I don't think so. I'm pretty sure my dad saw a completely different book from me and you. He told me to shelve it in general fiction. Yours would be non-fic, and mine would be horror."

His wife rapped her knuckles against the cover of the book, then set it down on the coffee table. "I'm sorry," she said. "I don't think I understand."

"That makes two of us, babe." Then Dan had another thought. "Do me one more favour?"

"Sure."

"Try reading it."

"Sure," she said, then saw his expression. "You mean, like, right now?"

"Yeah."

"...okaaay," she said, again, drawing the word out. She sighed, reached out for the book on the table, lifting it toward her again. Dan heard her mumble, "damn thing's *heavy*," before placing it on her lap. She gave him a quick, uncertain glance, then opened the cover and flipped to the first page of text. And then she just slowed down to a dead stop.

"Lee?"

She remained exactly in place. Book on lap, hand holding the cover and first few pages open, other hand on her belly. Dan consciously avoided looking at the text. Lila's head was angled down toward it, her long hair a curtain on one side. He got down on one knee, angled in, and looked at her face. She was breathing, but shallowly. Her eyes didn't move. Nothing moved, except her lips. She didn't blink. Not a twitch of a finger.

Fuck me.

He was sure that if he pushed her, she'd fall over like a statue.

Dan didn't push her over. Instead, he put a hand on her shoulder and gently shook her. "Lee," he said.

Nothing.

A harder shake. "Lila!"

Nothing.

He reached over, pried her hand off the cover, and closed it. Then he moved his hand to her cheek. It was warm as he gently angled her head away from the book and toward him. Her eyes didn't track like normal, sighting something, then sighting something else, working toward him. Instead, they simply remained staring, unseeing as her face moved.

What if she stays like this? That terrified him. Then, something worse. *What about our baby?*

He put his other hand on her other cheek, cupping her face with a slight pressure. He yelled loudly, "Lila! Baby! Come back to me!"

She blinked.

He watched her closely, saw her come back by quick degrees, her eyes finally looking around, finding him. Her mouth parting, her breath coming more normally.

"Babe?" he said.

"Thought you wanted me to read it?" she said. "Why'd you stop me?"

"I didn't."

She smiled. "Yeah, you did."

"Remember the other night when I spaced out?"

"Yeah."

"Yeah, you just did the same thing."

"I did?"

"What did you read?"

"I just got a couple of words in. 'The sleepy town...' and that's it."

"And I don't think you'll ever be able to get past that."

She moved to open the book cover again, and he put a hand over hers to stop her. "No," he said. "I don't ever want to see you haze out like that ever again."

He pulled the book from her lap and slid it back into the bag. "I think the less time we spend with this thing, the better."

"Again," she said, "you're kinda freaking me out, Dan."

He folded the top of the bag down, then rolled it down until it was tight to the book, as though trying to seal it in.

"Well," he said, "if it makes you feel any better, Lee, I'm kinda freaking myself out, too."

◆ ◆ ◆

"TELL ME WHAT you make of the cover."

"Pretty obvious," Lila said. "The first three pictures reference all that craziness from...what? Ten years ago?"

"More like seven. Late 1976. About a year after Mom's accident. I was just thirteen. I remember hearing "More Than a Feeling" and being blown away by it, probably the first thing that had really gotten through to me since we lost Mom. Then my dad coming in my room and telling me about all the disappearances."

"Yeah," Lila said, "that's right. I think my thirteenth birthday was the next weekend, so that would be right. Wow, almost exactly seven years ago." Lila's birthday was coming up soon.

She nodded in confirmation, then held up four fingers. "The two missing cops from the police car," she said, ticking off a finger. "Spooky Talia's mom in jail." Another finger down. "And the two others…older couple."

"Mr. and Mrs. Kovacs," Dan said. "She was a pain in the ass—"

Lila waggled a finger at him. "Swear jar." They were trying to curb the language before the baby arrived.

"Dammit!" Dan said, then clapped a hand to his mouth.

"Swear jar times two," Lila said.

Dan pulled out his wallet, dropped two dollars in a big pickle jar they had sitting by the coffee table. "So, anyway," he said, "she was a pain in the butt. Came in the bookstore all the time. Drove Dad nuts."

"That's the first three," she said, dropping the third finger. "And the last one's really obvious."

"Yeah," Dan said.

"Yeah," she said, and dropped the last finger and put her hand back in her lap.

It wasn't a topic of conversation amongst many in the town, and especially not from the roughly two hundred kids who didn't get killed or go missing from Clarington District High School. Lila and Dan had lost a lot of friends that evening.

In the span of about a half hour.

Lila had never been big on school stuff. She got through her days, then, in her words, "ran screaming from the building and never thought about it until I had to set foot in it again." School and Lila were never going to be friends.

Dan, while never a stellar student, didn't mind it. He did like Hassy — Mr. Hasselton who was always in charge of the sets for the musicals — and would try to help out when he could.

But that day, Dan's father was sick as a dog, and had received a particularly large book shipment and was demanding that Dan come right after school to help him get it unpacked, catalogued, and shelved. It was boring work, but his dad had to be sick if he was asking for help. Stan Holt was a stubborn SOB who never asked for help.

His father's flu probably saved Dan's life. Dan's and Lila's, because she was happy to run screaming from the school to unpack books. Very few survivors walked away from the high school that afternoon.

Dennis "The Toad" Bussik never spoke of the evening, claiming he had no memory of it. No one believed him, but it didn't matter. He left town six months later. No one had heard from him since.

Laura Davis and Tom Popper were the only teachers who walked away. They seemed to be a bit of an item when they came out, but that ended quickly. Popper ended up getting a woman pregnant, then ate a bullet Hemingway-style about a year ago. Davis, who was Spooky Talia's aunt, of all things, left town shortly afterward. Both of them, like Bussik, always claimed they could not remember any of it.

Marcia Mayer, originally thought among the dead, was found the next day, murdered some miles away in a scuzzy hotel in Oval Lake. There was speculation around Theo Clarke doing the killing, but there were just as many people who thought he was one of the ones who hadn't made it out. But that was it. Four people, possibly five. Two dead not long after, the other two not talking and now gone.

And that was what the last picture on the cover of the book, whether it was Lila's version, or Dan's, was referencing.

"You know that line I hate in books and movies?" Lila said.

"The 'I'm just one woman' one?"

"No, the other one."

"Oh, yeah, that one," Dan said.

"Yeah, well, I'm going to say it now."

Dan nodded.

Lila pulled a comically bewildered expression, threw her hands out, and said, "But what does it mean?"

Dan looked at his wife. "I get why you hate that line. But it's pretty appropriate here, huh?"

"It is."

"I guess…" Dan's voice faded off. "I think what it means is, this book, for whatever reason, is trying to remind us of these past two horrible events."

"Remind us?"

"You don't think so?"

"Well, is it to remind us," she said, "or is it to tell us?"

"Tell us what?"

"I don't know," Lila said, looking worried. "Maybe that it was responsible?"

There's a Book. A bad Book. You need to stay away from it.

Dan reached out for his pregnant wife's hands. "Babe, I gotta tell you something else that happened."

♦ ♦ ♦

OH, THESE DAMNABLE meatbags.

It had been so easy with the one in the school. Nyarlathotep had been able to reach out to him through the Book. Had been able to pull him in and make him say the words.

But these ones! The whelp. His father. His mate.

Try as Nyarlathotep might, there was always someone there to break the focus, to pull their soft minds back from the words. To shift their focus from the Book.

Still, there was another way. It would take more subtlety, and time.

Nyarlathotep had time.

All the time in the universe.

Chapter Nine

"Have you thought about what you'll say to him?" Talia says. The store is dark, and Talia sits cross-legged on the floor. We've got some music playing in the background. I'd never heard of the band, but Talia insisted on them, pulling her own damn CD from somewhere on her person. Something called Japan. Some album called *Quiet Life*. I expected to hate it, but it wasn't horrible.

But, to her question. Had I thought about it? "Yes and no," I say. "Lex and I talked about it." I go back to the conversation of only an hour or so ago.

So, good thoughts? Love?

Yeah. Love.

Then that's your starting point, hon.

Remembering the warmth of Lex's hand on my leg, I say, "I guess we just talk, and take it as it comes."

"No," Talia says. Rather bluntly, if I'm honest.

"No?" I say. "What do you mean, no?"

"You're planning on coming at it from the ooh-you're-my-daddy-and-even-though-I've-never-met-you-I-love-you-and-let's-connect-through-our-feelings sort of thing, right?"

Ouch. Real blunt, our Talia.

"I mean, when you say it like that…"

"What's the problem, Talia?" Lex says, obviously not quite as offended as I am right now. *Thank you for having my back, Lex.*

"Because these conversations don't seem to last a long time. They get cut off rather quickly, yes?" Talia raises her eyebrows at me for confirmation.

"Yeah," I say. "The first one was less than a minute before it cut off, and the second was just a couple of seconds before the phone melted.

"So time is of the essence," she says. "We need to get a few facts first, the need-to-know stuff, then if the connection remains, you can move on to the nice-to-know."

"What's the need-to-know?"

"You said that, in the first conversation, despite it being your first contact with him, it seemed like he'd believed he'd talked to you before. I'd like to know how many times before, and why he believes it was you."

"Okay," I say, "makes sense. I'd like to know that too."

I watch Lex reach over the sales counter and grab a pad of paper and a pen down and pull them toward her. When I meet her eyes, she says, "Taking notes." I give her a smile and a nod. I angle back to Talia. "Anything else?"

"I'd also like to know what the date and time is for him. Helps to get a better fix on how far the range is."

"I'm not sure I get what you mean."

"The Last Word was destroyed on—"

"The evening of Sunday, April first," I say. "1984. I was born at the end of the month, on the thirtieth."

"Right," Talia says. "You're reaching him, though, when you call. So obviously you're getting through sometime before that date. My question is, how long before? A few days? A few months?"

"Got it. Anything else?"

"If you can find out if he's doing anything on his end to make this happen, that would be helpful."

"You think he is?" Lex asks.

"No, I really don't think so," Talia says. "Seems like a

stretch for him to put something in play in the hope that his as-yet-unborn daughter will somehow magically reach back through time to contact him, doesn't it?"

Lex and I both nod.

"Still, it's worth asking the question."

Lex jots it down.

"That it?"

"I think we'll be lucky to get all of that before the call cuts, so yes, I think that's it."

Lex slides the notepad over to me. Her handwriting is ungodly chicken scratch, but I've learned over the months how to puzzle it out. The key is remembering that lower case *Rs* could actually be *Ns*, *CLs* could be *Ds* and so on.

Talia reaches out, rests her hand on the handset of the store phone. "Are you ready?"

No. "Yes." I turn the volume of the music right down.

"Then there's just one more thing to do," Talia says, and digs into one of her pockets.

♦ ♦ ♦

TALIA PULLS OUT a leather pouch with a drawstring, and hooks two fingers into the top to draw it open. She tips the bag and a tumble of teeth rattle out, clicking and bouncing across the counter top.

I see all sorts of teeth. Molars. Eye teeth. Smaller, lower teeth. But I also see what looks like teeth from different animals. Cat's fangs. Dog's fangs.

Then I see the vampire fangs.

"Talia?"

She's dragged the phone out toward the middle of the counter and is busy sliding the teeth into a rough circle around the base of the phone. "Protection," she says.

"So the phone doesn't melt?"

Talia stops for a moment. She looks distracted. She reaches down and plucks out one tooth. It's almost a couple of inches long, very sharp.

She stares at it intently.

Almost as though she's never seen it before.

"Talia?" I say.

She drags her gaze from the tooth. Looks at me, eyebrows raised.

"Protection," I say. "No melting phones, right?"

"Well, yes," she says, "that too, I guess."

"Then what else?" Lex says.

The tooth trapped under her index finger stops its slide toward the circle as she sharpens her eyes in Lex's direction.

"We're dealing with an arcane connection here, Lex," she says. "I have no idea where that connection comes from, where it passes through, and if anything can piggyback on it..." She slides the tooth into position. "The last time something got through, it didn't go well for the high school. I'd like to prevent a repeat performance."

"And the teeth help with that?"

"They do."

"Where'd all these teeth come from?" I ask.

Once again, Talia pauses, this time on a tooth I know came from the mouth of a vampire. Rory? *I wonder.* She says, "Trust me, Monica. You're better off not knowing."

I swallow. I nod. I shut up and let her do her thing.

When she finishes with the phone, she scoops a large handful of teeth and comes around to me. "Is this where you'll stand?"

I check my position against the phone, shift a bit closer, then say, "Yes."

Talia takes a knee and places a second circle around me. I try to not look at the teeth, but I find I snatch quick glances.

The teeth are very clean, gleaming white. There's a lot of them.

Look away, Monica, I think. *You're better off not knowing.*

It only takes a couple of minutes, then Talia's done.

She stands, pours the rest of her teeth back in the pouch. "That should help." She cinches the pouch closed. "You can dial your father whenever you're ready."

Chapter Ten

"**B**ABE, I GOTTA tell you something else that happened."

There's a Book. A bad Book. You need to stay away from it.

Lila searched his face. "And I really don't know how to say it without me sounding nuts."

"Okay then," Lila said, "you gather your thoughts and we'll get dinner out on the table before the cannelloni turns into burnelloni." She held out a hand. "Now, help a preggy lady up."

◆ ◆ ◆

HE PULLED THE dish from the oven. "As weird as this is gonna sound..." he started, then stuttered to a stop, just standing there, the cannelloni forgotten.

Lila waited patiently, though he could see the worry lines around her eyes, at the corners of her mouth. She just went on setting the table.

"Just gonna say it," he said. "Someone called the store the other day and claimed to be our daughter." He set the dish on the oven top and angled to see her reaction.

Lila opened her mouth to say something. Closed it again. Blinked. Glanced at him. Leaned on the table with both hands. Looked away. Looked back again. Narrowed her eyes.

She appeared more concerned than angry when she said, "Daniel Arthur Holt, are you fucking with me?"

"Swear jar."

"Fuck the swear jar."

"Times two."

"I don't have my purse…"

Dan pulled two more dollars from his wallet. "You owe me."

"Seriously, Dan," she said, "Please tell me you're just messing around."

"Wish I was, Lee."

"Says she's our daughter. *Our*" — she pointed from Dan to herself, back to Dan — "daughter."

"She did."

"Why would you believe her?" Lila said. "Because I'm getting the sense here that you actually did believe her."

He pulled the spatula from its hook. "She knows my full name —"

"Including the 'Arthur'?"

"Okay, no, but —"

"Then," Lila said, "*not* your full name."

"She knew Dad's name." He began ladling out the food onto the plates.

"Okay."

"And she knew how Mom died, and when."

"No offence, Dan," Lila said, "but anyone who's lived in this town for more than a few years probably knows all that too."

Which is fair, Dan thought.

"One other thing."

Lila waited. He finished loading the plates, picked them up, brought them to the table. Then he stood there, simply staring.

"What, Dan?"

"She said her name was Monica."

That slowed Lila down a bit. They had discussed, and decided, on calling their child after Dan's late mother if it was a girl. They were hoping it was a girl because they'd had very little luck agreeing on a boy's name.

But the whole naming it Monica thing? They'd both sworn to not tell a soul until it was time. Not even Dan's father, wanting to surprise him.

Lila sat down hard in the chair, then looked up to her husband. "Have you said anything to anyone?"

Dan drew an 'x' across his chest. "Cross my heart, Lee, not a word."

"Me neither."

"So…" Dan prompted. He sat down.

"So it's still a reasonably safe guess, Dan. I mean, my parents are both around. Your dad's around. Everyone knows you lost your mom eight years back. Would be a good guess to think you might name a daughter after your mom."

"Yeah, you're not wrong," he said. "But…"

"But who would be so damn cruel?"

"I don't know."

They both grew quiet then, and by unspoken agreement set to work on their food. Both ate in silence for a few minutes, lost in thought.

Lila speared some cannelloni with her fork, then pointed to Dan with it. "Okay, so she tried to wow you with some well-known facts," Lila said. "But, what did she want?"

"That was the really weird part," he said. He got up to refill his glass, and laid out the conversation as best he could remember it. By the end, Lila was laughing.

"You actually thought it was Jehovah's Witnesses?"

"Yeah," he said, sitting back down. "Little bit."

"What the heck are you supposed to be summoning?"

"No idea."

"But she specifically said to stay away from a book." She rolled her eyes then. "Pretty damn hard to do when you spend most of your life in a bookstore, if you ask me."

"See, that's the weird thing, Lee," he said, poking his fork toward her, making his point. "It wasn't 'stay away from the book,' it was more, 'stay away from the *Book*,' you know?"

"No, I don't."

"This…Monica…put a strange emphasis on the word. I can't explain it, and I can't say it like she did, can't get the inflection right, but it was obvious she was saying Book with a capital B. Like it's not *a* book, but *the* Book."

"Hence the whole Jehovah's thing." She smiled at him over the rim of her glass.

"Yeah." He smiled back. It was stupid, he knew.

"But she said it was somehow linked to the stuff in '76 and '81?"

"I could be wrong, but that's the way I took it, yeah."

"And you're telling me all this because you think that thing on our coffee table is *the Book*?" Lila leaned into the last two words, adding an extra oomph.

Dan glanced over at the book, safely hidden in its paper bag. "Yeah," he said. "I think I do."

Another few moments of reflection as they finished their dinner. When the plates were empty and their bellies full, Dan scooped up their dishes and took them to the sink. Lila knew better than to try and help. Since she'd gotten pregnant, Dan treated her like a fragile thing. It drove her crazy, he knew, but she also told him he was sweet, which was good. He started the water running in the sink, got the coffee going, then pulled down some containers to stow the leftovers.

Lila said, "You sure I can't help?"

"Positive. You sit on your cute little—"

"Careful. Swear jar."

"—*butt* and let me clean up," he said, smiling.

As he worked away, Lila said, "Tell me why."

"Why what?"

"Tell me why you think that thing on my coffee table is this *Book*." Again with the oomph.

He flicked a sidelong glance at her. "I know it sounds stupid, Lee," he said, chagrined.

"Stop that," she said. "Tell me why."

"Like I said, I think I've seen the same book as two different King novels. Neither of which exist. I'm sure Dad saw it as another book altogether. I bring it home to you, and you see an entirely different book, and I can't see what you're seeing. I still see *The Doors* by King."

"And why do you think it changes?"

"Because Dad doesn't seem to think there's been a book written since the late 1960s that's worth reading unless it's Norman Mailer or Arthur Hailey, and he *hates* Stephen King. I love the guy. You don't like horror, but your favourite read is…"

"Real murders."

"Right. *Helter Skelter* and all that Manson stuff." Dan shut the water off, and started washing the dishes.

"There's more to it than Manson, but yeah."

"So," Dan said, spreading his soapy palms out, "I can't speak for what Dad saw, but I saw one of my favourite authors and subjects, you saw your favourite subject. All from the same book."

"So?"

"So, it's gotta be this weird Book that she was talking about."

"No other explanation?"

"No," he said. "You have one?"

"I think you have to consider the source, my love."

"What do you mean?"

Lila stood, came over to stand behind Dan. She put her arms around his waist and leaned into him, her belly to his back. "Not sure if you've noticed, but this is a womb, not a phone booth. Not a lot of room in there."

Dan smiled, grabbed the dish cloth, dried his hands. *My baby's in there. Our baby.* He turned, put his own arms around Lila.

"And, though you may not have noticed, there's no phone lines dangling out of my lady parts, making it even harder for her to make outgoing calls to her daddy."

And Dan then realized exactly how stupid it all sounded.

He dropped his head, lightly meeting Lila's forehead with his own. "Dammit."

♦ ♦ ♦

LATER THAT EVENING, sweaty from a spontaneous lovemaking session, they both lay quietly, staring at the ceiling, letting the thoughts swirl around their heads.

Eventually, Lila reached out and ruffled Dan's damp hair. "What's going on in that furry mind of yours, slim?"

He turned toward her, put a hand on her belly. "I don't know what to do."

"In regard to what?" She placed her own on top of his.

"All of it," he said. "The calls. This Book." He took a breath, scrubbed his hand down his face. "I'm worried, Lee. I'm worried this thing might actually have something to do with all that bad shit that happened before. I mean, I can't explain what you and I are seeing. Can you?"

"I'm sure there's some explanation," she said, "…but…no, no I can't give you a plausible explanation."

"So, if that's the case, then doesn't that maybe open up— okay, maybe 'open up' is too strong a term, how about 'open the door a crack'—so doesn't that open the door just a crack that maybe…"

"No, Dan, I'm sorry," Lila said. "I can't explain what's going on with that"—she pointed vaguely to their living room—"but I can't get behind the idea that this child, the one still inside me, is somehow reaching out to you via phone calls."

"Yeah, I guess—"

Lila laughed. "You guess? You *guess*? Dan, I love you, but this is why I don't read your Stephen King shit. That is some Stephen King shit, right there."

"Swear jar."

She patted her naked body. "Sorry, left my wallet in my other birthday suit."

"You owe me."

"Not after the past hour we just had, mister," she said. They both chuckled.

"Fine," Dan said, holding up a finger. "You get one pass. This time."

"You're so kind."

"I know it, that's why you love me," he said. "But seriously, no disparagement of the King of Horror will be tolerated."

"You know what I'm saying."

"Yes, dear."

"Oh, you did *not* just 'yes, dear' me, Mr. Holt."

"Only if you did *not* just 'Mr. Holt' me, Mrs. Holt."

"Dan?"

"Yeah?"

"Did you feel that?" she said, a smile breaking like the sun across her face.

"I did."

"She just kicked, didn't she?"

"Yeah." Then both of them said, "Oh my god," at the same time.

All thoughts of anything but the miracle they'd made were forgotten.

◆ ◆ ◆

THE NEXT EVENING, after dinner, Lila was perched in her spot on the dining room chair while Dan did the dishes. The stereo was playing an album by The Alan Parsons Project.

Dan placed a plate on the drying rack. Lila said, "So, what are you going to do about this whole Monica-our-daughter-is-trying-to-warn-me-of-something situation?"

"Honestly don't know," he said, scrubbing at the next plate, wondering why Lila's were always messier and harder to get clean. "I don't even know if she'll ever call back."

"Well," Lila said, sipping at her coffee, "the way I see it is, she might not, but you should be ready if she does."

"Ready how?" He rinsed the plate, put it on the rack.

"Well, the biggest question right now is, she's claiming to be our kid, right?"

"Right." The jangle of metal on metal as he grabbed up the utensils to wash.

"So, have some questions ready to ask in case she does call back. Questions that will prove she's actually who she says she is, or more likely, blow serious holes in her story."

"Okay, good idea." He paused, considering. "What should I ask?"

"Gotta be something she can't know just by living in New Hope or the area."

"Maybe middle names? You and me?"

"Maybe." She considered. "Maybe the layout of our apartment?" She shook her head. "No, still kind of easy."

"Well, I've got two ideas. One's easy for us, one's more complicated."

"Easy one?"

"My nickname for you from our first date."

"Okay, yeah, you've never told anyone that one, right?"

"Nope, that was strictly a you-and-me thing."

"But it's something we'd tell our daughter, right?"

"Let's tell her — assuming it's a her — right now." Dan hung his dishtowel over his shoulder, moved toward her, and dropped to his haunches. He gently cupped Lila's belly in his hands. "Okay, honey, on your mother's and my first date, I kept calling her *LIE-lah* and she kept telling me it was *LEE-lah*. So, because I couldn't seem to get it through my head, I came up with a nickname for her."

"Only because I started calling you Dolt instead of Holt, cuz you couldn't get it right."

Lila's belly was jiggling slightly with her laughter.

"So, in my infinite wisdom, and definitively proving that your mother was the smarter and far wittier of the two of us, I decided to butcher her last name and twisted Pirsig into Ripgis."

"God, I hate that name."

Dan rose back to standing. "But it's you, my darling Ripgis." He kissed her on the nose.

"So," Dan said, bending to address her belly again, "if you're asked, now you know the secret names of Dolt and Ripgis."

"I'm thinking that's going to be the one that stumps her," Lila said, "but just in case, what's the complicated one?"

He pulled the cloth from his shoulder and wiped the suds off. "We could nail down our daughter's full name right now. Only you and I would know."

"Is that something you think we can agree on right now?"

"We were talking about two names we really liked."

"Your most beautiful woman and my most beautiful woman?"

"My third-most beautiful woman."

"Third?"

"Yeah," Dan said. "Marilyn Monroe's my third."

"Okay, who are the other two?"

"The second is Farrah Fawcett," he said. "But I don't think I can saddle my kid with a name like Monica Farrah."

"Yeah," Lila said, laughing. "Doesn't quite have a flow." She poked his chest. "And who's number one?"

"Oh," he said. "Just this hot little number, name of Lila Holt. You might know her as Pirsig. Or even Ripgis."

"Good answer, mister."

"I know it."

"Okay, so, Marilyn Monroe and Audrey Hepburn?"

Dan held up his hands, as though displaying the type. "Monica Marilyn Audrey Holt."

"Hmm," she said. "Close, but no cigarillo. Not crazy about 'Monica Marilyn'…how about switching them? Monica Audrey Marilyn Holt."

Dan did the hands thing again. "Monica Audrey Marilyn Holt."

Lila studied the invisible type. She said the name under her breath, then said it again. Then she smiled. "I kind of like it."

"Me too."

"We're settled?" she said, then dropped her voice an octave to sound official. "We have an accord?"

"The ayes have it, Ripgis."

"You know, you don't have to keep calling me that."

"You really hate it, don't you?"

"I really do," she said. "Almost enough to donate to the swear jar, Dolt."

"Fine. No more Ripgis."

"Thank you, Dan."

"Monica Audrey Marilyn."

"Yeah."

"Yeah."

Dan kissed his wife. It took them the better part of the evening to get back to the dishes.

Chapter Eleven

"Hello, thanks for calling The Last Word. This is Dan, how can I help you?"

And just like that I can't—

"Breathe," Lex says to me, then indicates the phone with one hand, while opening and closing her fingers with the other. *Pay attention to the phone and talk.* I look down at Lex's notes.

Date?

How many times talked to you before?

Doing anything his end to make this happen?

Okay, I can do this.

"Dad," I say, "it's Monica. Your daughter."

Once again, I hear his voice soften. "Hey, Monica. I'm glad you called."

"I'm sorry to rush this, but I don't know how long we'll keep this connection. I need to ask you a couple of questions, if I can?"

"Um," he says, and his voice is a bit deeper than I always heard it in my mind, "sure. Shoot."

"What's the date today?"

"Oh, jeez," he says, then laughs. "I'm terrible at not knowing…hold on…" —I hear him moving things around— "…just…looking for a calen…ah! Got it. December thirteenth. I should know that, my wife's birthday is—"

"In five days," I finish. "December eighteenth. She hates that it's just a week before Christmas."

"Yeah," he says, after a bit of a delay. "She does."

"Sorry, so what day is that?" I write down the date.

"Tuesday," he says. "It's a Tuesday. Busy day at the store, because—"

"It's new release day."

"Right again." He sounds surprised and confused.

"Okay, so it's Tuesday, December the thirteenth, what year?"

"1983," he says, and his tone says, "Everyone knows that." I think, *I'll be born in about four-and-a-half months.*

"Just a couple more questions, okay?"

"Sure," he says.

"How many times have you talked to me on the phone?"

"Twice," he says, no hesitation. "This is the second time."

"Was there one where it might have been me, but there was no answer?" *God, Monica, what a stupid question.*

"No," he says. "No cut-off calls."

"Thanks," I say. "Last question. Are you doing anything on your end to make this happen?"

"Well, no offence, Monica," he says, "but honestly? I don't even know what *this* is. Especially when you're asking the date and stuff. I mean…is the date different for you?"

"Yeah, Dad," I say. "It…uh…" Tears spring to my eyes.

My father says, very slowly, and very carefully, "What date is it for you, Monica?"

"It's still a Tuesday," I start.

"Okay," he says.

"But it's February twenty-eighth."

"Feb…what?" I know he's not questioning the date. He's questioning how I can be separated by months. He doesn't know the full story.

"February twenty-eighth, 2012, Dad."

"No."

"Yes." I swipe at my cheeks. "As crazy as it sounds, I'm calling you from just under thirty years in your future."

There's a long, slow exhalation of breath. I hear tapping, like he's drumming his fingers on a desk.

"Okay," he says, and now he's sounding…what? Angry? Frustrated? "My turn," he says. "What's your full name, Monica?"

"Monica Audrey Marilyn Danielle Holt."

There's a long pause, long enough that I think I've lost him. "Dad?"

"I'm here," he says. He's still got that angry, frustrated tone, but it's tamped down a bit. "You said Monica Audrey Marilyn *Danielle* Holt?"

"Yes. I know it's a mouthful." *Please don't ask me why Danielle is one of my names, Dad. Please don't.*

"I have an old nickname for your mom," he says.

"Oh god," I say. "Yeah…she told me this. I know she called you Dolt to stop you from calling her…god! What *was* it? It's like, her last name backward, but not quite…Gripsig? No. Sigrip? No. Sipgrip? No…" Nothing. Nothing was coming…

Then I had it.

"*Ripgis!*" I shout. "It's Ripgis!"

The last thing I hear from my father is, "Oh my—"

And then he's gone.

But the line is still open.

♦ ♦ ♦

"Dad?" I say. "Dad? Are you still there?"

Talia, who had up to now kept a respectful distance, now steps forward, her eyes very wide. I only catch the movement peripherally. I'm more focused on the phone, crushing it in my hand to prevent the sound of my dad's voice from falling three decades away from me.

"*DAD!*"

No response. But the line isn't dead. There's the open, airy sound of an ongoing connection.

I look wildly to first Lex, then Talia. I feel the tears I didn't know I'd started crying again slide down my face. "I think he's gone," I say.

Talia's eyes meet mine, then she looks purposefully at the phone. I look down, and then I take a step back, the coiled phone cord stretching as I pull.

I take another step back. The handset is still to my ear, the echo of the open line still a presence. But it's the phone that holds my attention.

The phone, and the teeth that surround it.

Because the teeth are drawing in, sliding across the surface in an ever-tightening circle, like some strange approximation of a mouth biting down on the phone base.

"The protection's been activated," Talia says. "Hang up the phone, Monica."

I ignore her. "Who's there?" I say, fighting to keep my voice level. "There's someone on this line. Speak to me."

"Hang up, babe," Lex says.

"Hang up the phone, Monica," Talia says again.

"*Talk!*" I yell.

~You think you can do anything, child? You cannot.~

"Dammit, Monica!"

"Who is this?"

~The one who takes your father, child. You cannot change it. It has already happened.~

Talia reaches out to pull the handset from me, but I spin away from her. "Tell me what you want. Why are you doing this?"

~I have what I want, child. I do nothing because it has all been done. Time's curtain has drawn tight against your interference.~

"*MONICA!*" It's Lex and she's stabbing a finger at the phone.

The teeth have reached the phone, and they're sinking into it, and where the surface of the phone is dimpling, a darkness is bleeding out.

It's only then that I realize how hot the handset is now. I let it go, and I have to shake my hand because my flesh is sticking to the plastic.

I hear that same dark, grating voice saying something else, but I can't make it out. Talia has swooped in and scooped up the handset. She slams it down on the base, then grabs the whole hot, bleeding mess and rips it from the counter and into the drawstring bag that held the teeth.

There's only three or four scattered teeth left behind. The darkness that bled out of the phone seeps into the surface of the counter, staining it black.

"Damn damn damn," Talia says. Her hands are cradled in her lap, palms up, fingers curled in.

Her hands are smouldering.

My legs give out and I drop on the floor beside her, then immediately bark out a yelp as I put my hands out to catch my fall. I pull them up and see the one that was holding the phone isn't much better than Talia's.

Lex drops between us. "Oh my god, are you okay? We gotta get you both to the hospital."

"No," Talia says. "Just...give me a couple of minutes, please."

She stands painfully, with Lex's help, then walks off to another part of the store.

Then Lex is in front of me, gently checking out the damage to my hand.

And I say, "What the fuck just happened, Lex?"

Chapter Twelve

ONICA'S VOICE DISTORTED over the crackling phone line, but Dan clearly heard what she said next.

"*Ripgis!*" she shouted. "It's Ripgis!"

He was barely aware of his next words. "Oh my god."

It's her. It's Monica.

The line quality changed then. It had been filled with the sound of her voice—*my daughter's voice!*—and the accompanying phone sounds...the almost far-off sounds of hand movement on the handset, the rubbing of the mouthpiece against chin, the higher tone of the phone sliding against hair and ear.

That changed, and the sound coming through was less dense. Less busy.

Then the phone got *hot*. Like a hot bar of iron had been set in his hand. Dan dropped the phone, the plastic clattering against the countertop.

That was new. The previous two times, the phone always got warm, even uncomfortably so, when Monica called, but never like this.

My daughter.

But Monica Audrey Marilyn Danielle Holt? What was *that* about?

The thought flew away from his head in the next instant, when he heard a strange sound, like hard plastic being stressed to its limit. He looked at the desk, trying to source the sound, but it wasn't until he caught the hint of movement from the phone. The base flexed outward, as though a clawed finger was pushing at it from inside. The surface distended, stretching outward to a sharp point, then there was a crack.

Dan jumped backward as a small white object appeared to tear through the strangely extended surface of the Bakelite base. It *tac tac tac*ked across the countertop, then came spinning to a stop.

The phone, having ejected the object, slid back to its normal shape, only a small dimpled imperfection to hint that anything had passed through its surface.

And the object itself, sitting about a foot away from the phone. Its sheer incongruity to its surroundings made it stand out, sharp white against the dark wood surface.

He reached out and picked it up. Long and sharp and curved.

A tooth.

PART TWO
OPENING CONVERSATION

"Old friends, like old swords, still are trusted best."

JOHN WEBSTER

SECOND INTERLUDE
1981 – CLARINGTON HIGH SCHOOL

THE WASHROOM REMINDED him of a sewer, dark and damp. Theo was sick and tired of dark and damp. It smelled of piss, sweat, and toilet mints. But underneath it all ran a familiar coppery smell.

Theo's feet made splashing noises on the ceramic tile floor. With all the damage, the flashlight cast large shadows behind the concrete remains, like a full moon on a graveyard. Theo couldn't see worth shit and he stumbled over rubble. He angled left where the urinals should have been. A couple remained on the wall, but the bowl part was missing. The broken porcelain glittered in the beam of Theo's flashlight like big broken teeth.

To his right, where the bathroom stalls used to be, it looked like a giant hand had flattened them against the wall. All the toilets were gone, pulverized into dust. Nothing left but the holes in the floor.

"What's going on in there?" The Toad's voice sounded tinny as it echoed off the walls.

"Nothing, man. Place is trashed."

"Is this where the thing came from?"

"Who the fuck knows? All I'm sure of right know is I'm about ankle deep in piss."

Laura was saying something else, but Theo cut her off. "Hold up. I see something. Give me a sec."

♦ ♦ ♦

NYARLATHOTEP IS RELEGATED to peering through the translucent barrier between their realms again. Its offspring, all'Gueroth—whom these low-brained idiots had named Swlabr, for whatever reason—was off doing the two things it lived for…ignoring its lineage and sticking its reproductive organ in anything it could find, spraying its inexhaustible seed in any moist hole.

It occurred to Nyarlathotep then that, from what he'd observed of this world through the untold span of time it had been aware of it, his offspring acted very much like the young offspring of these humans.

Insolence and stupidity spanned all the realms, it seemed.

And now, another player entered the game. This Thelonious Clarke child. He would bear watching.

◆ ◆ ◆

THEO SAW A shape. The only reason it stood out in the moist semidarkness was that it had a less jagged outline. Amid the carnage of broken concrete and twisted metal, this shape was smoother, more organic.

It looked somewhat human.

Theo moved over to the shape. It was against the wall where the sinks had been. One of the four mirrors that used to occupy the wall above those sinks remained surprisingly intact, and it reflected the beam of his flashlight at weird angles.

As he approached the shape, Theo became more confused. It looked human, but not completely. The other thing messing with his senses was the fact that the shape seemed suspended in mid-air.

Fuck. It's floating.

"What's happening?" The Toad asked, making the light in Theo's hand jig in surprise. His voice was distant and it echoed in the darkened washroom.

"Jesus! Shut up and give me a minute here!"

"Okay! Shit! Don't get your panties in a knot, fer chrissakes!"

But Theo wasn't hearing him anymore. The shape *was* human. And it *was* in mid-air.

And it was Stinky Pete Wilson. But then again, it wasn't.

Peter was smashed up. But it went beyond that. Pete was *changed*.

♦ ♦ ♦

NYARLATHOTEP COULD NOT command these soft, stupid sacks of blood and meat. It was one of the intractable laws that governed various realms. Whichever of the many beings who claimed to be the all-mighty creator of these seething dimensions seemed to possess both a strange and unknowable morality, as well as a startlingly rare sense of humour.

One of those two elements were in play, holding back Nyarlathotep from executing its will. The Black Man was displeased. Greatly so.

It could watch these stupid little children thrash about in their cage. It could—with much effort and great difficulty—push the Book into one of their kinds' hands on rare occasions. It could, with the right proximity, even talk through the Book.

In short, Nyarlathotep could, with great difficulty, *influence*, but it could not coerce or direct.

And the Outer God, for all its power, could not cross over to this realm unless one of these stupid children invited him.

And, despite the demon putting the Book in the hands of werewolves and children, the Book also had a strange and unfathomable sense of humour—shot with a bright streak of capriciousness—that made It favour the one least likely to win.

In this realm, those types were named after animals. Underdog. Dark horse.

The werewolves sat on their gift. Talia Davis had simply pushed things back and forth through the realms. Peter Wilson had been the first to pull a demon through and, despite all the influence Nyarlathotep had mustered, the Book simply buried that influence and pushed the child toward all'Gueroth instead.

Chapter Thirteen

After Lex dragged both Talia and me to the small bathroom and got cold water running over our hands, she ran like a madwoman to the pharmacy for supplies.

She wrapped our hands in gauze once she returned, Talia protesting through it all. She complained, but Lex got it done.

Now, the three of us are sitting or leaning against different areas of the back office of the bookstore, facing each other.

"What happened?" I ask.

"No clue," Lex says.

"Tell me everything you heard on the phone after your father cut out."

There isn't a lot to tell. I tell them how terrifying that voice was, and how it said I can't do anything to help my father. Then I tell them the last thing I heard it say.

"It said, 'I do nothing because it has all been done'?" Talia says.

"That, and, 'Time's curtain has drawn tight against your interference,' whatever that means."

"I know what it means," Talia says, "but there's something else there…"

"Feel free to elaborate," Lex says.

But Talia simply stands and leaves the office.

Lex watches her leave, then turns to me, palms out, and mouths, "What the fuck?"

◆ ◆ ◆

MY FIRST REACTION is to go after her, to verbalize my girlfriend's "what the fuck" question. And I even go as far as pushing off the desk to do so, but Lex pins me with her eyes.

"No idea what's going on, Mon," Lex says, "but when she does this, it usually means she needs some alone time. We should probably give it to her."

"Okay," I say reluctantly. "Then what do you, oh Magical Staff Wielder, make of this?"

"I left my Staff in my other pants' pocket, weirdo," Lex says. "But the whole 'what's done is done, time's curtain is drawn' or whatever? I think that thing is just telling you that we're thirty years too late."

"But, isn't that obvious?"

"I don't know," Lex says. "You've called your dad three times now and gotten through every time. You tell me if that curtain of time is really closed."

"You're saying you…I don't know…you think we can maybe go back and do something?"

"You and I went to an impossible place a few months ago to retrieve an impossible thing for impossible beings…"

"So why not go to an impossible time?"

Lex stands and saunters over to me. She puts her arms around my waist and pulls me close. "Babe," she says, "I honestly don't know. A year ago, I didn't know any of this existed. I wrote articles for people who'd read the headline and move on, and sang for old people trying to relive their youth. If you had come up to me with a stack of money, I would have absolutely bet against it."

"Your point?"

"My point is, what the hell do I know? I am, quite frankly, the worst judge of what makes sense now. Because, despite living it, it still doesn't make sense to me."

"I've been around for almost fifty years and it still doesn't make sense, Lex," Talia says from the doorway. "I don't expect you to have it all figured out in a few months."

"Jumped-up Jesus in a sidecar, Talia," I say, "how many times are we going to talk about this. Sneaking up on people? Not. Fucking. Cool."

Talia tosses off a nonchalant, "okay," that tells me this newest talk will change her behaviour not a whit. "I did some thinking, and a little bit of reading," she says.

"Wait, what?" I say. "What you have possibly read in the two minutes you've been away? And furthermore, what could possibly be in this store that would be of help with this?"

"You'd be surprised," Talis says enigmatically. "Regardless, I don't necessarily have a plan as of yet, but I have some thoughts I'd like to run by the two of you."

CHAPTER FOURTEEN

"A TOOTH?" LILA said.

Dan was holding it out so she could see it. She reached out to take it from him, but hesitated, and he completely understood why.

The thing was *huge*.

She paused for only a second, then picked it from his fingers, and he let it go reluctantly only because he didn't like the looks of it. In fact, he'd briefly considered not telling her about it at all.

Then he heard his father again, during a conversation they'd had when Dan had told him both that Lila was pregnant, and that he was going to marry her. His father had nodded, told him it wasn't necessarily the best way to start a marriage, but backed him completely. Then he said something that Dan would never forget for the rest of his short life. "Son," his father had said, "if you listen to nothing else I ever say, listen to this: don't ever hide anything from your wife. Not ever, no matter how small. Because as soon as you justify hiding something small, it becomes easier and easier to hide more and more. Got it?"

Dan had nodded, and his father finished with, "Always be honest. Honesty will hurt sometimes, son, but it was *always* hurt less than lies."

Those words had come back to him as he'd walked home from The Last Word and, one hand in his pocket, fingers wrapped around the strange thing, he knew he'd have to tell her.

Lila held it pinched between thumb and forefinger, turning it this way and that. It was at least a couple of inches long, half of it looking like it was external tooth, but the other half some sort of complicated root. She let it roll to her palm, then hefted it a couple of times. "It feels like it should be heavier."

"Yeah," Dan said. "I thought so too. But if you look at the sharp end, then the other end, it's actually hollow."

"Like a bird bone?"

"Yeah," he said. "But then again, no."

That got the infamous quizzical look from his wife.

"Look at it again," he said. "If you had to guess what kind of animal it came from, what would you say?"

"Too small for a bear," she said. "Too big for something like a raccoon. Dog? Coyote? Wolf?"

"Hollow?"

"Right," she said. "No." She pinched it again and twisted it this way and that. "What do you think?"

"You don't want to hear what I think," Dan said, a small smile on his lips but not in his eyes. "Because it's stupid."

"Oh, hon," Lila said, handing it back to him. She got that equally infamous grin that alerted him to incoming sarcasm. "We all have our shortcomings. You know I love you for more than your mind."

"Gee," he said, "thanks. Makes me feel a whole lot better."

"Seriously, though," she said. "You looked bugged. Which makes sense, considering the tooth, but what are you thinking?"

Instead of saying anything, he plucked the tooth from her fingers and held it up to his mouth. His upper lip was lifted, almost in a snarl, to bare his teeth, and he positioned the tooth to the right side. Like a fang.

"No," she said. "Come on, Dan, seriously? Vampire?"

"It's long, it's hollow, and it's sharp as hell."

"You really believe all that BS about the Vilni vampires?"

"Not really, no. But tell me what else makes sense."

"There's something," she said. "We just don't know what." She regarded the tooth again. "Tell you what. Dad's still got that full set of *Encyclopedia Britannica* at home. They're not too far out of date, 1977 or '78. He got them for me for high school. I think he might still be paying them off, so he'd be happy just to see me use them."

"You're not going to show him the tooth, are you?"

"Oh, hell no."

"Okay."

"So, all right," she said. "You've told me she called again. Then we got sidetracked with dental issues. Tell me, how'd it go?"

Shit, Dan thought, mentally slapping his head. *How the hell could I get sidetracked from that?*

"She passed…" And suddenly, Dan's throat felt like it had a hard lump of stone in it, blocking any further words from escaping. And his face got hot. And his eyes started leaking.

Lila stepped closer, put her arms around his waist. He took a shuddering breath. "Lee, she…ah god…" He swallowed hard, swiped at his eyes. Took another breath. "She answered every question, Lee."

"Really?"

"Every. Fucking. One."

"She got the Ripgis?"

Dan laughed through the tears. "Yeah, she had a bit of a time remembering, but she got it."

"And the whole name thing? Middle names and all?"

"Yes," he said. "And no."

"What's that supposed to mean? It's an easy yes or no. Not a combo." She pointed to her belly. "Are you pregnant? Yes. And no." She laughed. "See? Doesn't work."

"Monica Audrey Marilyn…Danielle…Holt."

"Danielle?" She squinted in confusion. "Where'd that come out of?"

"Don't know."

"But she got all the other names." Her eyes lost focus as she considered. "Weird."

"You think we change our minds?"

"Or do we name her that because she told us that's what it is?"

"How did she explain being able to talk to us from the womb?"

"She's not," he said. "She said she was calling from 2012. Last day of February, to be exact."

"No," Lila said. "Sorry, that's BS and I don't buy it. That's…what…?"

"Twenty-eight years, two months, and a few days into the future."

"We'd be in our fifties!"

"Almost sixty, Lee." Lila was proud of the fact that she avoided dastardly numbers at all costs.

"Nope," she said, shaking her head vigorously. "Not buying it."

"But babe, she even knew you called me 'Dolt' too."

"Okay," she said, throwing her hands up and backing away. "This is getting too damn *Twilight Zone* for me. Vampire teeth. Our unborn daughter calling us. From the future."

Dan couldn't disagree with her. She was right. "But," he said, "it's happening. What are we going to do with all of this?"

Chapter Fifteen

L EX MOTIONS FOR Talia to continue, rolling her hand. "Spill."

"We've gone through some unusual experiences, the three of us," Talia says.

"That's one way to describe it," I say.

"'Fucked-up shit' would likely be more accurate," Lex says, and I nod.

"I won't disagree." Tilting her head toward us, she says, "With that shared history in mind, I'll ask for your indulgence for a couple of minutes."

"Okay," we both say.

"Thank you. Let's start with the call. It may not seem like it to you, but we can extrapolate a lot of information."

"Such as?" I say.

"Such as, we knew we were talking to him in the past, but we didn't know how far in the past. December of 1983 is only four months from when the event occurred."

"And I was born."

"Right," Talia says. "Which brings me to my next point. He had questions for you. Your mother's nickname, your full name, and so on."

"I don't—"

Talia raises a finger. "Ah, but it's the nature of the questions. These aren't necessarily top-of-the-head questions. I think he put some thought into them. Possibly with your mother's involvement."

"So?" Lex says.

"So, he wasn't just randomly tossing questions out." Still leaning against the counter, Talia angles her body forward, hands on knees, to emphasize her point. "He was testing you. Remember, to him, at that time, you're an unborn child. Yet here's someone phoning him claiming to be that child. That's...whackadoodle."

"Whackadoodle?" Lex says. "Really? That's the best term—"

"Yes," she says, chopping a hand to cut her off. "My point is, he asked, and you had the answers." She leans back, crossing her arms. "Your father was a few years older than me, Monica, but I did know him. I was in this store when it was still The Last Word. And when I talked to him, I got a sense of the man he was. Trust me," she says, "you passed his test."

"You knew my dad?" I say.

"I did."

I stand, mouth agape, shocked that the thought had never crossed my mind before. The thought of talking to someone who had once stood on this very spot and interacted with a father I only knew through word of mouth...it makes me tear up. I feel Lex's hand grab mine.

"Wow," I say. *I'm gonna be picking your brain later, Talia. Maybe even asking for one of those memory injections you gave Lex.* But for now, back to business. "You're saying you think he believes I'm who I say I am."

"Correct."

"Fair enough," Lex says, motioning to me. "He believes her. So?"

"Well, this time, something different happened, didn't it?"

"The second voice."

Talia nods. "My first question to you, Monica, is, do you recall ever hearing that voice before?"

"Oh *hell* no," I say. I definitely would have remembered that particular growl.

"I only ask because it sounds like it knew you."

"Why do you say that?"

"What it said to you," she says. "Your father's gone, you can't change it. Time's passed. You can't do anything."

I tilt my head back, close my eyes, and rub my fingers against my forehead to forestall the oncoming headache. And then it hits me, as Talia knows it would. *Of course. "Your father."*

"It knew Dan's my dad."

"Yes."

"But there's still something bugging me, and I can't put my finger on it," I say.

"What do you mean?" Lex says, giving my hand a squeeze.

"Something about that voice. Not sure if it's the voice…or what it said…"

Talia nods, encouraging me, but I've got nothing. "…or how it said it, perhaps?"

I hold my finger up. She's got something there. Like, we should get it…but it's still out of reach. "No, I got nothing."

Talia says, "You talked to your father in 1983."

"Right," I nod.

"And yet, that second voice —" And then I had it.

"Talked to me about what had *already happened,*" I say, excited now. "It's talking to me from a different time. Talia, you're a freakin' genius."

"Hardly," she says.

"Okay," I say, forcing myself to calm down. "So I know *what's* bugging me, but why?"

"Let's look at what it said…do you feel like it was warning you? Pushing you away?"

"Maybe," I say. "But neither feels exactly right. It was more…"

"Bullying?" Lex says. "Or challenging?"

"Yeah," I say. "Yeah, Lex, more challenging than anything. Almost like…like maybe it was trying to goad me into trying? 'You can't do this, so don't even try.' Nyah nyah nyah."

"And I think we all know that telling Monica Holt that something can't be done is as good as getting it done, because Monica doesn't really respond well to that kind of message."

"Hey," I say. "It took a long time, but I finally got you, didn't I?"

Lex flashes her brightest smile. "You did."

"Very well," Talia says. "We're in agreement. This second voice is trying to goad you into trying to do...something. I don't think saving your father is its end goal."

"What is?"

Talia gathers her things into her bag as she says, "Let's get some dinner and discuss it. We have much to talk about."

Lex groans and says, "Just going on the record with this, Talia. You're killing me, but the only reason I'm going along with this is because I'm starving."

"Noted," Talia says, drily. I can't help but laugh at the two of them, despite the situation.

◆ ◆ ◆

NEW HOPE ISN'T necessarily known for its higher-end eateries. After we went through the frustrating "what do you feel like eating?" dance for a few minutes, Lex just mumbled "fuck it" and we ended up at Annie and Ambrose's place, the Cozy Pine Inn.

Lex had a soft spot for the place. So do I. First, it's because Annie and Ambrose are my aunt and uncle, but there's a more important reason. It's where Lex and I met back up and finally got together. Literally got together right down the hall in the room on the far right.

Lex gives me a knowing smile as we walk into the dining room. She leans in close, her breath warm in my ear as she says, "You're blushing, beautiful."

I make to protest, but I notice Lex has a slightly flushed look about her as well. Obviously, we're thinking the same thoughts.

"Ladies," Talia says, "I'd suggest you two getting a room, but that would only slow us down."

I feel the heat of a new and improved blush hitting my face. "Oh my god," I say. "Can we just sit down and order?"

"Yes," Lex agrees, "can we?"

Ambrose glides up and gives us a warm smile. "Ladies," he says in his friendly growl. As per usual, the badger-like hairpiece is perched precariously and incongruously on his noggin. "Good to see you." Then he turns to Talia and the wattage dims considerably. "Ms. Davis."

"Mr. McDonald," she says. "I trust you're well." I don't know Talia that well—I truly don't think anyone does, Talia being the most opaque person I've ever encountered—but the way she says those two words, it's like she's not only *not* trying to be confrontational in any way, but actively trying to soothe any discord from Ambrose as well.

It seems to work. He doesn't get any friendlier, but I think I see a microscopic loosening of his shoulders, an infinitesimal relaxing around his eyes and mouth. Even the badger seems to stand down a fraction. He mumbles out, "Fine," almost as though against his will and better judgment. But it seems to crack the ice somewhat.

There's no need for Ambrose to give us menus. We all order from memory and he heads off to get us our drinks and put the food order in. As he walks away, Talia looks at his retreating back a little wistfully.

"Sorry, Tal," Lex says. "I keep forgetting…" She doesn't finish the sentence.

But Talia does. "That I disappeared his father?" She turns back to us. "He'll never forget, nor should he," she says. "I just don't want to torment him with the memory of that every time I come in."

"Yeah," Lex says. "Sorry."

"Shit," I say. "Does *anyone* in this town have a decent memory of their father?"

The three of us stare at each other and, as if on cue, we all shake our heads no. It's grim, but it serves to lighten the mood a touch.

"Speaking of fathers," I say. "You knew mine?"

We wait a moment while Ambrose and his badger return with our beverages. Coffees all around. When he's out of earshot again, Talia answers.

"I did," she says. "I was not a frequent customer, but I was a regular one. In fact, if I have one claim to fame in the history of The Last Word bookstore, it's that I was the one who first asked for the Conan novels to be brought in."

"You," Lex says derisively, "are a Conan fan?"

"Not particularly," she says. "But it's a fact that the two Howards—Howard Phillips Lovecraft and Robert E. Howard— were friends, and Robert occasionally incorporated Lovecraftian monsters and demons into some of his own stories, with Lovecraft's blessing. And not just Conan stories. I was trying to get my hands on anything related to those beings, whether fictional or factually accurate."

"And...?"

"Very little of it was helpful," Talia says. "One of the few things I've read from Robert E. Howard that has proven accurate..."— and here she points to Lex—"...is the Staff of Solomon."

"My Staff?" Lex says. "Really?"

"Read his Solomon Kane stories," Talia says. "It's in there, though severely de-powered."

"Huh, who knew?" Lex says.

"I did," Talia says without a trace of irony or sarcasm. "There's something else, too."

"Uh oh," Lex says.

"This one's...not so positive."

"Okay, you're worrying me, now," I say.

"Talia, fucksake, you gotta learn to stop hesitating and drawing shit out," Lex says. "Just fucking say what you need to say."

Talia gives Lex a small nod and says, "You both know that everything that happened with me back in the seventies was due to the Book." We both nodded. "What I haven't told you up to now was that the Book was delivered directly to me through my babysitter, Marcia Mayer."

"The one who was—"

"Yes, one of the casualties of the high school…thing."

"Okay, and this is relevant because…" Lex says.

"Because of where she got the Book from."

"Oh," I say. "Oh, shit."

"The Last Word?" Lex says.

"Your father thought he was doing a good thing, Monica," Talia says. "Marcia was a lovely, kind girl, and she was looking for a gift for both Alex and me. I remember she brought Alex a stuffed Dino the Dinosaur from *The Flintstones*." Talia gently touches her coffee mug, as though the memory is just behind it. "That was my sister's favourite show." Lex and I say nothing, only nod. She stares off into her memory for another moment, then blinks. "Anyway, yes, Alex got Dino, and I got a Dr. Seuss book. *Oh, The Thinks You Can Think!* Dan sold it to her, and she brought it to me."

"Only, it wasn't a Seuss book," Lex says.

"No," Talia says. "I truly believe neither Marcia or your father knew that they'd handed off a weapon of mass destruction to a very young, very angry girl."

"The Book came from Dad's store," I say.

"Let me be clear," Talia says. "The Book didn't *originate* there. It was placed there. I don't know if it was done so through Its own will, or through the will of another. But It was placed there strategically."

"So, did Peter Wilson get the Book from The Last Word as well?"

"I can't say. I know the Book told me it would go to him, so it had him picked out long before the transfer. But how that transfer happened, I don't know. I'll probably never know. All I can tell you is, I had possession of the Book until around the end of April of 1981. Then, one afternoon, it felt like someone tore my insides out. And the Book was no longer mine. It was Peter's."

"I almost want to say sorry, but…"

"But it's not appropriate," Talia says. "To be honest, those five years with the Book are quite hazy. I felt like I'd regained control of my mind once It left, so it wasn't a bad thing."

"You still miss It, though, don't you?" Lex says.

I can't read all the emotions in Talia's expression as she holds Lex's gaze, but her words chill me.

"Imagine being raped, but experiencing the best orgasm of your life," Talia says. Then, quietly, softly, sadly, she says. "I'd be lying if I said I didn't miss It."

Not one of the three of us has anything to say for a time after that. We stare at the table, at the walls, out the windows. We look at anything but each other, and I try to keep the storm behind my eyes in check.

Finally, thankfully, Ambrose delivers our food, and it seems to, if not break the spell, at least lessen it somewhat. We can look at each other again.

As we tuck into our meals, Talia stops for a moment. "I must tell you, Monica, that, despite my…reputation…as Spooky Talia, your father was nothing but polite and enthusiastic and helpful with the strange young girl who came into his store."

I smile at that. Everything I've heard about Dad is that he was a nice guy, a kind guy, and it was good to have these values reinforced.

"Your grandfather, Stan Holt, was…not a fan," Talia says. "So I always dealt with Dan instead."

"So you dealt with Dad," I say. "But, did you ever really talk to him?"

"Oh yes," she says. "There was one night where I waited until the store closed, and talked to him very seriously about the Book. Because I found it again. In The Last Word."

Chapter Sixteen

Despite the worries about the Book, life had a way of pushing matters aside, no matter how troubling they could be.

Lila's birthday came and went. Then it was Christmas. Then New Years, and then 1983 turned into the fabled year of 1984. There were doctor's visits for Lila, and more stuff to buy for the baby. The room needed painting. There were things to do, people to see, tasks to complete.

The days passed.

And, through it all, the Book bided Its time.

◆ ◆ ◆

"Look who it is!" Dan said, after looking up at the ding of the door opening. "As I live and breathe, it's my favourite customer."

A cold gust of late January air followed the customer in before she shut the door. "I'm sure you say that with every single customer who comes in here," Talia said drily.

"Not true. I have never once called Mrs. McKenzie a favourite customer."

"Okay," Talia said. "Fair enough."

I wish, just once, I could get this kid to smile, Dan thought. "And what strange and wonderful tome brings you into our fair shop today?"

Talia pulled a piece of paper from a pocket and slid it across the counter.

"*Another* Lovecraft?" Dan said. "You really like his stuff, huh?"

Talia shrugged her shoulders. "Not particularly."

"Then why...?" He put up a hand. "Nope, never mind. Don't answer that. Ours is not to question why." He waggled the note in the other hand. "It'll be the usual. About a month or so."

"Thanks," she said. She waved a finger in a circular motion. "Gonna look around."

"Please do," Dan said. "Buy lots. Reading makes you smart."

"You saying I'm dumb?"

"What? No!" Dan was instantly mortified. "God no! I'm sorry, I didn't mean—"

In the same dry, emotionless tone, she said, "It was a joke, Mr. Holt."

A joke. She'd actually joked with him. It caused him flop sweat and horror, but she'd joked with him. *Still not getting her to smile, though.* "Yeah, right, I knew that."

"Sure," she said, and turned away to head over to her usual area: science fiction, fantasy, and horror.

Dan picked up her note and transcribed it over to the order book.

♦ ♦ ♦

ABOUT TEN MINUTES later, Talia was back.

"Found something?"

She nodded, and slid the book across the counter to him. "I'll take this one."

"No prob—"

Dan froze. *Oh no. No no no.*

The book was *The Doors*. The book he'd left at home this morning. The book that could not be on his counter right now because he'd left it at home.

He'd left the fucking thing at home.

What the hell?

He reached out, tentatively at first, then forcefully, grabbing the book, and turned and tossed it on the back counter. "Sorry," he said. "I can't… It's not…"

Say something, dumbass, he thought. *Use your words.*

"Sorry, a customer asked me to put that aside for them. Huge King fan."

"King?"

"Stephen King."

"That's not a King book, Mr. Holt."

Dan stared at Talia for a long two seconds, only breaking the gaze when he realized his mouth was open and nothing was coming out. He turned to the back counter, looked at the book.

The Doors. Stephen King. The man in the desert facing four doors with those scenes behind them.

Everybody sees a different book.

He turned back to her, shaking his head. "Right," he said, feigning confusion. "Sorry." He tapped a forefinger to his temple. "Order brain. Ignore me."

"So, I can buy—"

"*No,*" he said, far too sharply. He softened his tone. "No, sorry, it's not a King book, but a customer did call and ask me to set it aside for them."

"What if I said I'd pay twice as much for It?" Talia said. "You could order them another one."

"I…sorry, Talia," he said. "I can't."

"I'd really like to buy that Book today, Mr. Holt."

"I get that," he said. "I know you…like that…author. But—"

"What author?"

"Pardon?"

"You said you know I like that author," Talia said, quite reasonably. "What author?"

Fuck.

He did the only thing he could think of. He pointed to the book on the back counter and said, "That author."

They regarded each other for another long moment. Dan placed both palms on the front counter, mostly to hide his shaking hands, and thought, *Please please please, Talia, just let it go.*

Talia, with another shrug, said, "Okay, Mr. Holt." Then she did something weird before turning toward the door. She reached over and patted his hand.

"I'll make sure I get that Lovecraft ordered for you."

She raised a hand in acknowledgement and left the store without another word.

Fuck.

♦ ♦ ♦

THE STORE CLOSED three hours and sixteen minutes later, and it couldn't come soon enough for Dan. He kept looking at that damned book on the back counter, sometimes running different scenarios of how he could have handled Talia better, and the rest of the time just ensuring the fucking book was still there.

Because he knew he'd left it at home.

When he'd ushered the last customer out of the store, killed the lights, counted the till, and done everything else required to close down the shop for the day, he went back to the counter, pulled out a bag, picked up the book and slid it in, then tucked it firmly under his arm. It was heavy as hell, far heavier than a book of that size should be.

Then he set the alarm, left the store, locked the door, and turned to walk home.

Talia was standing three feet in front of him.

"Jesus!" he said, dropping both his keys and the bagged book.

"Sorry," she said, not sounding sorry at all.

Dan took a knee to pick up the dropped items. "You scared the everlivin' shit out of me, Talia."

"What's in the bag?"

He stood, tucking the book under his arm again. "Huh?"

"The bag under your arm. Looks like a book. Which one is it?"

"Oh, nothing," he said. "A new horror novel. Graham Masterton."

"You sure it's not *Callahan's Lot*?" she said. "Or *The Doors*? They're both by King, right? Or is it *New Hope, Old Disappearances*, by Danika Hilliers? Or is it *Soft Kiss, Hard Death* by Raymond Chandler? Or *The Original of Laura* by Vladimir Nabokov?"

What? Dan hadn't heard those last two before. It superseded the jolt of surprise he'd gotten with the mention of the first three titles.

"They're what your father sees when he looks at It," she said. "One of those two."

"What?" Dan said again, stupidly. "I don't—"

"The first time I saw It, I was eight years old. My babysitter Marcia Mayer had picked me up a book from The Last Word. It was called *Oh, The Thinks You Can Think!* and it was supposedly written by Dr. Seuss. That's what you saw when you sold It, what Marcia saw, and what I first saw. I think It was learning then, and stuck with actual titles. Lately, though? We all see what we want to see, though some, like Peter Wilson and Theo Clarke, saw it for exactly what it was."

There was a bench just a few steps down the sidewalk. Dan pointed to it and said, "I think I have to sit down."

"You want to get a coffee or something instead?" Talia asked. "We've got a lot to talk about."

"What're you, fifteen? Aren't you a little young for coffee?"

Talia smiled then. Actually smiled.

"We've got a lot to talk about, Dan."

Chapter Seventeen

"WHAT DID YOU talk about?" I say.

"We went across the street to the coffee shop that is now called How You Bean?, and talked about a lot of things. Even you." She looked down at her coffee cup, raised it, and said, "You live long enough, you come full circle in your life. As it is with the father, so it is with the daughter."

Lex, with knife and fork in hand, leaned forward over the table, and said, "Talia, tell us everything."

◆ ◆ ◆

TALIA TAKES HER time, paints a picture of the original setting. The counter was there, there were a few paintings on the wall from a local artist there and there and there. She and Dan sat at a table just over there. He ordered a large coffee, triple triple. She took a large coffee, black.

"Blech," I say. "Three creams, three sugars? That's disgusting."

"Yeah, and your huge dollop of chocolate milk and mound of brown sugar is so much better," Lex says. Yeah, she got me.

Talia tells Dan Holt of how she initially came across the Book, how her babysitter brought It over as a surprise. "I remember her saying how she saw It in the bookstore and 'just knew' it was the perfect book for me."

Then she talked to him about the next several months. How the Book sunk its claws into her, showed her things, taught her things. Bent and twisted her mind.

"I told your father how, in the summer of '75, I was a normal—if somewhat angry—eight-year-old kid. Pissed that my father had left and, in my stupid kiddie brain, blaming my younger sister Alex for it." She pauses then, lightly touching her glass. "She would have been almost forty now, if I…" She doesn't finish the statement.

All three of us know how it ends.

"Then I tell him who I changed into, far too quickly," she says. "I can't even imagine what was going through my mother's head, listening to her not-quite-ten-year-old daughter talking like a miserable, forty-year-old asshole."

"Try having a dad who wants to fuck you," Lex says.

"I did," Talia says, shocking us both. And then, unbelievably, she waves the thought away to continue her narrative. She talks about hurting her sister, the cops, her mother's arrest, her time with the neighbours, her father's triumphant, if short-lived return.

And then, for the first time from the only person who truly knows what happened that day, she tells us what she did next.

"There's this other place," she says, holding a hand palm out beside her, as though pressing against a wall, "and it's both unreachable, and right…"—she pats her hand against that unseen wall—"…right here." She draws her hand back, her fingers curling in as though from the cold. "There are very few—at least on this side—who can make an opening to it."

I watch Talia as she looks to that place that only she can see. There's such a sadness about her. It's always defined her, but right now, it's almost a visible aura about her.

Still looking at that empty space, she says, "I was nine years old, and I was a monster."

Lex leans forward, puts her hand on Talia's. "No, Talia, you weren't. You were nine years old, and you had a monster who fed you far too much power and knowledge, and pushed you to do things you normally wouldn't do."

A faint smile ghosted her lips. "Thank you. But I hurt my sister before I even knew about the Book."

Lex's tone is forged iron. "You. Were. A kid." She squeezes Talia's hand. "Show me one kid who never did a single stupid or cruel thing."

"But I—"

"You were a kid, Talia," Lex repeats. "Let it fucking *go*."

She squeezes Lex's hand in response. Takes a sip of coffee. Ignores the meal congealing on her plate. She holds her palm up once again, and says, "There are very few who can open a passage to that other place, but I am one. Most who can, can only open a hole in a specific shape to allow a being through. For example, the demon that was brought into the high school in 1981, that was by someone who had a one-time opportunity and could allow only one thing through."

We nod our limited understanding.

"I am, on the other hand, essentially a master key." She raises her other hand parallel with the first. "I can open a passage at will, and move whomever, or whatever, I want through to it."

"Like your mom?"

"And the police officers. Sydock and, I'm sorry to say, Ambrose's father. Mr. and Mrs. Kovacs, and their dog. My sister, as well, but that was more of an accident. She was caught up in my wave of anger."

Lex winced at that.

"Your father as well?"

"My father was the catalyst," she says. "Lex, your father was sexually inappropriate with you. My father was…inappropriate with both my sister and me."

"That's what caused…"

"The anger, yes. I did horrible things when I was angry, and I wanted to punish my father. So, I did."

"You were a child. With a monster feeding you power. And another monster that wanted to do things to you that no father should do," I say.

Talia nods. I'm not sure if she's agreeing, or just doing something to make me stop talking.

I feel Lex's hand on my thigh, squeezing. She's as terrified as I am to hear what comes next.

"I said I can send things to that other place." She pauses, sighs. "I should also tell you I can also pull things from that other place to here. It's what I did to my father. Sent him over. Brought him back. Again. And again. And again. I wanted him to suffer, and I ensured that he did."

Talia stops then. She looks down at her food, picks up her fork, spears some pasta, and puts it in her mouth. She chews mechanically, while our minds chew on the information we'd just been fed.

Lex's brain can sort and categorize and organize much quicker than mine. One of the many things I love about her. She says, "Tal, you say you're a monster—"

"I *am* a mons—"

"Just listen to me," Lex says. "You were nine, going through something no one, child *or* adult, should ever experience. And your sister suffered through it as well."

"My sister suffered much," Talia whispers.

"But your father?" Lex slaps the table with her palm. "He was a grown-ass adult who obviously knew better. If there's a monster in this story, Tal, it ain't you. You were angry, and you lashed out, and yes, innocent people paid for that, but the monster here? It's your father." And then Lex's eyes well up. "Just like mine, Tal."

She gets up, moves around to Talia, who's eyes are also shiny with brimming tears, and wraps her in a hug. "You're not a monster, Talia. You're just a scared little girl, just like the rest of us."

Talia leans into the hug, squeezing Lex back. Then she puts a hand out and I take it.

"Thank you, Lex," she says. "Thank you, Monica."

"We love you, Talia," I say, and Lex echoes me.

Then Lex breaks away and says, "Okay, ladies, break it up before we become even more the talk of New Hope than we already are." She scoots back around to her place at the table, picks up her knife and fork, and digs into her steak. Around a mouthful of meat, she waggles her knife and says, "Talia, you were telling us about your talk with Monica's father…"

◆ ◆ ◆

"YOU KNOW," TALIA says, "I honestly think this entire story was far easier to tell the first time around."

"Probably," Lex says, still chewing. "Don't care." She waggles her knife again. "Continue."

Talia gives me a look and I shrug. "Can't live with her, can't dump her."

"Nope," Lex says. "I won't go."

"You two…" Talia says. It's unusual to hear some warmth creep into her voice, but I've heard more of it today than probably ever before. Come to think of it, never before.

"Anyway," Talia says, "after I got through my history, I moved up to Dan's history."

"The high school?"

"The high school."

"What did you tell him?"

Talia then fills us in a little more on the tragic story of Peter Wilson, known back then as Stinky Pete. She explains how he'd pulled a demon through, and gives us a bit of a blow-by-blow of what happened in the school—enough that I decide I'm completely finished eating for the day—then she tells us about the next owner of the Book.

"Thelonious Clarke," Talia says. "Theo."

"The guy who everyone thinks killed his ex-girlfriend."

"Okay," Talia says, holding up a hand in pause. "There's a story there. But the short answer is, no, Theo did not kill Marcia Mayer."

"Then who did?" I ask.

Talia looks over to Lex. Her face is the saddest I've seen it. Lex drops her utensils. "What?" she says.

Talia opens her mouth to speak.

Lex says, "Mar. See. Ah." The she says, "When I was in his head…when he first became aware…" Lex drops her head. "Oh god, no."

"Marcia Mayer was impregnated by the demon that came through to the high school. It actually impregnated a lot of people, but Marcia was the only one who survived the entire ordeal. The gestation is…relatively quick. Theo and Marcia were running away from town. Maybe they'd seen too much, I don't know. But sometime between them landing at the motel and Theo leaving again, the thing inside Marcia finally clawed its way out. Either Theo had left her behind prior to that, or he got lucky and it came out while he slept. Him not moving would have been the only thing that saved him."

"Wouldn't the Book?"

"One thing you'll learn very quickly is that, while the Book hasn't met an underdog It didn't like, It's also fickle. I doubt very much It would have saved Theo."

"What happened to that thing?" I ask, still not getting it.

"It became—"

"Marcus Hedges." Lex said. "My dad."

Then she runs for the washroom to puke. I follow.

◆ ◆ ◆

IT TAKES LEX about twenty minutes to compose herself. Even my Aunt Annie bustles in to the washroom at one point to see if she can help.

By the time we come back out, Lex looking a little more haggard and worse for wear, we see something that shocks us so hard that we can only stop and reach for each other's hands.

Talia is still at the table where we left her, but now Ambrose is sitting in a chair next to her, the two of them facing and leaning in toward each other, elbows on thighs.

And they're talking.

Hell, Ambrose even has a thick, calloused hand over Talia's own. He's patting it.

We stand there long enough that Annie swings by, and taking in the unbelievable scene, puts one arm across my shoulders and the other across Lex's. After a few moments, I hear quiet sniffing.

A few moments later, Ambrose happens to look around and sees us. "Oh geez," he says, and quickly stands. He does a piss-poor job of surreptitiously wiping his eyes, and says, "I gotta get back to work."

Then he hesitates, literally tottering between walking away and moving in toward Talia. Ultimately, he moves toward her, leaning down and giving her a kiss on the top of her head. He whispers a thank you, but his voice is gravelly enough that we all hear it.

He stands, looks at us a bit guiltily, then points vaguely over his shoulder and says, "I'm gonna…I gotta…" Then he walks away, adjusting the badger with one hand and swiping at his eyes with the other.

We get a last squeeze from Annie and she follows him. We rush back to the table and sit down.

"So?" I say.

Talia turns to Lex. "Are you well?"

Lex bats a hand at her. "I'm fine, I'm fine. Spill."

"I had an opportunity to try and make amends to an unintended victim of my actions, and I took it."

We stare at her.

"The details of which remain between Mr. McDonald and I," she says. Then a smile—increasingly less rare, it seems—crosses her lips. "We came to an understanding."

We continue to stare at her.

"We're fine, Ambrose and I," she says.

And, as though to prove her point, Annie brings out a pitcher of beer and three cold mugs. "Thank you for what you did there, Ms. Davis—"

"Talia," Talia says. "Please."

"Okay, thank you, Talia. You've just healed a very old wound, and both Ambrose and I appreciate it." She points to the beer. "It's far too little a gesture, but…beer's on the house. Amby would come and tell you himself, but…" She runs her fingers down her cheeks. "He's gonna be indisposed for a bit."

Talia lays a hand on Annie's arm. "No thanks necessary."

"Still…thank you." Then, tearing up herself, Annie turns on her heel and scoots toward the kitchen.

"Well," Talia says, reaching for the pitcher, "that went better than I expected."

♦ ♦ ♦

LEX AND I sit back down and Talia studies Lex. She says, "I know I asked, but…seriously, are you okay?"

Lex isn't, that's obvious, but she nods perfunctorily and gives us a "let's get on with it" look.

"Do you want to know more about Marcus now, Lex?"

Lex shakes her head. "Eventually," she says, "yes, I will. But this isn't about me and my dad today. Let's focus on Monica's."

I can't even imagine the storm that's got to be roiling around in her head right now, but still, she's more worried about me. Have I mentioned lately how much I love this woman?

Talia gives a short nod, then says, "All right. Moving the narrative forward a little, there's the high school event, the…" — she glances at Lex — "…the aftermath, but that doesn't come to a head until around about the death of Lex's mother." Dabbing her finger in the condensation on the side of the sweating mug, she says, "In the meantime, Theo left, and took the Book with him, but that only lasted a couple of years. I'll tell you the same thing I told your father, Monica: the Book has a long history with this area, and It always finds Its way back somehow."

"I'm getting that impression," I say.

"So what do we do about it?" Lex says.

"Well," Talia says, "let me tell you about the conversation I had with your father, then we'll get to that."

Chapter Eighteen

AN AND TALIA were seated toward the back of the coffee shop, Talia with her back to the wall for good sightlines throughout the store.

Both had massive mugs of coffee in front of them. Talia was rapidly consuming a comically large apple fritter. As she chewed, she looked around. The shop had a tropical beach motif going on, with a painted mural of a palm-treed beach facing a blue-green ocean.

She narrowed her eyes, swallowed, and said, "I don't get it."

"What's that?"

"Why the beach scene?" She indicated the mural.

"Because of the name of the place," Dan said.

"Brew By You?"

"It's a pun," he said. "The coffee shop near you, so…um…brew…by you…coffee near you."

"Still doesn't explain that," she said, pointing to the mural.

"It's a pun on the song?"

She stared at him, chewing.

"'Blue Bayou'?" he said. "Roy Orbison?"

"Who?"

"Oh, please. Okay, um…Linda Ronstadt?"

"Never heard of her."

"You don't listen to music?"

"No," she said. Taking another bite, she tapped her forehead with a sugary finger and said, muffled, "Got enough noise going on in here."

Jesus, kid, Dan thought. *What have you been through?*

She shoved the last of the pastry in her mouth, chewed, and swallowed. "Anyways," she said, and Dan tried to hide the wince, "we didn't come here to talk about beaches and Roys and Lindas."

Dan smiled, took a sip. *Still too hot.* "You're right." He set the mug down. "Can I start?"

Talia motioned for him to continue.

"I'm gonna tell you something that's gonna sound like a serious load of fuckery," he said, "but just hear me out, okay?"

"Fuckery's kind of my thing, Dan." *True enough.*

Dan gave her a high-level overview of the calls. When they came, and more importantly, who they came from.

"Your daughter?"

"Yeah."

"You sure about that?"

"She passed both sniff tests," he said. "Well, mostly." He explained about the nicknames, and Monica's middle names.

"Danielle?" she said, her brows furrowing.

"Yeah, not sure where that came from."

"Obviously from your name."

"Yeah. No. I know that," he said. "But why my name? Why not tack Lila's in there, or something?"

"Not sure," Talia said. Dan tried to read her expression, but couldn't. For someone so young, she had an uncommonly good poker face.

"Oh, and with that last call?" He stopped, dug into his pocket, pulled out a small wad of tissue, and unwrapped it. He set the object down on the table between them.

Talia's eyes widened. Dan actually watched her eyes dilate. Her mouth fell open, just a fraction, but enough to blow by the poker face filters. She reached out a hand to pick it up, stopped inches short.

"It's okay," Dan said. "Pick it up if you want."

Still her hand hesitated, then she slowly withdrew it. Her eyes, however, never left its gleaming surface. "Where," she said, and the reverence in her voice caught him off guard, "did you get this?"

"The last call? The one with the names and dates? After it finished, the phone spit this out."

"When you say, 'spit this out'…"

"I mean the base of my phone on the front counter stretched out like it was fucking taffy, and then this popped out, skittered about a foot across the countertop, and the phone went back to normal."

She stared at it.

"You're probably thinking it's from a dog or someth—"

"It's a vampire tooth."

"Oh…uh…well, good job at beating me to the plot twist," he said, "but…yeah, I was guessing that. Of course, everyone knows there's no vampires, so…"

Head still bowed over the tooth, Talia looked up at him through her eyelashes. "Oh, trust me, Dan, there's vampires."

"Okay." He scratched at his chin. Rubbed his neck. "Sure there is."

"They're likely not important to this particular conversation, aside from this." She nodded at the tooth. "But they exist. Stay away from Vilni if you can."

"Got it. No Vilni."

Still transfixed by the tooth, she said, "Tell me why this is important." She said it like she already knew the answer, but wanted to hear what he was going to say, regardless.

"I'm only making the connection because, on an earlier call, she said something about an evil…no, I'm wrong, she said there was a 'bad Book' and that I needed to stay away from It." She'd said something else then too. What was it? Dan couldn't remember, and the thought flew away when Talia spoke.

"She said that?"

"Yeah, I kind of forgot that whole conversation until now because, well…I thought she was trying to use her Jehovah's Witness Jedi mind tricks on me."

"What's a Jedi?"

He gave her a look. "Not important, has nothing to do with what we're talking about."

"Okay," she said, dubiously. "You know exactly what she was talking about now, though, right?"

"Yeah," he said.

"That Book," Talia said. She didn't have to point. They both knew exactly which one she was talking about. It was currently wedged under one of Dan's legs. He was terrified to set It down somewhere It might be forgotten.

Or that It just might disappear when he wasn't looking at It.

"Yeah," he said. "This Book." It was strange how, since meeting this strange girl, when they talked about the Book, Dan could *hear* them capitalizing the term. Not the *book*, but the *Book*. That extra little oomph on the *B*.

"It's evil, Dan," she said. "Your wife's pregnant, right?"

"Yeah, she is."

"Then none of the three of you should be around It." *I asked Lila to read it*, he thought.

It's fine. She read three words and spaced out. It's fine.

It had to be fine.

Talia gave Dan a very abbreviated history of her relationship with the Book, and then a condensed version of what happened two years ago at Clarington High.

"It was St…Peter Wilson?"

"The Book looks for two things, Dan. Some sort of mental anguish, and someone looking for help out of a bad situation. They do tend to go together."

"But that's just it," he said. "I mean, sure I'm worried about being a dad, but…"

"No. That's why the thing hasn't glommed on to you or your wife. You're reasonably balanced. It got me because I was angry at everyone, and I was desperate to retaliate, even though I didn't know who to aim it at. Pete just wanted his asshole father out of the way."

"What about Theo?" Dan said. "He seemed relatively okay. A little intense at times, but..."

"No, Theo wasn't in anguish until the Book put him there. And he definitely wanted out of that situation. But he also had a surprise in store. He's one of the few who actually bent the Book to his will." She stopped then, opened her mouth to say something, closed it again. Stared at the painted ocean for a second. "That was something I couldn't do. Still can't."

"So, where's Theo now? Can't we, I don't know, give It back to him for safekeeping?"

"No," she said. "He had It. It moved, either through Its own will or through the manipulation of another. Whatever the case, it means he wasn't strong enough to hold It, or he found a way to rid himself of It—"

"In which case we don't want to saddle him with It again."

"Right," she said. "Or someone stole It from him, or—"

"Not sure what that means."

"That Book has been a part of this area for a very long time, Dan." She took a sip, closed her eyes for a moment, relishing it. "God, I love a good cup of coffee." She opened her eyes again to see Dan watching her. "Anyways—"

"Ugh," Dan said.

"What?"

"You keep saying *anyways* and it's not a word."

"Sure it is. Anyways. It's a word."

"*Anyway* is a word. *Anyways* is an abomination. Just like *irregardless*."

"Okay," she said. "I *know* irregardless is a word."

"It's not," Dan said. "But that's not important now. Carry on."

"*Anyways*," she said and Dan sighed, "yes, the Book has been in this area for about a couple of hundred years or so."

"Two hundred years? Did anyone even live here two hundred years ago?"

"Not a lot, but you'd be surprised at who...and what...was here then."

"Okay," Dan said, head still spinning.

"It might have even had a role in that boat that sunk in the early 1900s."

"The *Mayflower*? Really?"

"Wouldn't surprise me." Another closed-eye sip. "My point is, sometimes the Book leaves — or is taken away — but It always seems to somehow find Its way back."

"And you're saying It might come back of Its own free will —"

"Or someone or something keeps bringing It back."

"Okay," Dan said. "I think I cut you off, though. You had one other option for how the Book would end up back here?"

"Yes," she said. "The last option is, Theo's dead."

"Oh shit."

"Right. And if he is, that would release the Book to find Its way back to No Hope."

Dan sighed. "I hate that term. It's New Hope, Talia. I know maybe it hasn't been the best for you, but this town's given me a lot to be thankful for. The store. My wife. My kid. It can be a hopeful place."

"And a hopeless one, as well," Talia said. "But I won't argue the point. You're right, you have a lot to be hopeful for. So, I think we need to ensure it stays that way."

"And how to you propose to do that?"

Talia nodded to the Book trapped under Dan's leg.

"We have to destroy the Book. Kill it, somehow."

Chapter Nineteen

"Obviously, you failed at that. Killing the Book," I say. "Is it because you didn't have the Staff of Solomon to help?"

"No," Talia says. "Something much more basic than that."

She squeegees more condensation from the side of her mug with the pad of her finger. "The problem was, I was wrong."

♦ ♦ ♦

"I think you're gonna have to explain yourself on that one," I say slowly. Slowly, because I'm also scared where that explanation may lead.

"Let me tell you what happened, so everyone's on the same page," Talia says. "Do you even know what happened that day?"

"No," I say. "Just that my father and grandfather were killed. Mom couldn't tell me much. All I really know is, The Last Word was there on the morning of Sunday, April the first, 1984." I take a breath. "But, by that evening, my grandfather was dead and so was my father. My mother was now the owner of a gaping hole in the ground where the store used to be. And, aside from some vague conjecture from the New Hope residents, no one knows what happened. And the only person that might…"—I looked pointedly at Talia—"…disappeared and—

aside from a quick pit stop for Kayla—didn't turn back up until a few months ago."

Talia nods. "Okay," she says. "That's the basics. Let me fill you in."

And then she tells us.

CHAPTER TWENTY

OVER THE NEXT week, Dan and Talia met after the store closed, sometimes at the store, sometimes at Dan and Lila's apartment.

They tried the obvious things first.

They set the Book in the barbeque, doused It in lighter fluid, and threw a match on top of It.

They stepped back and grinned at each other at the satisfying *whoof* of the Book going up in flames. They watched the cover blacken and curl inward, then the pages catch and curl and crisp to ash. It went quickly, but hey, It was an old book, right?

They gave It ten minutes. There was still quite a bit of Book for the flames to eat, but it was working. Dan gave It another good soaking with the lighter fluid, then they went inside to give Lila the good news.

Lila was sitting on the couch, hands absently rubbing her belly. *Dallas* was playing unseen on the television, J.R. Ewing no doubt plotting something devious.

"I think that's the end of that," Dan told her. "That thing's crispier than a bucket of Colonel Sanders's finest."

Lila gave him a wan smile.

"What's the matter, babe?" he said, sitting down beside her. "Thought you'd be—"

Lila pointed to the television.

On the screen, Dan and Talia were setting a volume of the *Encyclopedia Britannica*—Volume Fourteen: Libi to Mary—on the barbeque. The three of them watched as Dan soaked it with lighter fluid, then step back and grin when the match was tossed and the screen briefly flared to white as the book went *whoof.*

"What. The. Hell," Talia said, turning back to Lila.

Then Lila pointed lower.

The Book leaned against the television stand. Perfectly fine.

♦ ♦ ♦

THEY TRIED TEARING the pages out.

That turned out to be *Encyclopedia Britannica*, Volume Twenty-Three: Vase to Zygo.

♦ ♦ ♦

THEY USED STAN Holt's shredder. They borrowed a friend's wood chipper. They took a small boat out to the deepest part of Lake Kwanashishing. The Book was in a wooden box weighted with stones. They dropped It over the side.

Nothing worked.

No matter what they did, no matter where It was left, no matter how destructive they got, the Book was always waiting for them, propped against the television stand, when they got back to Dan and Lila's home.

Dan was going to purchase some explosives when Talia and Lila called a time out.

"I think we can keep escalating the physical destruction all we want, Dan," Talia said, "but I don't think It cares. It'll just keep shrugging them off every attempt and keep coming back here."

"Then what can we do?"

"I think we have to go in a different direction," Talia said.

"What does that mean?"

"It means, if the tiger you've been hunting has killed the hunters who came at it with knives and arrows and traps and guns, then it's time to stop sending hunters."

"What do you send instead?" Lila asked.

"How about a fucking T-Rex?"

◆ ◆ ◆

THE NEXT FEW days were spent researching. Dan made a lot of long-distance calls to libraries only for the staff to either misunderstand what he was looking for, or utterly refuse.

Talia dug around the archives of the area libraries. Dan never asked how she got to and from them, as some were a couple of hours away by car, and Talia never offered.

Of the two, Talia had the greater luck. True to her previous statements, there were some surprisingly helpful sources and glimmers of information. At least twice, Talia had found information that led to other information, that ultimately led to a surprisingly impressive amount of information. Nothing that could be considered a treasure trove, nor even complete, but conclusions could be made and theories at least partially confirmed.

After four days, Talia met with Dan and Lila back at their apartment.

◆ ◆ ◆

"YOU SURE THIS is the right thing to do?" Dan said. It was Sunday, the morning of April first. The Last Word was closed Sundays, so they'd have the entire day today to get done what they needed to accomplish.

"As sure as anyone can be when dealing with magical books, ancient demon gods, and multiple universes," Talia said.

Lila sat in the kitchen, a tall glass of water in her hand. Dan knew she really wanted coffee, but his unborn daughter had decided to make the merest whiff of coffee disgusting to Lila. She gagged so badly that all coffee was removed from the apartment, and Dan popped breath mints before coming home from work.

"But," Lila said, "do you think it's the *right* thing?"

Talia was as strange and mysterious as she could possibly be, but one thing Dan could say about her was there wasn't a hint of bullshit about her. So he wasn't surprised with her answer.

"I honestly can't tell you it's the *right* thing, Lee," she said, "but I firmly believe, based on everything we found out, that it's the *only* thing we can do."

"There's a lot of space between those two goalposts, Talia."

Talia didn't try to hide the unease in her eyes when she said, "I know."

Dan didn't want to linger on that note. He knew how anxious Lila was about this. Last night, the two of them laid in bed, conscious of the third person there with them—Lila had lately begun calling her "pre-Monica"—and she'd been on her back, staring at the darkness of the ceiling as she said, "Look, I know this is going to sound terrible, but…"

"Just say it, Lee," Dan had said.

"You're going to be a dad soon. In a matter of weeks."

He reached out a hand to caress her belly. "I know, babe."

"She's been through this before. She's…seen and done stuff I can't even imagine. And she's barely old enough to drive. And she looks like she hasn't even seen the far side of puberty yet."

"But like you said, Lee. The things she's been through…"

"The things she's done, Dan," Lila said. "She wiped how many people off the face of the earth? Her entire family included?"

"You know her," he said. "She's not like that anymore."

"Yeah, I know. It was the Book, It influenced her, It twisted her mind."

"But who else has the knowledge that she has?"

"I don't know, Dan. Have we checked enough? Have we run down every avenue? You're the guy who reads all the horror and comics, is there a real-life Dr. Weird we can contact?"

"Dr. Strange, honey."

"Whatever. You know what I mean."

"I don't know."

"It's just that…"

"Say it, Lee," Dan said. "Just say it."

"What if her mind is still twisted by that thing?" she said, and a tremble entered her voice. "What if, all the time she's been talking about something manipulating that…evil, horrible thing, what if it's been her?" Her breath hitched. "What if she's just going to do it again? Wipe someone…wipe you off the planet?"

"Lee, honey…"

"No, don't, Dan," she said, the words sharp, cutting. "Just don't. You're my husband. The father of my child." She turned on her side toward him, touched his face. "I can't lose you. I need you. Monica needs you."

"I know. And I need both of you," he said. "You are the best thing that ever happened to me, Lee. After Mom died, I was lost, and I had no way out of the woods I was wandering through. Dad couldn't help, my friends couldn't. But you found me and led me out."

"Dan…"

"I'm just saying, honey," he said, and he placed his hands on each side of her face, the warmth of her filling his palms, "I probably need you more than you need me. I love you. I love that I'm going to be a dad. I'm not leaving you. No way."

"But Talia—"

"—has her issues, but overall, if I'm going to have a partner in this, I don't think I could do better than her."

"And that's my point," she said, putting her own palm over his. "Why do you have to be involved?"

"Because the B…"—he saw her eyes flash, even in the dark. She didn't like to refer to it directly—"…that infernal thing keeps showing up on our doorstep. Either the store or here. It's *my* problem. Hell, Lee, Marcia Mayer got the damn thing from The Last Word and gave it to Talia. It started there."

"It started two hundred years ago. She told you that."

"You know what I mean."

"You have so much to lose, Dan. What if it goes wrong?"

"What if it doesn't? You're right," he said. "I know what's at stake. And believe me, I don't want to bring our daughter into a world where that thing exists." He moved his hand, stroked her cheek. "But you know I also can't ask a fifteen-year-old girl, no matter how good her resumé is with this stuff, to do this for me. You get that, right?"

Lila hesitated, and closed her eyes for a moment as his fingers played lightly on her cheek. Then she opened them and, with a shuddering breath, said, "I do. I get it." Then she brought up her own hand to cover his once again. "But I also hope that you get that I need you to come home. Because, if you don't, then I may get lost in those same woods you were in. With no one to lead me out. Okay?"

"Okay," Dan said, ignoring the heavy stone that seemed to settle in his chest. He tried to lighten it by telling his wife he loved her, but somehow that only made the stone feel heavier.

◆ ◆ ◆

THEY'D SPEND MOST of that Sunday morning going over the plans and reassuring Lila everything would be fine. It was mid-afternoon when Dan and Talia unlocked the back door to The Last Word and entered the quiet store. Dan disabled the alarm and automatically reached for the lights. Talia touched his arm and shook her head. He nodded, and left the store dark.

Dan navigated the dark back half of the store with ease, having grown up dodging boxes and wheel carts and everything else that washed up on the shore of the backroom. He was not surprised that Talia had no problem finding her way either. Nothing she did surprised him now, despite the short time they'd known each other.

In the business end of the store, they moved in front of the cash counter and stopped. The street visible through the storefront windows was quiet, with only the odd passing car to break the scene.

Dan reached into his bag and pulled out the Book. "You ready?" he asked, his mouth going dry.

"No," she said, casting a wary eye on the Book, "and neither are you, but let's get this done."

♦ ♦ ♦

AFTER REALIZING THE Book could not be destroyed by conventional means, and then researching other possible solutions, they'd decided to do the unthinkable.

Just like Stinky Pete Wilson had done less than three years earlier, Dan and Talia were going to summon a demon to help them with their problem. However, instead of calling a lesser demon like all'Gueroth, they were going to the source.

An Outer God.

The father of all'Gueroth.

The Crawling Chaos. The Black Man. Arioch. The Stalker Among The Stars. The Faceless God. The God of a Thousand Forms. The God of a Thousand Names.

Nyarlathotep.

◆ ◆ ◆

"SO, HOW DO we go about summoning the God of Eleventy Billion Names?" Dan asked.

"Before we do anything, Dan, three rules."

"Okay, hit me."

"First, you have to treat this entire…event…with respect. You refer to him only by his name, and nothing else."

"Okay," he said. "Got it."

"Second, no matter what happens before we're done, no exclamations or uses of any other gods' names. No blurting of Christian gods, or sons of gods, if you know what I mean."

"You may have to remind me about that one on occasion. It's a bad habit of mine."

"I know."

"Okay. Respect. His name. No calling on the Great Kazoo, or—"

"Which brings us to number three," Talia said. "No humour. We have to remain serious, focused, and respectful."

"Dude sounds like a real Debbie Downer."

Talia shot him a look sharp enough that he threw up both hands to ward her off. "Just getting the last bit of sarcasm out," he said. "Serious, focused, respectful from here on out."

"Thank you."

"Rephrasing my original question, how do we go about summoning this particular Outer God?" Dan said. "How did Peter Wilson do it?"

"You probably don't want to know how Peter Wilson did it." She pointed to the Book in his hand. Dan wanted to put It down, but Talia asked him to be in contact with It at all times. Said the last thing she wanted was for them to get all prepared, only for the Book to whisk Itself away. She did not, however, want any contact with It herself. She told Dan she'd had quite enough of the Book, but from the look in her eyes, Dan figured it was like a junkie desperately turning down one last hit. It wasn't really done willingly, but only out of a sense of personal safety and survival. She knew her limit.

"With Peter, the Book didn't have a lot of time, so It made him jump through a lot of hoops. Without a deeper knowledge and understanding, he had to resort to complex incantations."

"And we don't?"

"No," she said. "It had more time with me, and gave me a lot more information and experience. It's the difference between someone needing to put something together who's never done it before, and requiring an instruction manual to lead them step-by-step through the process…"

"That would be Pete."

"Yes," she said, "…and someone who's studied the assembly process for a lot time, and had a lot of practice with it. No instruction manual, no step-by-step."

"And that would be you."

"It would."

"So, what do we do?"

"I've pushed living beings through the thin wall that separates our reality from other ones. And I've pulled them back through to this side. But I've never tried to pull something like an Outer God, so I'm going to ask you to hold onto that Book, and join hands with me. I need to draw from you."

"So I'm basically going to be some sort of transformer in the middle of an extension cord?"

"Basically, yes."

"Okay," Dan said. Then, after a thought occurred to him. "This gonna hurt?"

"It's going to very likely hurt," she said. "And it will also be the most terrifying and unpleasant thing you'll ever experience."

Dan didn't trust himself to answer. Instead, he just blinked, swallowed, took a breath, then did the bravest thing he'd ever done in his entire short life.

He held his hand out for Talia to take.

♦ ♦ ♦

SHE DIDN'T TAKE his hand immediately. Instead, she closed her eyes, took several deep breaths, and widened her stance a bit, as though getting ready for a fight. Then she opened her eyes, glanced over to him briefly. From her pocket, she pulled a small pouch with a drawstring. She opened it, and emptied the contents into her palm.

Dan couldn't make out what the objects were at first, only that they were white and pearlescent.

Then he understood.

Teeth.

He reached into his pocket and pulled out the tooth he'd been carrying with him now for months. He had no idea why, but it made him feel better somehow. Protected. He held it up, pinched between thumb and forefinger.

She didn't say anything, but her eyebrows knit together in question. "It showed up after the last call with—"

"Your daughter," Talia said. "I remember."

He twisted it this way and that. "I kind of see it as a good luck charm, somehow. Maybe it'll help." He offered it to her.

Talia stared at it for quite a while, then gently plucked it from his fingers. She thanked him, and set it in with the others.

Dan had a lot of questions, but like Talia, decided to hold them for now. And then the thought flew away from him as the phone rang.

◆ ◆ ◆

DAN STARTED TOWARD the phone, then stopped.

"Not really the time to be fielding customer questions, Dan," Talia said.

But the phone continued to ring, and it was insistent. Dan didn't *want* to answer it, but he felt compelled to.

"Dan?" Talia said.

"I…" He looked at the phone. Then he broke and strode to the counter, with a mumbled apology on his lips. He heard Talia huff out a frustrated breath behind him.

◆ ◆ ◆

"HELLO?"

"Hi, um…"

"Oh, crap," Dan said. He was rattled. "Sorry. Should have said, 'Hello, thanks for calling The Last Word. How can I help you?'"

The line went quiet for a moment, but Dan heard breathing. He actually heard the caller's breath catch. "Hello?" he said. "You still there?"

"Yes, sorry, you said I'd reached The Last Word?"

"Yes, you did!" He looked over to Talia, who rolled her hands to get him to wrap it up. He turned back to the phone.

"Sorry, can I ask…" It had been months now, but Dan was fairly certain he knew the voice. "…can I ask who I'm speaking to?"

"Sure. It's Dan. Dan Holt." Then the caller almost sounded as though they were strangling. There was noise, but it was panicked-sounding. He said, "Hello?"

"Dan Holt?"

"Yep, that's—" *Yes*, he thought. *It is her.* "Wait a minute. Is this Monica? My daughter Monica?"

"Dad?" she said in a voice so small it sounded like it came from a child.

"Monica," he said, relief and concern washing over him. "Monica," he repeated. "Honey, what happened to you?"

That tiny, child's voice again, so full of pain and longing. "What do you mean?"

Dan didn't understand the question. He'd talked to her a couple of times now. He said, "I was starting to think you weren't going to call me anymore."

He heard a sharp intake of breath.

And then the line went dead.

◆ ◆ ◆

HE DROPPED THE phone. It was hot to the touch. "Jesus Christ," Dan said, resting his elbows on the counter and sinking his head low enough that his hands encircled the back of his neck.

"Dan, I *told* you not to use—" Talia's tone was chiding, but gentle.

"That was my daughter," he said, his voice low and aching. "That was Monica."

"I got that," she said. "What did she say?"

"Not much, we got cut off." He lifted his head, turned to her. "But honestly? If I had to guess, it was like she'd never talked to me before."

"So, this was probably her first call."

"You think?"

"You never mentioned that she seemed surprised to be talking to you in the previous calls."

"Yeah, not that I can remember."

"Then they've come out of sequence," she said. "Time can be funny like that."

"You think it means anything?"

She put a hand on his shoulder. "If it means anything, Dan, I think it means we need to ensure you get to see your daughter."

Dan nodded.

"Let's get this done."

◆ ◆ ◆

TALIA WALKED BACK to middle of the open area in front of the cash counter, bent and scooped up her teeth, and closed her fist over them. She assumed the same wide-legged stance as before, then closed her eyes and took a few deep breaths.

It only took her a few moments, but then she was ready. She reached her right hand to Dan and he took it with his left, the Book clutched tightly in his other hand.

As soon as his hand made contact with hers, a scourge of electricity ran up his arm, feeling like it both numbed and sent an explosion of tingles and muscle tremors from wrist to bicep. Her grip tightened to a clutch, and a keening worked out of her throat.

The Book grew heavier in his grip. It shook and vibrated and he squeezed It tighter.

Every single muscle in her neck was delineated, as though she was fighting against her head being pulled off. The teeth crunched weirdly in her other hand as she ground them together. Her breath, initially slow and measured, had quickly scaled up to a pant. Her jaw muscles clenched, her forehead grew shiny with sweat, the panting turned into grunting gasps.

Then, it was just that, for a long time. It could have been two minutes, it could have been twenty, Dan didn't know. Time could only be measured by the tremors of her hand in his, and by the sounds squeezing out of her constricted throat.

Finally, there was a shift in the air. A harsh snap as the air grew thicker, heavier, then it was cold inside the bookstore. Frigidly cold. Dan's fingers were numb from the pressure and the temperature. The Book burned with aching cold in his hand. Talia's face tightened into a clench-toothed grimace, and a grunt of pain slid past her lips, the breath fogging.

He wanted to ask her if she was okay. Terrified of breaking her concentration, he remained silent, enduring the crushing pain of her hand grinding the bones of his together.

As though reading his mind, her head turned slowly toward him and he swore he heard the bones of her spine creaking against each other as she did. She pushed her eyes open and, still through clenched teeth, said, "Get…ready…he's…coming."

There was nothing to really prepare, so instead, he opened his fingers, then readjusted his grip on her hand. He squeezed the Book tighter. Their breaths hazed the atmosphere in the small space.

And he waited.

♦ ♦ ♦

HE DID NOT wait long.

Dan was about to turn, having caught a flash of movement from the corner of his eye, but a hole tearing itself into being in the air not six feet away from him made him forget everything else.

The hole, like the screen of an old tube television in reverse, started with a single tiny point, which spread outward left and right in a line that was, improbably, both sun-bright and nightmare-black at the same time. As it widened, the sound was...terrible. Like souls torn from living bodies. Like stars dying. Like the universe collapsing. Like hope vanishing.

Whisper-soft and ear-breakingly loud, the wail from the hole made his bowels loosen and tears fall and freeze on his cheeks. If it hadn't been for Talia wrenching on him, he would have dropped the Book.

The hole then opened top to bottom, widening obscenely in a desecration of birth. The dark light that shot through the opening stabbed at his eyes and he turned his head this way and that to try and escape the physical pain of its impact. He couldn't breathe, couldn't think, couldn't move. He was losing it, losing his sanity, his mind threatening to erase itself simply to avoid processing the profane desolation that bombarded it.

And then the terrifyingly tall Man of Black stepped through the opening.

◆ ◆ ◆

THE BLACK MAN stepped into the store from elsewhere, and stood, hunched over, to survey his surroundings. Satisfied, he rose to his full height.

The ceiling rose with him, accommodating his height. It flexed like it was an inverted trampoline. It bowed up, at least three feet above his head.

The bookstore had twelve-foot ceilings, Dan knew. The Black Man had to be a foot taller than that. And yet, the room allowed him to stand upright. *Or he's literally bending it to his will.*

Dan's sanity was on shifting sand, but he was somehow holding it together. *For now.*

Dan could not look directly at the Black Man, his eyes, his mind, rejected the difficulty of trying to make sense of the blasphemous being sharing the room. The figure warped and bent with artificial darkness as any light that reached the Outer God twisted around or away from him. Dan caught flashes of darkness. His skin was the darkness between stars. His robes were the heart of a black hole. Dan sensed movement near his head, glanced that way and, in an eye-watering moment, realized the Outer God had smiled at the two of them, his teeth angular, sharp, and black. The tongue that darted out to wet his foul lips was an eclipse.

And then the Outer God spoke.

"Natalia Glenda Davis," he said, and his voice was a threnody, both beautiful and malevolent. "Daniel Stanley Holt." He nodded, and Dan's heart quaked in his chest at the pull of this thing uttering his name.

"Nyarlathotep," Talia said. Her voice was high, but carried force. *She's fifteen years old*, Dan thought, *and she's got more balls than any man I know.* "You have been called to complete a task of our choosing."

Nyarlathotep's head bobbed back in surprise. "Indeed?" He opened his palm toward her. "Please, do proceed."

"You will remove the Book from this universe. Whether it is through destruction, or relocation, either will do, but you will complete this task."

Nyarlathotep laughed then, and Dan felt galaxies die.

"That may have been your intent, young one," he said, and despite the tone of his voice, he sounded joyful. "However, I have no intention of being ordered about by a whelp and her lapdog."

He then did something surprising. He sat down cross-legged in front of Talia and Dan. Books and shelves fell over themselves to shift away from the being.

"You're wondering what I'm doing," the Black Man said. "I'm waiting for what comes next."

"What—" It was all Talia got out.

Then the front door opened.

And Stan Holt stepped in.

♦♦♦

"Dan?" Stan said, obviously confused. "What's going on?"

"Oh my god, Dad!" Dan barked. "You gotta leave! Now!"

"Talia?" his father said, still not getting it. He turned to his son. "Is that Talia Davis?"

"Stanley Walter Gene Holt," Nyarlathotep said in his pleasing, happy tone. "Three is a much better number than two, isn't it? Now we have…" —he indicated Stan, Dan, then Talia—"…the father, the son, and the holy ghost." He clapped his hands. "Lovely."

"Dad," Dan said, "why are you here?"

"I called Lila. She said she was worried…"

"Goddammit."

Talia said, "I said, no mention of deities."

Dan stabbed a finger at the Black Man, still smiling, still cross-legged on the floor. "He just referenced—"

"I don't care," she said. "Enough." She turned quickly to Stan. "Mr. Holt, please stay by the door if you will not leave." Then, back to the demon in the room. "And you, Nyarlathotep. You will do as I command. The Book—"

"—is of little importance to me," the Black Man said. "It was simply a means to an end. I put a problem in front of you, and you foolishly attempted to solve it. And you lapped up every pathetic little splash and dollop of information I laid out in front of you."

Dan then realized the enormity of their error. "Oh, shit."

"Oh, shit indeed, Daniel," the Black Man said, laughter rumbling from his chest.

"What do you want?" Dan said.

Nyarlathotep leaned forward until he was inches from Dan's face. Dan closed his eyes. His entire body trembled with pants-shitting fear. The Outer God stank of cabbage and cinnamon and dread and despair. His bladder released, and he simply didn't care anymore. "I want nothing, innocent child," the Black Man whispered, and the sound was profanity. "Literally, I only want nothing. I exist merely to exist. I serve the great Azathoth, who slumbers at the centre of everything. Great Azathoth is comforted both by the dancers, pipers, and drummers who play for him, and also by the knowledge that his first-born is the force of his will in all things and all worlds."

He leaned back. "What do I want? I want to complete the will of my father and, if given the opportunity along the way, to plant the seeds of uncertainty, of confusion, of ignorance, and to reap the chaos that blooms from them." He studied his nails, picked at something trapped beneath one. "For now, it serves the purposes of both Azathoth and myself that I sow those seeds here."

The Black Man finished with his fingers and gave Talia a massive, black-toothed smile. "And for that, I thank you. You opened the door to bring me here."

Talia's voice was thunder as she bellowed, *"I BROUGHT YOU HERE TO DO MY BIDDING. YOU WILL DO AS YOUR SUMMONER COMMANDS."*

"No," Nyarlathotep said calmly, "I do not believe I will." He crooked a single ebony digit at Stan, still standing by the door, as though to entice him closer. "Come," he said. Dan's father fought to stop his forward motion as he slid across the floor to the demon. Dan watched in helpless frustration as panic gripped his father as much as the unrelenting will of the Black Man did.

Stan could only yell, "No! No! No!"

And when the older man was easily within reach, Nyarlathotep stretched out a casual hand. It was a massive black shadow wrapped in a glove of twisted darkness as it engulfed the whole of Stan's head.

Then the Black Man clenched his fist.

The sickening crunch of bone grinding against bone, and flesh rending to tatters, filled the room. Blood and saliva and cerebrospinal fluid and brain matter leaked between the demon's fingers

Enough that, in his fear, Dan lost control of his body.

He dropped the Book.

♦ ♦ ♦

"OH DEAR," NYARLATHOTEP said, clasping a black hand to his chest, "you've dropped your Book, Daniel."

A small movement of a gore-streaked black finger on his free hand sent the Book spinning off to a corner of the bookstore. Talia had time only to cry out, "No!" before that same black finger flicked in Dan's direction.

Dan lifted off the ground and hung in space, his feet peddling weakly for purchase and finding none.

Still, his eyes were locked on his father, prone and leaking on the carpeting of the store he'd worked at his entire life. "Dad," he whispered.

"...is gone, boy," the Black Man said. "As are you, in mere moments. As will she be, moments after you." He indicated Talia, who stood, clutching her collection of teeth in frustration and fury.

"What do you want from us?" Dan choked out.

Nyarlathotep smiled then, a wide, dark, malevolent smile that sucked all light and hope from the room. "Me?" he said, placing long fingers to his chest. "I'm afraid the answer will disappoint you, boy." He stepped closer to Dan, leaning in until Dan coughed on his fetid breath. "I am Nyarlathotep," he said. "A Lord of Chaos. I exist only to exist. If there is sanity, I push it to insanity. If there is logic, I break it to illogic, I see order and I demand only sweet chaos. I will destroy everything and when I am gone there will be nothing." He reached out and cupped Dan's jaw in his massive hand, the skin so cold it burned. "Sweet, beautiful nothing."

He let Dan's face go and stepped back. "But I didn't say I wouldn't enjoy the process."

He stood to his full height then, the roof bowing above him once again, and he swept his arms out to each side, throwing his head back and laughing as Dan rose into the air.

And then, he disassembled.

◆ ◆ ◆

THE BLACK MAN dropped his hand from Dan's face. The hand had been so cold that its absence felt like a fire on his jaw, any warmth too much for his overloaded nerves.

That feeling of heat lasted only a second, and then was forgotten as Dan felt his body rise from the floor. He hung in the air like a puff from a dandelion. Nothing was within reach for him to anchor himself. Talia made a move to approach him—

And then his world, his universe, was pain. Shocking, brain-shaking agony firing through every cell. He felt his vision narrowing and realized he was passing out.

Until he wasn't.

Nyarlathotep had flicked another finger. "Can't have you shutting down when we're just getting to the fun part, can we," he said in his terrifying, melodious voice.

Dan's vision was…strange. He couldn't move his head to look around, but he also couldn't even move his eyes, couldn't blink. He was having trouble seeing properly, everything seemed doubled. Sounds were strange.

The Black Man laughed. "You are confused, boy. I understand. Let me help you." He took a step back. "Let me allow you to view yourself through my eyes."

It felt then as though he'd blinked. Everything went dark…no, not right…everything went *away* for a moment, and then he could see again.

Through Nyarlathotep's eyes.

At any other time, the most strange and terrifying thing would have been *how* he saw. Everything was more red-shifted. Everything, near and far, was so sharply focused Dan could have counted the individual pages of a closed book. Everything had a strange glow or aura about it. He could see beyond the walls of the store if he tried.

But worse than all that, what flooded into his mind as he took in anything, living or not, was an instant awareness of whether it was threat or weapon, whether it was to be used or could be destroyed. The instinct bombarded him.

At any other time, this would have been the worst aspect of this new experience.

But then Dan looked out of the other's eyes, and he saw himself.

♦ ♦ ♦

It took a beat for Dan to understand what he was even looking at. The reddish form before him was vaguely human-shaped, but then again, not. It simply didn't make sense.

Nothing that scattered could possibly be alive.

And yet, the heart still beat. The lungs still worked.

He knew, because he could see them clearly.

Dan had seen exploded-view diagrams before. Drawings of complicated machinery or systems that had all the parts separated out, as though the illustration caught it in mid-explosion.

That was Dan right now.

He was a living exploded-view model.

At the centre, all his organs were separated out from each other, so each one could be seen clearly, while all the connections, though stretched, remained in place. Outward from that were the bones of his skeleton. Outward from that, the overlaying muscles and tendons, each pulled slightly away from each other. Outward from that, the skin, separated raggedly, bracketed the muscle.

His head was the same, with the brain at the centre, the skull cracked in half and pulled away from it. Eyes and ears jutting out farther still. Jaw separated and down to mid-chest, with the tongue hanging on by the root and all his teeth out in front like some small asteroid field.

And yet, his organs continued to work. His eyes still saw. His brain still functioned.

He couldn't speak. But the Black Man seemed to know what he would have said.

"This is what I do, boy," he said. "You are a complex, organized system. Quite ridiculously complex, when you compare yourself to me. I am merely dust and mud, arcanely molded and given sentience. A simple system."

The Black Man moved toward Dan's form. He raised a finger and, in a weird doubling, Dan saw him push a raggedly-clawed nail through his eye, while also seeing the nail come at his eye.

"Simple is better. Chaos better still." He swept a hand through the field of floating teeth, caught them, and tossed them at Talia. "For your collection." He laughed.

"Daniel," he said then, "I give you my greatest gift." He spread his black hands. "I return you to chaos."

Dan had a brief moment of unbridled panic, and he heard Talia scream, "No!"

Then he caught a glimpse of his body separating, flying to all the corners of the room.

And then he was gone.

◆ ◆ ◆

"YOU FUCKING *BASTARD*!" Talia screamed, falling to her gore-streaked knees on the gore-streaked floor.

Dan was gone. Simply *gone*.

She looked down at her blood-sodden hands. No, not gone. He was everywhere in the room, sprayed over every surface.

Nyarlathotep broke him apart, but then he *atomized* Dan.

And now, the Outer God was turning his sights on her.

She had to do something. Quickly.

Talia reacted without thinking. She thrust both hands out toward the Book, summoned It to her as easily as she would pick up a glass. It slapped into her outstretched palms and she threw her head back and screamed as the feeling of both a body-shaking orgasm competed with the feeling of all her bones becoming white-hot.

She fought past both the pain and the pleasure, but drew on both as she took control of the Book and commanded It to carry out the first of two tasks.

The first had to happen now. *Now.*

She stood. The Black Man, somehow *not* covered in Dan's mortal remains, was still turning toward her. He looked down at her hands.

Saw the Book.

"Oh," he said. Then the bastard smiled.

"Nyarlathotep," she said, facing him directly. She thundered, "**GO.**"

There was no noise, no final words from Nyarlathotep.

Just a rush of wind.

◆ ◆ ◆

TALIA FOUND HERSELF still holding the Book. And it was raining.

The store was gone. Simply *gone*.

Roof, walls, floor. Gone.

What remained was a roughly circular divot in the ground, deep enough to expose part of the foundation and the ground underneath. The buildings to either side still stood, though the siding of each was warped and discoloured.

Talia hung about fifteen feet above the newly exposed sub-layer, Book in hand.

Nyarlathotep was gone.

She closed her eyes and breathed a sigh of relief. She stayed there for a few moments, letting the cold rain cleanse her, the remains of Dan Holt sluicing down into the ground below. Then she followed the rain down to the newly exposed earth, her eyes not opening again until her feet touched the cold, wet dirt.

She had two more tasks, both exceedingly painful.

◆ ◆ ◆

ON THE GROUND, in the space where The Last Word had existed until moments ago, Talia was standing below street level. Where once was a building, now there was only a pit.

She looked down to the Book, once again in her possession.

At one point, she'd longed for this. Prayed for it. Dreamed about it.

Now that she had the vile thing in her hands again, she could only think of how she wanted It as far away from her as possible.

It had caused all this.

This destruction.

This waste.

This death.

That's all the Book was. A tool of death.

Still, It whispered to her. Promised her. Threatened her. Enticed her. Terrified her.

She had to get rid of It. But this banishment, unlike Nyarlathotep's, would require thought. She had to not only put It someplace safe, but also someplace where It couldn't manipulate itself back into use again.

It had to go away.

But to where?

The rain pattered against her skull, and Dan's blood slowly sloughed off her and soaked into the ground as she turned the problem over and over in her mind. A snatch of a thought came to her then.

Theo bent the Book to his will.

Then she realized she'd been asking the wrong question.

Not, to where? To whom?

She held the Book aloft, high above her head. The rain refused to hit It, the drops curving around It, bending away from Its abomination as the light had turned from the Outer God. She turned her face to the weeping sky, then fastened her gaze squarely on the Book.

She knew exactly what to do with It. Knew, despite the vague nature of her command, that the Book would be sent where It would be incapable of manipulating anyone, of hurting anyone, of whispering Its secrets.

Once again, forming the precise command in her mind, holding it there for a few critical moments, twisting it this way and that, looking for mistakes, for structural flaws, for loopholes. She found none.

"Book," she said, facing It directly. Once again, Talia thundered, "**GO.**"

As before, there was no great sound.

There was only a small rush of wind.

And then the Book, too, was gone.

♦ ♦ ♦

Talia sobbed then.

Maybe it was for the loss of the Book one last time. Or maybe it was for the loss of a friend. Dan had been a good man.

Maybe it was just for herself.

She climbed out of the pit and, streaked with mud and bits of Dan's blood, soaked to the skin from the rain, she turned in the direction she needed to go.

One last thing to do, she thought.

PART THREE
DIFFERING OPINIONS

"I believe in the purpose of everything living,
That taking is but the forerunner of giving;
That strangers are friends that we someday may meet..."

FAITH
EDGAR A. GUEST

Chapter Twenty-One

TALIA STARES DEEP into her beer mug, as though the answers to the universe might be lurking there, and then finally raises her eyes to mine. "I told your father he needed to destroy the Book. And I got him killed, Monica." A tear slid from her eye and down her cheek. "I was too young, too stupid, and I am the reason you never met your father. I am the reason he never got to meet his daughter."

She stops talking then, but her eyes continue to search mine, and mine search hers. Somewhere in there, Lex's hand grabs mine again, but she doesn't say anything.

Talia and I have had our moments. There's been times I wanted to kick her ass, but there's also been times I wanted to—and did—hug her.

Right now, god's honest truth, I have no idea how to react. So, I don't. I remain very still. I don't cry, because what's done is done, and it's thirty years in the past, there's no changing it. I don't get angry because I can see from Talia's face, from her posture, from every signal that's coming off her, there was no malice there, she'd never wanted anything bad to happen. She was trying to do good, and bad came from it.

Just like back when she was a child.

Just like a few months ago, with Lex.

The three of us remain quiet for a few minutes, each processing our own thoughts and reactions. It isn't an awkward silence, more a contemplative one.

Eventually though, someone has to say something. "Okay," I say roughly, and clear my throat. "Okay. Thank you for your honesty, Talia. I want you—no, you need to know—I'm not angry. I'm sad, but not angry."

She nods. "Thank you," she says.

Lex is tentative, not wanting to be insensitive, but her curiosity is obviously prodding her onward. She says, "May not be the right time, and Monica, tell me if I'm overstepping, but I have questions."

"Probably the same as mine," I say, and motion for her to carry on.

"Okay, first," Lex says, turning to Talia, who has gone back to searching her beer mug for the secrets of the universe, "you banished, Nar…Nyar…"

"Nyarlathotep," she says, distractedly. "Though we shouldn't be saying his name."

"Right, names have power. So we've seen," Lex says. "But where did you banish him *to*, exactly?"

"I will tell you, but it will make no sense to you."

Lex repositions her elbows on the table, as though bracing herself. "Try me."

"I banished the Black Man back to a previous prison, a planet named Abbith. It's a truly desolate, forbidding world."

"There's…" I say, then stop. I take a drink, try again. "I'm a touch lost. Abbith?"

"Yes," Talia says. "It's—"

"It's a planet that revolves around seven stars behind Xoth," Lex says. Then she cants her head to one side, squinting.

"Ah, right," I say. "*That* Abbith." I look over at Lex. "I mean, how could we forget Abbith, right?" But Lex isn't picking up what I'm putting down.

She still has that puzzled look on her face as her mouth pops open and she says, "Abbith. Very dark, very barren, very quiet world. The only life there are metallic brains, possibly the most formidable intellects in the known universes. They carry the secrets of the universes."

"Metallic brains," I say.

"Yes," both Talia and Lex say.

"The secrets..." I say, rather dubiously, "of the universes..."

"Even better," Talia says, "they share them with no one, especially not the Outer Gods." And Lex nods.

She fucking nods at what Talia says.

Like she understands it.

"I warned you it would make no sense to you."

"You said that to Lex. Apparently, that's not the case," I say.

There's a faint tremor in Lex's voice as she says, "Yeah, Talia. How do I know all this? You didn't..."—she waggles her fingers over her head—"...you know...inject me with knowledge or something again?"

"No," Talia says. "I didn't. I suspect it's your Staff. Or having crawled around inside the head of your father."

I place a hand on Lex's to stall further questions. "And you're probably right," I say. "We'll figure it out." I stop. Breathe. "May I ask a couple more things related to what you just told us?"

"Of course," Talia says.

"Okay," I say. "Okay." I glance at Lex, and she nods for me to continue. She's obviously got enough to mentally chew on her own right now anyway. "You said, after it was all done, that you had one last task."

"Yes," she says. "After it was all done, my mind was

◆ ◆ ◆

NUMB, HER BODY struggling to push forward through rain that had increased in intensity to driving sheets, Talia kept a hand out, using buildings, trees, telephone poles, anything to keep her upright and moving toward her destination.

The apartment of Dan and Lila Holt.

It was normally a brief walk from one location to the other, but it felt like it took Talia hours to move herself from one place to the other.

But somehow, she did it. Somehow, she found herself at the door to the second-floor apartment. Somehow, she raised her hand, curled it into a fist, and knocked on the door.

And somehow, she managed to stay conscious long enough to tell Lila everything, and to completely destroy the woman's world.

◆ ◆ ◆

"YOU WENT TO see my mom?"

"Of course I did," Talia says. "She'd just lost her father-in-law, her husband, and the family business. I wasn't going to walk away without warning her of that. She deserved that respect."

I nod.

"She let me in, and immediately bustled me into a hot shower before I could tell her anything."

"Sounds like Mom," I say. "Care first, all else comes after."

"When I came out, she bundled me into a big fluffy bathrobe—"

"My dad's," I say. I still have it.

"—put a hot cup of coffee in my hand, and then I told her everything."

"All of it?" Lex asks. "Even the Black Man?"

"Even the Man of Black, yes."

"How'd she take it?"

"As you'd expect," Talia said. Her gaze was downcast yet again, her body here, but her mind back in the eighties. "She cried. She sobbed. At one point, we had to stop and we just held each other's hands. I distinctly remember her rubbing her belly, and each time she did, I could only think of how sorry I was to that unborn child." She raises her head, meets my eyes. "To you."

I can only nod again.

"It was very late when we finished talking. I remember your mother stood, still with one hand on her belly. She told me she was going to bed, then told me I could sleep on the couch if I wanted, but if I didn't mind, she'd prefer I use her bed."

Lex and I both look at her.

"She'd just found out her husband was never coming home, Monica," Talia says. "I think she just wanted to have someone close by one last time. It was strictly companionship, nothing else."

I nod yet again. "I understand." I reach out for Lex's hand.

"One last thing," Talia says. "We were in bed. Lila was on her side, facing away from me. I wasn't even sure she was still awake, but I told her that, once her daughter was born, she must tell her that there will come a time when she needs help. And when she does, she can think of me. I promised your mother that I would protect you and would never let anything harm you."

"She told me that," I say, surprised. "She said, 'If you're ever in need—serious need—call for Talia.' And, eventually, I did."

"Yes," Talia said. "You did. And, across the decades, I came."

"What?"

"As I said, I wasn't sure if your mother was awake or not when I told her that. However, within minutes, I knew she'd heard it. I knew she'd passed it along to you sometime in the future. And I knew when you called, because I felt it as I lay in your parents' bed that night. And, when I heard it, I began the long journey of coming to you."

I know my face is scrunched up as I regard her, take in what she just said, and try to process it. "But I didn't even think about you for a very long time. I didn't call you until just a few months ago. At Lex's mom's funeral."

Lex's head swivels around to me. "What?"

"That funeral," I say. "It was awful. Your brother…"

"Yeah."

"And you just seemed like you needed help. Help I couldn't provide."

"Ah, Monica," Lex says.

"So, I cashed in my Talia card," I say.

Lex waggles a finger between Talia and me. "So, is that weird little secret you two have had?"

I nod.

"You called Talia," Lex says, eyes wide with disbelief. "No shit."

"And I heard that call back in 1984," Talia says. "So I came to you."

"From…"

"From the moment I heard you." She smiles. "Your mother fell asleep with me beside her. When she woke, I was gone. From that moment until Lex saw me at the edge of the graveyard, my only goal—with only one real detour—was answering that call."

"And you did that by…meeting with Lex?" I say.

"Lex is your protector. As am I. It made sense to determine whether we were going to be at odds, or work together. Thankfully, you chose well."

"I did, didn't I?" Lex and I share a smile. Then something she'd just said sunk in. "You said, 'one real detour…'"

"Kayla," Lex answers. "You were there after Ray…"

"I was," Talia says, and the three of us let that go.

◆ ◆ ◆

THE THREE OF us sip on our beers in silence, Lex and I digesting all of the stuff that Talia has fed us. It's a lot. Too much.

Still, each fact leads to more questions.

"So…"—Lex sets down her beer with one hand, swipes at her mouth with the other—"…the Book…"

Talia waits for the question.

"Where'd you send It? Where'd It go?"

"That's a somewhat complicated question," Talia says. "I knew the Outer God could manipulate from afar—"

"Even from Abbith, with all those mechanical brains?" I say.

"*Metallic* brains, hon," Lex says.

"Yes, even from Abbith," Talia says, nodding. "He'd done it before, pushing the Book into the hands of the someone who could possibly aid him in his escape."

"Okay, so…"

"So it wasn't enough to simply send It someplace," Talia says. "What single place in all the universe would be safe from his influence?"

"Heart of a star?" Lex says. "Black hole?"

"Perhaps," Talia said. "And if either of those thoughts had crossed my mind, I may have chosen them instead. I was thinking of the next keeper of the Book."

"All right. Can't send It anywhere without worry," I say. "Where'd you send It?"

"The answer isn't 'where,' but 'when' and 'whom.'"

"Talia," Lex says, "for chrissakes, just tell us. Spill."

"The command I used was necessarily vague, only because I didn't know exactly when, nor did I know exactly who, I was sending It to. So I can only tell you I threw It forward in time to find the first person who could control the Book, instead of anyone the Book could control."

"You used the Book to imprison Itself?"

"I asked It nicely, but I was also rather forceful."

"I'm sure that made all the difference," Lex said drily.

"How did you know such a person existed? Someone with the strength to resist It?"

"I didn't."

"So..." I shake my head. "I'm confused..."

"If there was such a person, it would fall into their hands," Talia explained. "If there was not..."

"It would just keep going?"

"That was my thought."

"So, do you know who has It now? Or...um...whenever they are?"

"I do not."

"Does it matter?" Lex says. "It's gone. Good riddance."

"It's not that simple," Talia says. "As I said, I was wrong back then. I made mistakes."

"Do you know where you went wrong?" I say.

"I do."

"And do you know if there's any way to correct it?"

"Yes," she says. "There is. It's difficult and complicated, but there is."

"And do you know the right way this time?"

"Yes."

"You're sure?"

"Very." She runs a slow finger around the lip of her beer mug. "But to fix it, we need a few things, including someone other than me who has wielded the Book. And we need at least a couple of more people to assist."

"And..." My voice falters then, as my throat constricts. I drop my gaze to the table as I clear it once again. "And if we get all these things, all these people...is there any way that...some of the previous mistakes might be...corrected?"

"If you're asking if I can bring your father back," she says, "I believe the answer is no."

My turn to nod.

"However," Talia says, "I do believe it's entirely possible for you to meet him."

Okay, that stops me cold.

CHAPTER TWENTY-TWO

THE PLAN WAS to give Talia a day to…do whatever it is that Talia does when she's not around us. She told us she'd meet us at our home when she was "ready"…whatever that means.

I even made her promise to not just suddenly be in our living room.

And then Lex and I went home. To wait.

◆ ◆ ◆

I PASS THE next day desperately trying to focus on my bookstore customers. I probably give them ten percent of my concentration, while the other ninety percent is chugging over everything that was talked about last night.

I go through pain, and sorrow, and loss, and wonder, and fear, at speeds varying from all in a few seconds, to dragging through one or two in an hour.

It's a long, emotional day for me, and I crave the numbness that alcohol would bring me. But I'm through with that. I'm through with running from who I am, what I think. There's a lot of shards in me, a lot of things broken and scattered, and while I haven't even begun to sweep them up, I'm at least okay with the mess, and learning to tiptoe through it.

My father was scared, but he faced the demon head-on. No flinching.

I owe him the dignity — the legacy — of a daughter who is just as tough.

I somehow get through the day, do the day-end duties, and even spend an extra half-hour straightening the shelves, reordering the misplaced books.

Then I head home to wait and see what comes next.

◆ ◆ ◆

I PARK THE car, reminded, as usual, of the time Lex and I first came down the driveway, back when she'd just learned she was inheriting the place.

She'd wanted to renovate, not just to bring the place into the current decade, but also to confront, then deal with, and finally erase the ghosts of her past, the ones that had initially made her run out that front door, up the drive to the highway, and away from this place for many years.

Lex had initially run from her demons, but then she too finally had the courage to face them head-on.

My father, Talia, and Lex. Now, it was my turn.

I twist the key to kill the engine, reach over to gather my purse and keys, and get out of the car.

"Good evening, Monica," Talia says.

As per usual, I drop all my shit as I jump back, yelling, "fucksake!" It's a word I've picked up from my better half.

Apparently this is all rather amusing to Talia, as she simply stands there, a small smile playing over her lips as Lex flings the door open. Apparently, I'm also rather loud when I yell.

Lex, instantly clueing into what just went down, says, "She just show up and scare the shit out of you? Again?"

"Yes," I say, glaring at her. "Again. Fucksake."

"You made me promise not to show up in the house," Talia says. "I did not show up in the house."

"Thanks," I say, stooping to pick up all my dropped shit. "Fucksake."

"Language," Lex says.

"Is there coffee?" Talia says, totally ignoring my agitation and Lex's amusement.

"There will be in moments," Lex says.

Talia and I make our way to the door. I mumble, "I'm really starting to think you do that on purpose, lady."

"Me?" she says. "No."

And, oh my god, just like that, I realize Talia threw down some sarcasm. It probably feels close to what Dorothy felt moving from sepia Kansas to Technicolor Oz.

It doesn't dampen my agitation, but it does layer it with a slim icing of respect. I pat her on the ass and say, "Get in the damn house."

♦ ♦ ♦

"SO?" LEX SAYS, once we're sitting around the kitchen table.

"I have to reach out to the last known wielder of the Book."

"Who's that?"

"Thelonious Clarke. Theo."

"And why him? Didn't he do a lot of bad stuff?"

"I thought so, originally. Because the wielder before him, Peter, truly did. But Theo? No, he saved the town. I found that out in the brief time the Book was back in my hands, back when…"

"…when The Last Word was destroyed. When Dad died."

"Yes."

"And why do we need him?"

"As far as I know, he held the Book last. Before It fell into my hands, and then the hands of the person I sent It to. I'm hoping that, together, we can get to the person I sent It to."

"Why can't we just go to that person, instead? The one you sent It to?"

"Because, through the Book, Theo and I share a common thread. Not a link, but we're now woven into the same tapestry." Her hands clawed at the air weakly. "But whomever It went to afterward, the Book holds no sway on. I can't get a sense of them."

"All right, then it's Theo we go for," Lex says. "Any idea where he is?"

"A place where he really hoped he could disappear," Talia says. "He tends bar in a town that literally doesn't have a name, nor a place on any map."

"How do we find him?"

"We use your Staff, Lex. It will take us to him."

"How?"

"Through my connection with him, and by you asking your Staff nicely to move us there."

"Asking It...nicely," Lex says.

"These artifacts, if you haven't noticed as yet, always respond more to polite requests rather than stern commands."

"I'll have to give that a shot."

I look at each of these women, both so important to me. "When do we start?"

Talia smiles at me, then looks at Lex, who looks confused for a moment, then her eyebrows jump and she says, "Oh! Okay, let me fetch the Staff."

♦ ♦ ♦

WHILE LEX WENT off to our bedroom to pull the Staff from under the bed — she kept it under her side like anyone else would keep a baseball bat, because, "You never know when you're gonna need it, babe," — I asked Talia how this was going to work.

"First things first," she says. "Do what you'd do if you were leaving your home for an extended period of time. Because you may be."

I make a couple of calls, first to the Muracks, then to Colum asking for coverage, telling them I was being called away for some family business. Technically, it isn't a lie.

Lex comes out with the Staff—I never cease to be surprised by the thing. It's very tall, with a cat's head carved into the tip. Runes run down Its length, and It ends in a very sharp point.

I don't like to think of that point, because that's what I drove into my ex's chest to kill him. It had to be done. It was a mercy.

Still…there's a dark, dark corner of my mind that lets the shadows bleed out when I go there too much.

We finish our prep, then Talia tells us to head outside. We exit out the back door and she leads us to the middle of the backyard, halfway between the house and the beach that offers a stunning view of the wide, northern half of Lake Kwanashishing.

"I don't like to do this stuff indoors," Talia says. The story is still fresh about what happened to my father's bookstore, so I understand. Lex nods, getting it as well.

She gets Lex to hold the Staff of Solomon in her left hand. I hold her right hand, and Talia's left. Talia has only to grasp the Staff to complete the circle.

"I will find Theo and firmly place him in my mind." Lex and I nod. "Lex, if you could request that the Staff look into me, find that thought, then take the three of us to him."

Lex nods again.

Talia gives a tight, quick nod in return, then closes her eyes and drops her head, chin to chest.

She stays like that for a long time. Long enough that Lex and I give each other at least three wide-eyed "what's going on?" glances, and one matched set of shrugs.

Then Talia takes a deep breath, raises her head and, eyes still closed, she reaches out for the Staff.

As soon as she touches It, a cold fire sweeps through me. My arms tingle, my lips go numb, and there's the taste of copper in my mouth.

Lex's hand flexes on the Staff, her fingers tighten and her knuckles go white.

And then, we're not in our backyard anymore. Instead

Chapter Twenty-Three

WE'RE IN A room about the size of our living room/dining room/kitchen area. Maybe thirty feet on the long side. Rough wood floors. Rough wood panelling. Mix-and-matched tables and chairs. A bench along two of the walls, tables pushed up against them. Along the back of the wall is a bar, with a couple of what could only be presumed to be regulars propped up against it.

Behind the bar, prominently displayed, is an old sign from a carnival. *This is a dark ride.*

The room's ambient noise drains away. One of the two guys at the bar says, "Ain't never seen these'n's before. New guys?"

The other man seems only to stare into his beer, and rather morosely at that. "Yup," is all he says.

Guy's a human Eeyore, I think.

Despite three people just randomly appearing in a room of about fifteen people, despite the cessation of talking and drinking for a few moments, no one seems surprised at our entrance. No one seems to find that the least bit strange.

Which is strange.

The first speaker turns back around. "You ever seen 'em?"

The woman behind the counter says, "No." But she had already stopped moving and stands, both hands on the bar, very still. I feel like she could be a second away from launching herself over the bar to attack us.

This is a dark ride, I think.

Talia drops my grip and moves to the bar. "May I speak to Theo?"

The first speaker says, "Who?"

The woman says, "Shush, Willie, the women are talking." She turns back to Talia and says, "Who's asking?"

"Talia?" I hear from behind me. "Talia Davis?"

We all turn to the door to the place. I see that it leads outside, but I can't see much beyond it. *That's the exit*, I think, *good to know*—realizing when popping into the middle of a building, it's difficult to determine exactly how to get back out by conventional methods.

Then I focus on the man who had spoken. Tall, with hair pulled back into a loose ponytail. Unshaven, with a neatly trimmed Van Dyke. I'd had to learn the term, because Lex gets pissed when I call them goatees. Apparently, that's the incorrect term, according to Encyclopedia Hedges.

Talia ignores the woman at the bar—at great personal peril, according to my gut—and crosses the floor to the man. "Theo," she says, looking up at him. "You've aged very little."

Theo makes eyes at the woman behind the bar, then pats the air in a stand down motion. "Could say the same about you." He smiles. "One of the few side benefits of that fucking Book, huh?"

"I need to talk to you," she says.

He nods, looks over her head, addresses the room. "Drink 'em if you got 'em," he says. "You have two minutes to scoot."

Groans.

"Yeah, yeah, yeah," he says. "One night off ain't gonna kill any of you. Trust me, your livers will thank you in the morning."

Glasses, bottles, and mugs are raised, and throats work convulsively to empty them. On the way out, Theo slaps a few on the back. Guys with names like Red and Blind Willie and

Greasy Eddie. The woman behind the bar remains still and tense.

Interesting place you have here, Theo, I think. And I'm silently thankful that Red, the human Eeyore, is only Red, and not Red King. I know he's dead, but still…

As the last of them stumbles out into the thickening evening, Theo gestures to a table. As we sit, he pulls another over and beckons the woman behind the bar to come out.

"You want anything to drink?" he asks.

"We're good," Talia says, though I could have used a Coke. I let it pass.

We all sit. The woman comes over, stands defensively beside Theo, a hand protectively on his shoulder, like he'd be the one to protect. I've seen what these former Book buddies can do, so, while I'm thinking, if anyone's gonna do the protecting, it's Theo, I'm also looking at this half-pint at his shoulder and realizing she may be some sort of badass herself. He glances up at her, says, "It's okay. Stand down, soldier. At ease."

She gives him a sharp glance, but nods. She sits down, but in no way does she stand down.

Theo chins in our direction. "Who're your friends, Talia?"

She introduces us. When she's done, Theo leans back, tilting his chair on the two back legs, and puts his arm around the woman. "And this suspicious fireball is my wife, Rainer."

She gives him the side-eye.

"Easy, dear," he says. "I went to school with Talia. She was a little younger than me, but she's had her own shit with the Book."

I start at the nonchalance. "You just toss that out?"

"What?" he says. "The Book? Yeah, Ray and Sam know all about the Book, and all the shit I went through back in the day."

"Wow. Okay." It had taken Talia quite a while to open up to us in regard to her own shit.

"Besides," Theo says, "Ray here used to hunt werewolves. Back when there were werewolves to hunt." There was an unmistakable pride in his voice.

I swallow hard. "Werewolves," is all I can say. Lex grabs my hand.

"Yeah," Rainer says. "Problem with that?"

"Like hubby said, stand down, there Buffy," Lex says. "Her husband was one."

Rainer turns her frankly terrifying gaze to me. "I know he's dead, but—"

"How do you know that?" I say.

"Because she"—pointing to Lex—"said 'was.' But also because Sam exterminated every last one of those furry fucking assholes."

"What?" I say. "How…?"

"When?" Lex asks. "When did you exterminate them?"

"Not me. Sam. And it was about eight years ago."

"She killed her husband six months ago."

Rainer abruptly stands, knocking her seat back, sending it skittering across the floor. "Not. Fucking. Possible."

Lex turns to me and, with one look, she conveys that she wants to educate this woman on a thing or two and am I okay with her talking about it. I nod, squeeze her hand.

"He was attacked by werewolves outside a bar in Vilni. About eight years ago. I think he was infected only hours before your 'extermination event.'"

"So, he would have turned after it was over," Rainer says, righting her chair, holding the back of it as she considers this. Finally sitting again. "He survived for eight years. Fuck me."

"Vampires had him most of that time," Lex says. "Long story short, I hit him with this"—she touches the Staff—"and knocked the fucking wolf out of him, and my girl here ended him."

Rainer's eyes soften then. She looks at me differently. Looks back at Theo. Then Lex. Then me again.

Then she reaches out and gently takes one of my hands. "First of all, I'm sorry you had to go through that. I know exactly what it's like to lose family to wolves, and worse, I know what it's like to kill family because they're a wolf. So, I'm very sorry."

I can only mutter a quiet "thank you." I swipe the tears away angrily. I'm sick of crying over this.

"And also, I'm sorry we didn't get the job done that would have prevented you having to go through that."

I don't trust my voice now, so I can only nod my thanks this time.

"And finally," she says, giving Lex an admiring look, "where the hell has that Staff been all my life?"

Theo's been staring at me through all of this. Then he suddenly leans forward, angling toward Talia. "It just clicked. Holt. Monica Holt. Dan Holt's daughter? The Last Word bookstore Holt?"

"Yes," I say.

"So he went ahead and married Lila? Took over the bookstore?"

"Almost," Lex says. She opens her mouth to say more, but Talia cuts her off.

"That's actually why we're here. Because of Dan, the bookstore, and the Book."

◆ ◆ ◆

WE END UP talking well into the evening. Rainer eventually went off and made coffee, but ultimately, everyone realized the story was just too big to relay in a single evening, so Theo worked out sleeping arrangements for the three of us.

The following morning, I'm up early, my internal alarm clock now no longer dulled by alcohol, and prodding me awake at the ungodly hour of five, telling me I have to get into The Second-Last Word to get shit done.

I make my way downstairs to the bar area, and decide to take a look around the place we've landed. All I know is what I could glean from the quick, out-of-context references of the previous evening, when experiences and stories were flying fast and thick.

I open the door I'd seen Theo come through last night, and take in the scene. What I see brings a single term to mind. *One-horse town.* I step away from the door and down the three steps to street level. The entire town is quiet, the streets still rolled up from the night before. A light mist hangs over the town, fogging the few lights still on.

It doesn't look like there's much in the way of industry here. From what I understand, the town is far enough north that lumber isn't a viable way to make a living. I see what looks like a dry goods store a hundred years out of date. A post office. A barber shop. A clothing store. A hardware store. No sign of a school.

Basic necessities. No luxuries. No kids.

It seems to me this is a place where people *exist*, rather than live.

It only takes a few minutes to walk the length of the main street. The buildings peter out very quickly at each end. Behind the businesses, there's a smattering of maybe ten or twelve rough houses.

Maybe twenty-five people here? I realize about fifteen or so were in Theo's bar last night. *Half the bloody population?*

I remember another small town from a few months ago, that Lex and I passed through.

The town where my ex killed everyone.

And then I killed him.

Not a good place to go, Mon. I change direction, both mentally and physically, and head back toward Theo's bar, thinking I'll take a walk around the back of the place.

As I walk past the front of the building, I see, for the first time, a weathered board with some faded writing above the door. I have to come up to the steps to make it out.

It says, *Abandon hope, all ye who enter here.*

Between that and the "dark ride" sign inside, I get the distinct impression that Theo's a bit of a pessimist.

I move around to the side of the building and toward the back.

That's when I see Rainer sitting cross-legged on the ground, completely naked, watching the sun rise through the desolate, barren ground that extends for miles past the building.

And I think, *What sorcery is this?*

♦ ♦ ♦

RAINER DOESN'T TURN around, doesn't show any sign that she's aware of me, but as I round the corner and realize what I'm seeing, she says, "Good morning, Monica."

Looking at her naked back, the swell of her buttocks on the ground, I can only stammer, "Good…uh…good morning, Rainer."

"My friends call me Ray," she says. "There's coffee ready to brew inside, and some juice, bagels, bread, and eggs in the fridge, or cereal."

"Okay." I swallow. I'm rather uncomfortable talking to a woman sitting comfortably naked in her backyard.

"Give me a few minutes, and I'll come in and get a little less disrobed." Then she chuckles, and I can only do the same.

I head in for breakfast.

♦ ♦ ♦

I HAVE THE coffee brewing, a bagel toasting, and I'm sipping on some juice by the time Rainer comes in from the backyard. She pulls a robe off a hook just inside the door and covers herself up nonchalantly.

I want to ask what the deal is with the whole naked sitting thing, but I let it go.

Which leaves me feeling awkward, with nothing to say.

Rainer pulls out a chair and sits across from me. She pours herself a glass of juice and asks, "You and Lex, have you been together long?"

"We've known each other since high school, but we didn't get together until a few months ago."

"When Lex's mother died?"

"Yes."

"And then the truth about Marcus came out?"

I set my glass down quickly. "You know about Marcus?" We hadn't gotten that far last night.

She nods, brings the glass to her lips.

"How?"

"Aside from my now-retired wolf-hunting role, I can also pick up a lot about someone through touch." She holds up one of her hands, studying it as though it was her first time seeing it. "Please don't think I was trying to spy on any of you. I know I was rather guarded when you first appeared, but this place is pretty much a magnet for weird. When I brought the coffee out last night, Lex happened to make contact with me as she took the cup. I'm sorry, I'm usually more careful with that."

"You're all a unique bunch," I say.

"'*You're* all'?"

"Well, yes," I say. "Theo's used the Book to defeat a demon. Talia's another veteran of the Book. You hunted werewolves and can pull information from someone with a touch. Lex is half-demon and has the Staff of Solomon."

"And you?"

I'm uncomfortable with this line of talk, so I say, "I just run a bookstore."

"I think you undervalue yourself, Monica," she says. "You've faced a demon, a werewolf, and several vampires. And you're still here to talk about it."

"Only because I have friends in high places," I say.

"I think you just have not yet had your moment to shine." The statement makes me think of possibilities again. I shrug and say nothing. But there's some activity behind me. Talia, Lex, and Theo all enter the kitchen. "Who needs a moment to shine?" Lex says.

Ray indicates me with her glass of juice.

"Why not?" Theo says. "Misery loves company."

"Theo!" Rainer says.

"What?"

"Not helpful."

"Shit," he says. Then, to me, "Sorry, Monica."

"S'okay," I say.

Everyone heads over to assemble their morning beverages and meals. Rainer says, "Talia?"

"Mmm?"

"I'm still rather unclear on all of this." Talia stops what she's doing and turns around. "Can you lay it out for me again?"

"We're going to go back to when the Man of Black—"

"Can we call him something else?" Theo says. "Every time you say that, I think Johnny Cash."

"Man *in* Black," Lex says. "Not Man *of* Black."

"I know, still."

"What do you suggest?" Rainer says. "God of a Thousand Faces is just ridiculous."

Theo holds up a finger. "God. Of a Thous…Goat. Let's just call him Goat."

"Equally ridiculous," Rainer says, rolling her eyes.

Talia, who is a black belt in the art of dragging out information delivery, actually seems to be getting impatient. She starts again, as though ignoring Theo, saying, "We're going back to when *Johnny* was summoned. With the extra...what's the word...?"

"Oomph?" Lex offers.

Talia purses her lips and nods once. "As good as any. With the extra oomph that we'll bring—"

"You mean Lex and her Staff, and the one who controls the Book."

"I do. With them, we should have enough...oomph, as you say...to make him do what we need him to do."

"Destroy the Book, go away, not kill Monica's loved ones."

"Exactly."

"When you put it like that, it sounds..." Rainer trails off.

"Crazy?" Lex says.

"Foolhardy?" Theo says.

"Impossible," Rainer finishes. "Why revisit something that happened so long ago?"

Talia leans back against the counter, heels of her hands propped on the edge. Her eyes take on a faraway look for a moment as she considers the question.

"You were saying something as we came in. About Monica not yet having had her time to shine."

Rainer nods.

"You're correct," Talia says. "I don't think she has. But, I haven't either. I wiped out my family, and broke or wiped out others' families as well, when I was just a kid. I promised Dan Holt that I would help him rid the world of something very bad. Instead, I got him killed. Monica's mother lost her husband and father-in-law, Monica lost a father. And Dan lost a daughter he never got to meet. And that bad thing? It lives on."

"Then," Rainer says, "if I've got this straight, you're asking a bunch of people who have mostly fought their own demons and darknesses—and who, I might add, somehow managed to deal with all that shit and move on—you're asking us all to now dive back in, do it again, and in the end, possibly die, possibly change the past, and very likely fuck everything up, one way or another. Have I got that about right?"

Everyone is silent, as each considers her words. I see slow nods around the room.

Finally, Talia says, "Yes. But the reward is the destruction of a lot of those demons and darknesses."

"If we win," Rainer says.

Talia nods. "Yes," she says. "If we win."

"People," Lex says, standing up and leaning on one hand while pointing with the other. First at Theo. "Book owner and demon killer." Then Rainer. "Werewolf hunter." Then Talia. "Book owner, righter of wrongs." Herself. "Staff keeper, threatener of wolves and vampires." Then me. "Absolute badass."

"And Advisor," I say. "Don't forget, Glory called me Advisor."

Lex gives a heart-melting smile that I know is only for me. "Advisor, sure. But still an absolute badass."

She then looks each of us in the eye, then says, "How can we lose?"

But even I can see that she's going for that locker room speech the losing team gets at halftime. Not even sure she's buying what she's saying.

♦ ♦ ♦

"SPEAKING OF BOOK owners," I say, "Theo, I haven't seen It. Where's the Book?"

He and Rainer share a look that worries me. Then he says, "Well, to be fair, I haven't seen the Book in a bit."

Lex's head whips around to him. "What?"

"Bit of a story," he says.

◆ ◆ ◆

THEO PUSHES OFF from the counter, ambles over to the table, and takes a seat. He rubs a thumb over a knot of wood in the tabletop. Flicks another glance at Rainer. I watch her give him a nod.

"After all the shit went down at the high school, I left No Ho—um, New Hope the same night. Me and Marcia. We spent the night at a motel in Oval Lake. When I woke up the next morning, Marcia was…"

"The thing inside her birthed itself," Lex says.

"Yes," he says. "It escaped, leaving me with just her body." His thumb picks at the knot as a tear slides down his cheek. "I was young and stupid. I ran. I honestly don't know what happened with Marcia, or the thing that came out of her."

"We can go into more detail later, Theo," Lex says, "but the short version is, you're still blamed for killing her. And the thing that came out of her? In the span of a year or so, it grew, assumed the form of a human, called itself Marcus, and I'm his daughter."

Theo's thumb stops its rubbing. All the spit dries up in my mouth as his gaze slowly pans to Lex. I watch as he sees her in a completely different way. A quick check on Rainer shows she's pretty much in the same headspace as her boyfriend. Guess her touchy-feely voodoo didn't catch that fact.

Theo opens his mouth to say something. Draws air instead. His brows furrow. His mouth closes. Opens. Closes.

"I guess you could say Marcia Mayer is, in a way, my grandmother," Lex says. There's no trace of humour or sarcasm in her voice.

215

"Fuck. Me." That's about all he seems to be able to get out.

That shocks Theo's story into submission for the moment.

Talia steps into the silence. "We're all sort of inter-related here, Theo," she says. "Marcia was also my babysitter, and the one who—likely by Johnny's design and influence—brought the Book to me. I also believe that, during the high school attack, you fought alongside Laura Davis. She was my aunt."

Theo physically jolts at the mention of that name, and I wonder why.

"Haven't heard that name in a long time," he says.

"She passed away two years ago," Talia says. "Breast cancer."

"Laura was…she was a good woman. A wonderful human being," Theo says.

And then I have it. I can hear it in the sound of his voice, the look on his face. He loved her.

Damn.

Another awkward silence. Rainer extends a hand, sets it atop my shoulder. "Looks like we're the odd women out," she says. Turning to Theo, she says, "Babe, finish your story. Where's the Book…"

"Right," he says, and takes a deep breath.

◆ ◆ ◆

"Long story short," Theo says, "I found my ass in this town that isn't on any map. It has no name. No one pays taxes. And there was this building…"—he raises his arms to take in the place we were in—"…sitting empty. I asked a guy—his name is Blind Willie—what was going on with the place. And I've got to say, I'm shortening a roughly ninety-minute conversation down to a couple of sentences here. But he basically asked me, if I moved in, what would I do with it. I said I didn't know, and asked him what was needed. He nudged his buddy—guy named Red, who I've never heard utter more than a single syllable at a time—then told me the town needed a watering hole. He nudged Red again, and he said, 'Yup.'"

"So, you just…"

"I walked in the front door—which was unlocked, by the way—did some sweeping, did some chatting with some of the welcome wagon, got some beer in, and opened the place two days later."

Rainer smiles, shakes her head.

"What?" Theo says.

"The Book?"

"Shit!" he says. "Right." He scrubs a hand through his long hair, then says, "It followed me. I know, shocker, right? Over the next few months, I tried to…not sure if 'destroy It' or 'kill It' is the better term…but I tried to rid myself of It. Burned It. Abandoned It miles from nowhere. Threw It in Hudson's Bay. I tried so…many…things…" The exasperation bleeds out of every word. Talia nods along, likely remembering her and my father's equally fruitless attempts at destroying the Book.

"Bottom line, I couldn't shake It." He looks at each of us then. Meets each of our eyes in turn. "Then after all that, It just…"—he explodes his hands outward—"…fucked off."

"This would have been when?" Talia says.

"Early eighties," he says. "I wasn't too concerned with calendars, so I can't tell you more than that." Talia nods and he continues.

"I thought I was rid of It," he says. "It stayed gone for so goddamn long."

"Then what happened, babe?" Rainer prompts. I can tell she knows what the answer is.

"Then, just like the three of you yesterday, a woman and a little girl showed up in my bar about eight years ago." He looks over at Rainer and she gives him a smile. "Rainer and Sam."

"You mentioned Sam yesterday," Lex says. She addresses Rainer. "Your daughter?"

With those two words, I see something darken in Rainer's expression. Not anger. Sadness.

"Yes, my daughter. Not by birth," she says, and then an expression as sad as the one Theo had for Laura Davis passes across her face. "Another long story for another day. Let's just say that she basically became our daughter, Theo's and mine."

Lex echoes both my nod and my bewilderment.

"Okay," Lex says. "You and Sam walk into a bar. Sounds like the start of a joke."

"Furthest thing from it," Theo says. "Because when Sam showed up, so did that motherfucking Book. Again. After twenty-odd years."

◆ ◆ ◆

AND TALIA PUTS drops her head into her hands and says, "Oh no. Not another little girl. Please, no."

Chapter Twenty-Four

"When I sent that damnable thing forward, the last thing I wanted was to saddle another kid with It," Talia says.

"I…don't know if I'd call it 'saddled,'" Theo says.

Talia lifts her head from her palms, her eyes red, her eyebrows raised in question.

"The Book doesn't affect her like It does you and me, Talia," Theo says. "It doesn't rule Sam. *She* rules *It*."

"Seriously," Rainer says. "That Book is her bitch." Then she laughs.

"Speaking of Sam," Lex says. "Where is she?"

"Yet another long story," Rainer says, "but the short answer is, she's in the middle of nowhere."

"I thought that's where we were," I say.

"Yeah, um," Rainer says, "a different middle of nowhere."

"Makes this place look positively cosmopolitan," Theo says.

◆ ◆ ◆

THE CIRCLE IS bigger this time, and when we end up where we're going, the heat is a shock. I immediately feel the heat prickle my skin, and sweat popping. It's not stupendously hot, but the change from the very cool northern air of Theo's kitchen to the warm air of, it turns out, Centralia, Pennsylvania, catches my body by surprise. As does the fug of the air, and the riot of colour coming up from the ground we stand on.

The shock lasts less than a second. Instantly, I see a beautiful teenager running toward us. "Theo! Ray!" she says.

She doesn't seem to question the fact that we simply appeared on…I look down and it's only now that I realize all that colour is a road. It's been graffitied into something out of myth. Bifrost, the rainbow bridge that connects Asgard to Midgard. Or the Yellow Brick Road that leads to Oz. Or maybe the other Yellow Brick Road…the one that Elton John's mongrel said goodbye to. The road where the dogs of society were said to howl.

I look around. It's a terrifying place.

I've seen this before, I think, but the thought is sidelined as the teenager throws her arms around Ray, enveloping her. She's a good six inches taller than the werewolf hunter, and the two of them embrace laughingly. Then she all but jumps into Theo's arms, and he lifts her off her feet and spins her before setting her back down.

They're so in love, I think. *These three people who found each other through tragedy have become a family.* I try to nonchalantly swipe an errant tear away, but, as usual Lex catches it and gives me a light punch on the shoulder. But I see her furtively swiping at her own face.

I'm not sure if our tears are for the unexpected love that comes from tragedy, the love that found the three of them like it did Hedges and me, or if our tears are for the fear of what we're about to do, and the possibility that all this love could be torn apart.

◆ ◆ ◆

AFTER THE HUGGINGS and the how-are-yous and such settle down, Rainer manages to get out, "Sam, this is—"

The teen—Sam, presumably—immediately darts forward for a third hug. "Talia!" she yelps, and throws her arms around Talia, who stands somewhat stiffly and nonplussed.

Theo says, "She's a hugger."

Rainer nods in agreement.

"Yeah," Lex says, "Monica and I are, too. Talia's kinda not."

"Oh," Rainer says, and looks worried. "Sam! *Sam!* Down, girl. Dial it down a couple hundred degrees, willya?"

Sam eases up, then pulls back, still holding Talia by the shoulders, and regards her from arm's length. "Oh, fuck me sideways," she says. "Sorry!" She drops her hands and backs off.

Lex leans over to the still-confused Talia and says, "You *know* each other?"

Talia slowly turns her head, her eyes not leaving Sam until the last moment. As she shifts her gaze to Lex, she says, "No."

"Honestly, Talia, so fucking sorry," Sam says. "It's just that, well, the Book, am I right? Told me all about you. Like, everything. I feel like I fucking know you."

"The Book told you?" Theo says.

"Yeah, big boy," she says, grinning. "You too. You got some 'splainin' to do." She thwacks his chest with an open palm.

"Wait, what?" he says.

"Theo," Rainer says. "She's screwing with you. Again."

"Fucksakes, Theo," Sam says. "Really? You fall for my shit every time."

"So, you know me?" Talia says.

"Of course I do. You kicked the Book clear of that fucking Narly demon asshole and sent It to me, didn't ya?"

♦ ♦ ♦

I HAVEN'T KNOWN Talia that long, but in all the time I have known her, she's been the most steady, most calmest, most unflappable person I'd ever met. And yet, since we've joined up first with Theo and Rainer, and now with Sam, it's like she can't find her balance. Every time she gets a semblance of stability, along comes another whack and she's on her ass again.

I'm probably being a shit friend when I say that, despite the circumstances, I'm enjoying this far more than I likely should.

Sam, after seemingly threatening yet another bear hug on Talia, finally relents and Rainer finishes the introductions. That done, Sam says, "Let's get off Graffiti Road. It's easy to warp the lookie-loos around me, but there's a lot of us, so it'd be easier for us to go someplace more quiet."

She takes Talia by the hand — *and Talia lets her* — and walks us down the road a bit. She moves her head in a way that strikes me as familiar, but I can't place why. The road itself, aside from some debris and overgrown foliage, is mostly clear.

Until it's not.

Out of nowhere, we're standing in front of a campsite. There are two tents, a very comfortable folding lounge chair, two picnic tables — one laden with coolers, a camp stove, and other cooking tools. The other looks dedicated to just eating.

And off to the side, there's a series of small stones. Nothing special about them, except that they're stretched out in a line about four feet long.

"We could stay here," Sam says, "but they'd likely still hear us, so…" She lets the sentence trail off and angles toward that strange line of stones. "Step over these, okay? Don't nudge them, or step on them, please." She demonstrates by taking an exaggerated step over the line and…

…and she disappears, except for her trailing forearm hanging in the middle of the air, her hand reaching back, still holding Talia's. I watch, fascinated by the flexing of the muscles under the skin as she pulls to urge Talia forward.

Talia hangs back for a moment, regarding the disembodied arm, then pushes forward. She also disappears.

Theo says, "Everyone form a line and hold hands."

"Just like kindergartners at the zoo," Lex says.

"That's right, everyone listen to Miss Hedges," I say. "Grab hold of the rope."

"There's no rope," Lex says, sounding disappointed.

We join hands, and I watch, half excited, half horrified, as first Theo, then Rainer, disappears ahead of me. It's my turn and I'm careful to not disturb the stones.

I step into a place that's very familiar, and also one that I never wanted to see ever again. I'm about to swear, but then Lex appears and bumps into me, knocking me forward and cutting off my expletive.

Then she says, "Well, fuck me."

♦ ♦ ♦

"HEDGES," I SAY, because I can't say any more. It's the sounds and the smells of the place that hit me. I drop forward, breathing too fast, eyes watering. I've seen Lex have her panic attacks, but this one's a first for me.

Lex reaches out and grabs my hand. We're standing in an underground concrete structure. The sounds of our footsteps echo through the place, going away, then coming back at us. But those sounds don't come back alone. There's other sounds. Mournful wind. Crackling flames. Shrieks of pain. Cracks and growls of thunder. All of it distant, removed, but impossible to ignore.

"Close your eyes, Mon," Lex says.

Smells of damp concrete settle in my nostrils. Underneath and woven into that scent, however, is the reek of sulphur, and the fug of burning things: wood, grass, hair, meat. Everyone seems to deal with it, but I can feel my eyes watering.

It's not just from the sounds and smells.

The last time we were here, we agreed it looked like an abandoned subway system. Only, instead of regularly spaced stops that lead up to streets, this place has regularly spaced stops that lead to very different, yet equally hellish places. The last time Lex and I were here, we didn't explore too far, because we'd found the right exit, and Lex had found the Staff of Solomon.

Along the way, I thought I saw Lex die. We'd lost each other, and I had a moment—a brief, terrifying, mind-wiping moment—where I knew I'd be trapped here for the rest of my life. Then Lex pulled me back to her.

Remember that, Monica, I think, eyes squeezed tightly shut. Remember that Lex pulled you back and saved you. That she'll do that every time. Just like you would for her. Remember that.

I squeeze Lex's hand a little tighter, then take a deep breath of that concrete-and-smoke air, blow it out slow, then stand upright again.

"You good, babe?" Lex says.

I don't trust my voice yet, so I open my eyes and fill my mind with Hedges's face, and just nod. I can literally feel the grim line my mouth is making. She gives me a nod and a squeeze of the hand, and we both take in the rest of the place.

Theo and Rainer are looking at the structure more with curiosity than dread. Talia, as well.

Sam turns to us. "You know this place," she says, matter-of-factly.

"We do," Lex says, and the two words fall like a bad taste spit from her mouth. "Why are we back here?"

"Because the Highway to Hell is the ultimate place to hide."

I literally jolt. Lex had said pretty much the exact same thing the last time we were here, only months ago.

Looking around at the place, Lex says, "It may be, but Monica and I aren't fans. Let's discuss what needs discussing, so we can get the fuck out of here."

◆ ◆ ◆

"SAMANTHA," I SAY.

"Oh, fuck that 'Samantha' shit," Sam says. "Call me Sam."

"Fair enough," I say. I can't help but like this young woman. "I've gotta ask…why are you here?"

"So many avenues!" she says. "You mean physically? Existentially? I mean—"

"Why do you choose to live in that stinking hell of a town?"

"Centralia?" Sam says. "It's got a certain charm."

"It really doesn't."

"No, you're right," she says. "Place sucks balls. But it works for me."

"I don't understand."

Sam holds up a palm. "Yep. Nope. Totally get it. Sam's being obtuse." She waves a hand at the expanse of space. "Pull up some floor and I'll give you the short version."

When we're as comfortable as we can be in a space designed to house multiple portals to various hells, Sam remains standing, and starts talking.

"First things first, Talia, I was around the same age as you when the Book dropped into my hands. Almost nine. Mom had died a few years earlier, and Dad and I had finally, after a couple of years, started to find a rhythm. He was a good dad. Then, along came Jake, my babysitter, who was probably the best friend I've ever had. Then I lost her to a piece-of-shit werewolf who called himself The Fed. Then, that same piece-of-shit killed my father."

Rainer said, "I'm so—"

"Ray?" Sam said. "We've talked about this shit. Don't you dare try to apologize again, or I swear I'll come over there and get all Bookish on your cute little ass. And I don't want to do that to my newest mom, okay?"

Rainer smiled, nodded, then looked down. I saw the pain in that smile.

"*Anyway*," Sam says, "we get up to Theo's place in Buttfuck, Nowhere, and then I get a big-ass, evil-as-all-fuck, ancient, magical Book in my hands, and It immediately tries to rape my mind."

I sit up straighter at that.

"Yeah, I mean, probably better ways to phrase that, but It basically wanted to get in here"—she taps on her head—"and do the hokey pokey on me."

"Yeah," Theo says.

"Yeah," Talia says.

"I told It to go fuck Itself."

"And It just…did?" Talia asks.

"Yeah," she said.

"Just like I'd hoped."

"I can tell you, the Book was hoping for different."

"I'm sure."

"Anyway, we got to the wolves, shit was said, shit was done, wolves were squashed."

"And you all lived happily ever after," Lex says.

"Well, yes and no," Sam says, rocking her hand. "Life's not horribly exciting for the only kid in Buttfuck, Nowhere, but we got along. Theo's lack of knowledge of anything post-1981 provides endless hours of entertainment."

"Hate you," Theo says, with obvious love.

"Hate you more," Sam says with equal affection. "But the long and short of it was, I knew having the Book around wasn't doing anything good for Theo, or the town, so I decided to scoot, take It someplace safer.

"Here," Lex says. Then she says, "Sonofabitch."

"What, Hedges?" I say.

Lex stands and moves closer to Sam. Sam watches her warily as she approaches. Then Lex darts forward.

And wraps Sam in a rib-crushing hug. She's laughing and crying at the same time.

The fuck?

"It was you, wasn't it?" Lex says.

"Yeah," Sam says, a little sheepishly. "It was."

"Will somebody please explain what the hell they're talking about?" I say.

Lex finally releases Sam, and self-consciously pats at her shoulders and arms to straighten her clothes back out. "Sorry, Mon," she says. "I can't believe I didn't figure it out when we first ended up here."

"Figure out what, exactly?"

"When I got the Staff and you…when we got separated…"

"I remember."

"I never told you, but I was desperately trying to get you back, but nothing was working."

"Okay."

"And then there was someone else in the tunnel with me."

Sam cocks both thumbs at herself. "This guyyyyy."

"She's the one who made it possible to get you out."

I look at Sam.

"Sam saved you."

"I just helped you a bit, Lex," Sam says. "You did all the heavy lift—"

I engulf Sam in a rib-crushing hug of my own.

◆ ◆ ◆

"SAM, DAMN! YOU know how to make friends in the weirdest places." Theo laughs at us. "Not to bust up this party, but we really should get to the reason we came here."

"Fine," Sam says. "Be like that." Then she gives me a final squeeze, kisses me on the cheek, and says, "You're welcome, Monica. Glad I could help."

We separate, and Sam claps her hands. "Okay, fill me in on this genius plan of yours."

◆ ◆ ◆

"HOLY SHEEP SHIT, Batman!" Sam says, after finding out what we intend to do. "Good plan, but…"

"But?" Talia says.

"Tal," Sam says, "you should know this. It's not gonna work." If Talia takes offence, she doesn't show it.

"Why not?" Talia says. "What am I missing?"

"You've got a lot of the moving parts down, but this is Narly we're talking here," she says.

"You've heard of this thing?" Rainer says.

"Shit, yes," Sam says. "Hasn't everyone? He's like, I don't know, Darth Vader, and Hannibal Lecter, and Galactus all rolled into one."

Rainer mouths "who is Galactus" at Theo, and he mouths back "Fantastic Four."

Rainer only shrugs in a "yeah, well, of course" way.

"So, what's the problem?"

"The problem," Sam says, clawing both hands through her long hair to pull it back from her face, "is that Narly only listens to commands from us muggles when he feels like it."

"What's a muggle?" Theo mouths to Rainer. Rainer holds up a finger and gives him a squint that says, "Hold that thought, I'll explain later."

Sam stares at him wide-eyed. "Honestly, Theo, you're such a fucking philistine," she says. Turning back to Talia, she says, "While you're gonna have a fuck-ton of power there, between you, me, Theo, and Lex the Staff-wielder, you still need someone who holds the Power of Command."

"I imprisoned…Narly? Is that what you call him?" Sam nods. "I imprisoned Narly on Abbith with one word."

"Few things to unpack in that," Sam says, giving her a smile. "First off, totally tripping on hearing you call him 'Narly.' But, more importantly, it's easier to push something—or someone—away than to draw them toward you. And, most importantly, you were just sending him somewhere. There's a big difference between sending someone somewhere, and keeping them close by, and telling them what to do."

"So you're saying you can lead an Outer God to water, but you can't make him drink," Theo says.

Sam stops, stares at him wide-eyed for a moment, blinks, then says, "Fuck me. Yeah!"

"So, you're saying I didn't command him," Talia says.

"I mean, all respect pushing that fucker to the Planet of the Shiny Brains, Talia, but no. That was relocation, not command."

We watch as Talia thinks it through. Only she knows the exact way she used the Book that day, so only she can figure it out. Then, she obviously does. Her eyebrows rise, and she nods. "You're probably right."

"Dude," Sam says, putting a hand on Talia's shoulder. "Full respect, but I'm totally right." She drops her grip, but dips her head toward Talia and says, "So we're going to need that. A being that wields the Power of Command. Ya dig?"

Talia nods.

"I'm lost. Power of Command?" Rainer says. "What the hell is that?"

Monica and I look at each other.
A being that wields the Power of Command.
Because we know.
"Oh shit," Lex says.

Chapter Twenty-Five

"Sam," I say. "You sound like a great person. Theo and Rainer both speak highly of you. But if you are truly talking about what I think you're talking about—"

"Vampires," Sam says, far too matter-of-factly for my tastes, thank you very much. "I'm talking about vampires. Preferably more than one."

"—you're out of your fucking mind," I finish.

Lex raises a hand. "Seconded."

"You may not like what I'm saying, but..."—she tips her head toward Talia, standing off to the side and looking stricken—"...she knows I'm not wrong."

"There's no fucking way—"

"She's right." This from Theo.

We all turn to him. Even stricken Talia.

"Of the three of us, I owned the Book the least amount of time. But, aside from Sam here, I probably dug into its innards more than anyone." He squeezes his eyes closed, drops his head. "Had to, to fight that fucking Swlabr. Can't help but pick up a lot of other information along the way, whether I wanted it or not." He sweeps his hair back as he raises his head again. "Fucking Book."

"Got that right," Talia says. "Fucking Book." She walks a couple of paces to one of the platforms, turns, leans against it, and crosses her arms. "This is going to be a problem, Sam."

"Can't say as I've never dealt with a vampire, but tell me why?"

"Because a few short months ago, Lex, Monica, and I basically fucked them over."

"But good," Lex says.

"They want us dead," I say. "Only thing saving us is Hedges and her Staff of Doom."

"It can hold them back?"

"Honey," Lex says, "I can literally beat the werewolf out of a body."

"That," Sam says smiling, "I'd like to see."

"I did, not that long ago," I say. "Not pretty."

Sam gives me a look, then narrows her eyes to study Lex. "How—"

"Long story, Sam-I-Am," Rainer says. "Not the time. I'll explain when this is done."

Sam continues to stare at Lex. And her Staff.

"I think this is also the appropriate time to point out that I also used the Staff to command the vampires to stop attacking us and do as they're told." Lex turns to Talia for confirmation. "Power of Command, right?"

"Not...quite," Sam says.

"What do you mean?" I ask. I'm desperately hoping that we can talk Sam into this, because the alternative? It's not good.

"Your Staff—which is sick as fuck, by the way—gives you power over lower demons, obviously. Vampires and werewolves and likely a bunch of other ones you don't even know about yet, but Narly is a Big Bad, an Outer God. What I'm talking about here is using the Book, your badass Staff, the will of the three of us who have used the Book, as well as at least one vampire to join in and utter our demands. Normally, a vampire on its own wouldn't stand a chance, but we're the amplifier that will help get the job done."

"So, amplify me instead."

She shakes her head, and Theo and Talia are mirroring it. "The difference here is, your Staff gives you the power. It's external, the Staff is the source. The vampires have the natural ability to do it. It's internal. Easier to boost."

Hedges and I share a look. Lex says, "You're saying—"

"Listen, you need something to swoop in and destroy the town, you gonna get a flock of seagulls to come in and poop everywhere, or are you gonna bring in the fire-breathing dragon?" She pauses, squints, says, "And no, Theo, I'm not talking about the band."

"There's a band called Fire-Breathing Dragon?"

"Fucksake," Lex says. "Off topic. You're saying…"

"I'm saying, you want to get this done, you have no choice." Sam meets each of our eyes in turn. None of them happy with that last statement.

♦ ♦ ♦

I HOLD HEDGES'S hand tighter, close my eyes, and say, "What do we need to do, Sam? Talia?"

Talia's mouth is a grim line.

Sam says, "Pretty simple. We go to the vampires, just like you did with us."

"Does it have to be the Vjesci? The Vilni Vjesci?" I say.

"Yes," Sam says. "They're the ones directly impacted by this. No other vampires will care."

"Fine," I say. "We find the vampires who want us dead, and then…?"

"And we convince them they need to help us."

"That's…not going to be possible."

"It has to be," Sam says, and there's a note of desperation in her voice.

"Yeah, well," Lex says. "Unfortunately, not only did we dangle the Staff they've been wanting for a couple of centuries in front of their nose, and then we yoinked it away—"

"—and we killed their pet werewolf," I say.

"Right," Lex says, "so, we did all that shit. And then, just to ensure the cake was iced nicely, I also killed the Queen of the Vilni Vampires' pet soldier, the Red King." Her hands grasp an invisible ball, then separate quickly. "Blew him to atoms."

"I'm sure it was necessary," Rainer says.

Lex laughs bitterly at that. "Says the wolf slayer to the vampire slayer." She hefts her Staff. "No, Rainer, it wasn't necessary. It was a pure act of revenge. I didn't need to do it, I wanted to do it."

"Ah." She nods. And I see, right there, that she'd been in the same situation Lex had been in.

Talia says, "There may…*may*…be a way."

Lex leans on her Staff. Sam says, "Tell us."

◆ ◆ ◆

"YOU THINK IT'S gonna work?" I say.

"It's the only card we have left to play," Talia says.

"Okay, but do we really *want* to play that card?" Lex says.

"Seriously," Sam says. "Not sure I like that. That's not a bell you can unring."

"It's the *only* card we have left to play," Talia says again.

"So," Rainer says, "I'm with Sam, not sure I like it either. Do we play it?"

I say yes. Hedges says yes. Talia says yes. Sam says no, but hesitantly. Rainer's no is more emphatic. We turn to Theo. I know what he's gonna say.

"I say yes."

Huh, I think. *Guess I didn't know what he was gonna say.*

Sam says, "Okay. Monica, this is kinda your show. What's next?"

"Vampires," I say. "We go talk to Verdant Glory."

And I think, *Fuck.*

CHAPTER TWENTY-SIX

THE FIRST THING I notice is the change in smells. Before I register the coolness, before I register the darkness, before I register the grass under my feet and the stars above my head, I notice the rank stench is replaced with the smell of nature. Of trees and flowers and grass, a cool breeze gently drifting it to my flared nostrils.

Hell to heaven in one second flat.

Then again, Monica, I think, *this ain't heaven. Not really...*

I turn to see our ever-growing band each looking around, looking down, looking up, and breathing in the clean air. That's when I take in the rest. The coolness, the darkness, the grass, the stars. We're back in the same valley where we'd first met Glory and the other vampires, and, later, where they'd delivered Lex's father and a schoolmate of ours for punishment.

And it's where Lex had killed the vampire Rory, the Red King.

We stand that way for a couple of long moments, then I say, "So, where are they? Do they know we're here?"

Talia says, "Yes, they know." Turning to Lex, she says, "But the last time we were here, you banished them from this place."

"Oh shit," Lex says. "I did. Forgot about that."

I had too.

"You need to invite Glory...Chloe...back."

Lex goes quiet for a moment, eyes closed. Then she opens them, and nods. "It's done."

We hear her before we see her.

In a voice like the rumbling of distant thunder, she says, "You *dare* come back to this place?"

There is a figure coming toward us, shapeless in the dark, but coming toward us quickly. We turn as one to face her.

Then Chloe glides up to us, feet inches above the ground. Her childlike face is composed, but her eyes spark and dance with rage.

I think—but make damn sure I don't say—*If it wasn't for us, you couldn't come back to this place either.*

"I should gut you where you stand," Chloe says.

"You could try, Chloe," Lex says, and her voice is serene.

"You will not speak my name."

"Actually, Chloe Susannah Tyler," Lex says, "I will. So, enough with your silly reindeer games, because I have a proposition for you..."

Chloe's eyes narrow to slits. I hear the rumble of that godforsaken voice as she grumbles. She stares at my girlfriend for a very long time, completely ignoring the others.

She's got to know she's outgunned here. None of her group can help her. Yet still, the monster that appears to be a young woman appears angry only because she can't rip Lex's heart out.

Lex matches her, glare for glare. My woman is a badass. She makes me proud.

I wish I had half her courage.

Nobody moves. And I realize this is very likely the first time any of the rest of the group, aside from Talia, is seeing their first vampire. They hold their silence and allow Hedges to run with the ball. And Hedges allows Chloe the time she needs.

Chloe finally snarls and says, "Who is this meat you bring with you?"

Lex pulls one hand from the Staff, uses her palm to indicate each one in turn. "You know Monica and Talia. This is the slayer of all'Gueroth, this is the hunter of werewolves. And this is the Book wielder who exterminated all the werewolves."

We'd had a long talk about vampires and names before coming here, so none of the three are surprised.

"Thelonious Carson Clarke. Rainer Alica DeSantos. Samantha Lea Palmer."

Okay, that surprises all of us. Vampire lady somehow knows all of our names. *That's not good.*

Sam gives a slow, sarcastic clap. "Well played," she says. Chloe gives an almost imperceptible nod of acknowledgement.

"You did not exterminate the werewolf race, bitch. One survived."

"For a while," I say. "I got him." Hedges gives me a smile of encouragement. My voice barely shook when I said that.

The vampire gives each of us a slow, appraising look, taking her time, as though she's running the show here. Gotta give her credit, she doesn't rattle easily. "I will listen to what you propose," Chloe says. Lex draws a breath to start, but the vampire cuts her off. "I will hear it from her." She points to Sam.

It's obviously an attempt to throw us off guard, changing up the batter, last minute. But Sam takes it in stride. "No problem, fangs. Listen up."

Fangs? Holy shit on a popsicle stick, did she just refer to the head of the vampires as "Fangs"? I fight the smile. Lex doesn't even try.

Chloe ignores the slight.

Sam does a good job of summarizing what brings us all here, her words filling the silence all around us. Chloe simply watches her, unblinking. Once again, I am struck by the silence of the clearing. As soon as the vampire showed, all the night creatures ceased their chatter. Even the breeze seems subdued.

"…which is what lands us here, now." Sam finishes. Looks around. "In this weirdly quiet golf course, or whatever the fuck it is. Anyway," she says, giving her head a shake to bring her back to the present, "as I've said, we've determined your assistance, your Power of Command, is necessary."

"And in return?"

"And in return…" Sam pauses, draws a breath. I know she doesn't want to offer this, but we don't have much choice. "…in return, Lex will wave her magic wand there, sprinkle her pixie dust all over this area, and lift the barrier for all the Vilni vampires."

I'm watching Chloe carefully here, and I see it. I see the moment we have her. Her eyes widen fractionally. It's a sliver of a second's change, but I catch it. *We've got her.*

"We will be free to travel the planet as we wish," Chloe says.

"I'm not happy about it," Sam says, "but yes, you and your Clutch of bloodsucking fucks will have the run of the planet."

Chloe watches Sam, remaining quiet. It's an old trick, but a good one. Keep quiet long enough to make it awkward, and the other person will start talking.

Sam doesn't take the bait.

Really starting to like this young woman.

Succumbing to her own game, it's Chloe who speaks first.

She says, "No."

A beat of silence, and Lex says, "What? What the actual fuck?"

"I'm speaking with the child, Alexandra. You will hush."

"Fuck you, Chloe."

Sam raises a hand. She's got this.

"Tell me why, Glory." *Ah, she's smart, avoiding the real name, avoiding insult.*

"If you think about it for more than a second, child, I think you can figure it out."

Sam shakes her head.

"It was you who wiped out the werewolves," Chloe says. "You crushed them into the ground, and continued to crush them until they were unrecognizable scraps of meat and blood and bone."

Sam throws up her hands. "Guilty as charged," she says. "Sorry, but I spent some time with them. Werewolves are assholes."

"A fair assessment," Chloe says, unsmiling. "However, I have to question why, once you get what you want from me, that you'll not simply choose the same fate for our kind as well? Surely you believe vampires to be, as you say, 'assholes' too?"

"Haven't spent a lot of time with your kind," Sam says. "Can't say for certain yet."

"You're not convincing me that I'm mistaken."

"Probably not." She steps right up to Chloe and holds up her right hand, little finger extended. "Would a pinky swear convince you?"

The vampire stares at her. Sam stares back, pinky still raised, unperturbed.

Girl's got no fear whatsoever. Suddenly, I feel incredibly inadequate to the rest of this group.

"Jesus," Sam says, dropping her hand. "You're a tough nut to crack. Okay, well, howzabout you consider this: I would need the Book to accomplish that. I think you know that. That's not a Staff thing."

Chloe nods once, her eyes never leaving Sam's.

"So, when all this shit is said and done, there will be no more Book. It'll be gone, once and for all. The Staff will open up the world for you, and I'll have no way to crush your asses."

Chloe considers this.

"Or, you can just keep letting that big Outer God asshole fuck with you." Sam steps in even closer. And something shocking happens as she does.

Chloe leans back.

Away from Sam.

I shoot a glance to Lex, and she stares back at me, open-mouthed.

Sam seems not to notice as she gets right up in Chloe's face. "You *do* know he's been fucking with you, don't you?"

Chloe, off-balance, does not respond.

Sam's head shoots backward in surprise. "Holy shit! You *don't* know. Well fuck me sideways." She steps back, then walks a slow circle around the vampire. "Well come and listen to a story 'bout a man named...okay, not Jed, but Nyarlathotep."

The Beverly Hillbillies? *Really?*

"Way back," Sam says, "just over a couple of hundred years ago—and if you really need it, I can give you day and date, even the time down to the minute—Narly brought that particular infection we call the Book to this area. He'd had a three-way choice. He could have dropped It in the lap of a particular human in need, or he could have given It as an early Christmas gift to the vampires, or..."

She stops, and Chloe angles her head to watch the young woman. "...or he could give It to the underdog." She laughs then. "Heh, didn't even mean to make the dog joke, but yeah, he gave it to the werewolves. And their first act? To lock you up in a small area around Vilni, New Hope, and Carry's Cove. Not a lot of people around here, especially that long ago. Not even a lot of farm animals. Slim pickin's for creatures that live on blood, huh?"

She resumes her slow circle around the vampire.

"Then there was the Staff of Solomon." She pokes—actually *pokes*—the vampire, who snarls in response, but dares nothing more, and says, "That one's a little more complicated, because Narly hates that fucking stick. But, the dogs had the Book. So if he tossed the stick into Vamp-Land, the vampires could have pulled the ban—like you tried to do with your First...Ileen was her name, right?...just about exactly a century ago. Valda gave you two a good fight, but in the end, only two people walked away from that brouhaha, didn't they? And *some*one"—another poke—"used it to become the new First of the Clutch."

I know "Clutch" is the term for the group of vampires. I know "First" is the title for their leader. But who the hell are Ileen and Valda?

"But you've never been able to get your clammy little hands on either the Book or the Staff. Thought you were close there a few months back with the Staff, huh? But Lex and Monica kicked your asses."

"They did not—"

"Shush, Chloe," Sam says, finger to her lips. "*I'm* talking now. My point is, as long as that thousand-faced asshole is around, even imprisoned as he is, he's still fucking with you." Sam cups a hand to the side of her mouth and stage whispers, "Don't think he likes vampires much."

"What's your point, meat?"

Sam tosses her head back and her laughter rings through the clearing, high and sweet. "Meat. I like that. As though you're not." She pokes Chloe *again*. "Well, okay, undead meat, but whatever." She finishes her circle and stops directly in front of Chloe once more.

"My *point* is, you will never get *any*where as long as Narly is pulling the strings. And as the First of your Clutch, it pretty much falls on you to do the best for your fellow friends of the fang." Chloe stares hate into Sam's eyes. Sam's smile back. "So, you can help us, which in turn helps yourself. At the end of it, Lex will lift your travel ban, and the Book will be gone, with only my promise to not try to wipe you off the planet like snot off a toddler's face."

Sam holds out her hand. "Deal?"

Chloe regards the outstretched hand as though Sam holds a turd in it. "What are you doing?"

"I'm shaking with you to seal the deal," she says. "It's an old custom where each party shows they carry no weapons."

Chloe continues to stare at the hand.

Sam huffs an impatient breath. "Continue to get fucked by the supernatural being who's got you bent over the table, or take a chance on an unfucking with a group who's willing to pinky swear." She wiggles her fingers. "C'mon, fangs, it's the best offer you're gonna get all millennium."

"I despise you," Chloe says, but grasps Sam's hand.

Sam affects a southern drawl as she says, "Chahhhmed, ah'm sure." Then she drops her hand and wipes it on her jeans.

She turns to the rest of us, all in various stages of astonishment not only for what she accomplished, but also for what she got away with. With a vampire. Actually, the goddamn queen of the vampires.

"Okay, kids," she says, dusting her hands. "What's next?"

CHAPTER TWENTY-SEVEN

TURNS OUT, WHAT'S next is to spend the rest of the night in the clearing, bashing out a basic plan that lays out what we'll do, based on Talia's recollection of that evening, and of who is responsible for doing what.

It actually doesn't take long, but we try to attack the plan with a fusillade of what-ifs to poke as many holes in it as we can.

One thought occurs to me and, as the plans are discussed, the strategies nailed down, contingencies worked out, I find myself withdrawing from the conversation more and more as the thought expands in my mind, encompassing my full attention, pushing all other thoughts away.

I don't even know what the group is actually discussing when I blurt out, "Why are we even going to the bookstore at this time?"

"What do you mean?" Talia asks.

"Why don't we go back farther? Go back to when my father first discovers the damn Book? Or even just before Marcia brings It to Talia as a kid? Why this specific time and place?"

It must be a good question, because the conversation stops, and all eyes turn to Talia, who looks to both her Book buddies, Sam and Theo, for backup.

I can almost see the unspoken thoughts and conversations flying back and forth between the three of them. Finally Sam and Theo nod at Talia, and she addresses the rest of us.

"I'll admit, it seems logical to go to a less…chaotic…time and place," she says, speaking slowly, as though working out the logic for herself a moment before she provides it to us. "But it's not that easy."

"Of course it's not," Lex says.

"Never is," Theo agrees.

"We have to land in that exact time and place—and I need to stress, we need to land in a specific second—because that's where all the moving parts come together. The Book is not only there, but It's also opened the door and is holding—sort of—Narly in check. And Narly is there. We need him there, and still gaining his footing in our world." She looks around the group. "To be clear, in all the crap that's happened over the years, this is the first time the Book and the Outer God have been in close proximity. It went south the first time, we're ensuring it doesn't this time."

"But the first time *is* this time. They're the same time," Rainer says.

"You're not wrong," Talia says. "Long story short: we go to that time and place, or we don't go at all."

And, as the sun is just about ready to peek over the horizon, and Chloe gets visibly antsy, Theo stands, arcs backward to stretch, and says, "Ladies, I think it's time."

That's when my throat goes dry.

Because I'm about to meet my father.

PART FOUR
PARTING WORDS

"What we call the beginning is often the end
And to make an end is to make a beginning.
The end is where we start from."

"LITTLE GIDDING"
T. S. ELIOT

Chapter Twenty-Eight

"GET…READY…HE'S…coming," Talia said through gritted teeth.

She felt Dan readjust his grip on her hand. She watched his knuckles whiten as he squeezed the Book tighter.

Moments later, a hole tore itself into being in the air just in front of them.

As the opening grew, Talia heard the sounds from the other side, both somehow ear-splitting and as soft as the beat of a butterfly's wings. She hummed to herself, just to drown out the awful sounds. "School's Out" was no match for insanity that tore through the opening.

Dan was close to losing it, and she tightened her fist on his and yanked his hand to bring him around. He couldn't drop the Book.

The hole then stretched and a stabbing absence of light, a painful dark, bled through and Talia felt Dan slipping away. No human mind was built to encompass all the sanity-shredding opposites that hammered at them.

And then the Black Man—Nyarlathotep himself—stepped through the opening.

◆ ◆ ◆

THE BLACK MAN stepped into the store from elsewhere, and stood, hunched over to survey his surroundings. Talia tried not to shrink back as he rose to his full height, looked down, and smiled at the two of them. She couldn't help but stare at his sharp, black teeth, like obsidian daggers. He slid his tongue over them, then he jutted his jaw toward her, as though he was about to say something.

Instead, he froze.

Where there had been just Dan, and Talia, and Nyarlathotep, now there were seven more people in the bookstore.

"Do not speak their names, beast," Talia said.

The *other* Talia. An older Talia.

It's me, the younger Talia thought.

♦ ♦ ♦

OH MY GOD. OH MY GOD.

It's my father.

I literally have no idea what to do next.

♦ ♦ ♦

WE'RE HERE, THE older Talia thought. We did it. We made it.

She remembered this scene. How could she not? It was burned into her brain, and she traced the lines of those memories often. What had happened. How Dan and his father had died.

How she had failed.

When they shifted from the clearing, the sky brightening, the air cool but comfortable, to The Last Word bookstore, almost three decades earlier, and Talia felt the shocking cold of the room singe her lungs with her first breath, when she saw the massive, monstrous form of the bastard she had narrowly overcome—overcome, but not beaten—just rising to his full height, remembered the ceiling wowing upward to accommodate him, the light bending around him to clothe him in darkness, revealing individual details yet somehow making the whole indistinct and hard to hold focus on.

When she saw and felt all this, and saw the tear in reality knitting back together behind him, she knew precisely what he was about to do. He was going to pin Dan and her earlier self down by uttering their names.

She would not allow it.

The older Talia stepped forward. "Do not speak their names, beast," she said.

Sam was right behind her. "Ugly fucker, isn't he?" she said.

◆ ◆ ◆

AS PLANNED, LEX jumps forward and swings the Staff of Solomon like a baseball bat, catching the Black Man mid-thigh. For a moment, I think Lex has somehow missed him, and I yell, "Hedges!"

Lex yells back, "Not now, Mon. Little busy."

I realize then that I saw the Staff swing, but the arc of the swing goes too far to have solidly hit the demon's leg. Then I clue in that the darkness blows around the Staff like smoke, trying to evade Lex's swing, but it can only move so far. The Staff actually strikes several inches *inside* the volume of the demon's thigh, as though the demon was insubstantial.

The Black Man's scream, however, proves he is not. His bellow shakes the building to its foundations. "You bitch!" he spits.

"Gotcha, asshole," Lex says, and brings the Staff around for another swing. "Let's see if we can knock the Outer God right out of you." She swings in and up, and it again goes further than it should have in its trajectory, passing through where the demon's balls should be. Again, he screams, and swipes at her, but she dances away.

As Lex keeps Nyarlathotep busy, the older Talia moves to her earlier self—there's three decades between the two, yet it looks like ten at most—and says, "Talia, no time to explain, but what you and Dan are planning will not work."

The younger Talia seems to get it immediately, which impresses the shit out of me, and she gives a brief nod. "What do we need to do?"

"Get Dan out of the way, then follow our lead."

♦ ♦ ♦

TALIA SAW HERSELF—older, with an older Theo and what could only be a vampire, and several other people she doesn't know—approach while one of the others waded in to attack the demon with…was that the Staff of Solomon?

The older Talia let her know her plan wouldn't work. She didn't argue the point. Older Talia, older Theo, they obviously knew something she didn't. She stood from her kneeling position and pulled Dan up with her, and they retreated.

"What's going on?" Dan said, his grip on reality obviously tenuous at best.

"Reinforcements," Talia answered, as she watched her older self dart toward the door, calling back to one of her group.

So many questions, she thinks, but knows now wasn't the time.

She and her older self would just have to make sure they got through this alive so she could ask her questions, and she could answer them.

On the back of that, another thought arcs across her mind, a comet of realization: *Older me is here. I made it out of this alive. Which means someone else didn't.*

Dan.

They're here to save Dan.

I got Dan killed.

Then the younger Talia forcibly pushes that panicked thought to the very back corner of her mind, ignores all the other thought-comets that flash across it.

◆ ◆ ◆

THE ELDER TALIA doesn't wait for her younger self — *my god, this is getting confusing* — to move. I see the younger one nod, and the older one keeps moving, angling toward the bookshop's front door. She calls out, "Rainer! Here!" over her shoulder, and Rainer's on the move.

The woman moves like a panther. She's at the elder Talia's side in a second.

Just as the door to The Last Word opens, and a man looking very much like an older version of Dan steps in and stops.

"Holy Mother of God," he says.

"Fuck your motherless god," Nyarlathotep snarls, "that worm holds no power here." He swings a dark fist in an arc, sending books fluttering like panicked birds as he attempts to hurt Lex. But Lex is never where he wants her to be.

That's *my* woman.

I whiplash my head around between Lex and Talia with Rainer. I hear Dan yell, "Dad!" but Rainer's got her hands on the taller man's upper arms and she's twisting him around and hustling him out of the building again as he protests inarticulately. I hear her calling him "Stan."

The street is dark, but a streetlight makes the falling rain glow as she gets him outside and pulls the door shut behind her.

And I think, *One life saved.*

One more to save, and one Outer God demon to kill.

◆ ◆ ◆

TALIA STOOD BESIDE Dan, the Book still clutched in his hand. Her elder self turned from the bookshop entrance, searched the room briefly, then yelled, "Sam!"

A girl not much older than Talia herself, easily a teen, ran over. "Dan, Talia," the elder one said, "this is Sam. Talia, you have to take the Book and work with Sam to slow down the demon."

Talia didn't understand. How would this girl be able to —

Sam held out her hands, and the Book was there.

Talia cut her eyes to Dan.

He still held the Book.

Two of them? she thought, then realized. *Ah. Older Talia. Older Theo. Older Book.*

"Dan?" she said and held out her hand. He searched her face stupidly, still in a daze, then realized her hand was outstretched. He hefted the Book and gave It to her. She held It tightly in both hands, felt the muscles jump in her forearms as the Book began whispering to her.

~…yessss…Taaaaliaaaa…~

She felt something close to an orgasm run from her arms to her crotch to her forehead, and she gasped.

~…it'ssss beeeen soooo lonnnng…~

It took everything she had to pull herself together. She could have simply sat down and just held the Book.

It would have been enough.

But she couldn't.

The girl named Sam said, "Fuck, no wonder everybody wants the fucking thing if It does *that* to you."

Talia didn't understand. Obviously this Sam had felt the same…

Not the time, she thought. *Save it for later.*

"Follow me," Talia said, and angled around the corner of the bookstore, toward the fantasy and horror sections.

◆ ◆ ◆

THERE WAS SO much noise in the bookstore, but Talia did her best to try and ignore it. When they were huddled off in the corner, Talia turned to Sam.

It was the first time she'd really had a chance to notice her. Taller than Talia, willowy, but not skinny. Very pretty, just a hairsbreadth shy of beautiful. She also had a way of looking at Talia that, had Talia been anyone else, they would have found unnerving.

"Okay," Talia said, to get the ball rolling, "I think we should—"

"Sorry, Talia," Sam said, "but I'm going to respectfully ask for you to let me run this particular play."

"I've known the Book for years," Talia said.

"I know. Probably about eight or so. Since 1975? '76?"

"Yes."

"And I've been fucking with It for a decade," Sam said. "Ever since you sent It forward to me when this whole thing"—Sam hooked a thumb over her shoulder to the screaming and yelling behind her—"went pear-shaped."

"Went...what?"

"Never mind. The point is, I have better control...*total* control over the Book."

"How can that—"

Sam reached out and pulled the Book from Talia's hands. There was an audible sigh of disappointment that slipped from Talia's lips before the realization of what the other girl had just done landed.

Sam had pulled the Book—*her* Book—out of her hands.

That shouldn't have been possible.

"How did—"

"Take It back." Sam proffered the Book. Talia grabbed It, felt the tingle and the snap of muscles again, but try as she might, she could not pull the Book from Sam's grasp.

Sam said, "Unless I let It go…" — she released her grip, and then It came back into Talia's possession — "…you would never have been able to get It back."

"I gave It to you?"

"You did. If we hadn't shown up, you would have done that in about three minutes, after Dan and his father were both dead."

"Oh."

"Yeah."

Talia took the briefest moment to consider, then looked into Sam's unnerving eyes and said, "What should we do?"

Sam smiled.

♦ ♦ ♦

I FEEL FAR too exposed and useless for anything, but then I realize maybe there's one thing I can help with.

I run to the all-too-familiar door of my father's bookstore — *my* bookstore — and go through it.

My overextended brain fully expects morning, but it's evening. I expect the warmth of summer, but it's raining. I expect the street view of 2012, but it's the street view of 1984. Just down the street, I see Rainer trying to hold back the man who'd entered earlier.

Stan Holt.

My grandfather.

I run to them because I can see Rainer's holding back. If she's fought werewolves, then one senior citizen shouldn't give her a lot of trouble, yet I see her struggling.

It's different when she's worried about not hurting them, I guess.

"Stan!" I say, and skid to a stop on the slick sidewalk. "Stan, stop. You can't go in there."

"And who the hell are you to tell me that?" he says. "It's my store! I have a right to—"

"I'm Monica Holt."

"I don't care if you're..." Then he pauses, just briefly. "Monica?"

Then I remember that I share my name with his wife.

"Yes," I say. "I'm...and this is gonna sound weird, but...I'm your granddaughter."

"Oh for chrissakes," he says, and makes to push past Rainer.

Rainer says, "Goddammit, man. *Listen* to her. *Look* at her. She looks just like her father."

Really?

He doesn't cease his struggles so much as slows them down as he squints at me. I angle my face a little more toward the streetlight, and say, "My father is Daniel Holt. Daniel Arthur, named after your dad. My mother is Lila Holt, originally Lila Pirsig. They named me after your wife. My grandmother."

He stops moving altogether. Stares at me harder.

"I can go on," I say. "Want me to tell you about the time you got drunk and tried to water ski up the beach and somersault onto a couch?"

"Oh my god," he says. Then, after a tentative step forward, he says, "How?"

"It's a very long story, but for now, you should stop fighting this young lady and thank her. She just saved your life."

"I...uh..." He swivels to Rainer. "Um...thank you..."

"You're welcome," Rainer says, smiling.

"And now, can you please go and be with my mother? She's terribly worried right now, and could use a friendly face."

"Monica?"

I nod, and I feel the tears well up. "Grampa."

He takes another step forward, brings a trembling hand up to touch my cheek, then his face crumples and he's hugging me. Hard. I hug him back just as hard.

My grandfather. I take just a moment to just *be* here, to feel the realness of him under my hands. To feel the coarse grey whiskers against my cheek. To smell him. To hear and remember what his voice sounds like.

My grandfather.

"Okay, Monica," Rainer says. "I hate to break this up, but we have to get back in there."

I pull away, nodding. I swipe at my tears and sniff. My grandfather does the same, and we share a small laugh.

Without a word, he squeezes my hand in his own, then turns and heads off to my mother's place.

My mother, much younger than I am now, I realize, is only a short walk from where I'm standing. And she's pregnant.

With me.

Goddamn.

♦ ♦ ♦

OUTSIDE, WHILE WE had been talking to Stan, the world was quiet, peaceful. A wonderful, small-town evening, with light rain making the street shiny and engulfing the town in soft patter.

As soon as Rainer pulls open the door to The Last Word, we're assaulted by sound and light. I have no idea how the sound doesn't carry outside the bookshop, but it doesn't.

Rainer's expression is grim as she waves me in behind her.

♦ ♦ ♦

NYARLATHOTEP IS BELLOWING in both rage and pain. He's no longer cloaked in darkness, instead he's bathed in brilliant light, and it makes him seem even darker, the black-hole darkness of his skin a negative shape in the glare.

But that black hole skin is peeling and flaking and smoking like the worst sunburn ever. I tear my eyes away from him and see Talia—the younger Talia—standing near me, to the demon's right. Her arms are outstretched, her head is thrown back, and she's literally *glowing*. On the far side of the demon, Sam mirrors her, arms out, head back, and glowing as well.

They're working together, working the Books, and bombarding Nyarlathotep into submission. And they're both screaming.

Off to one side, a shrouded figure stands.

"Okay," Talia, our Talia, says, "this won't hold for long. We do it now."

With no hesitation, Lex steps directly in front of the flailing, screaming Outer God and points the Staff of Solomon directly at his head. "All of you," she yells over the din of demon wails, Sam's and Talia's screams, and thousands of sheets of paper swirling and flapping and flying around the room.

Rainer steps over and wraps a hand around the Staff. She beckons to my father, who stands on the other side of It. He reaches out gingerly at first, then decisively, grabbing the Staff, his hand just in front of Ray's.

Theo is next, standing just in front of Rainer.

Then older Talia shouts, "Sam! Talia! Now!"

The room goes completely white, all details lost as they overload the light. I blink, then squeeze my eyes shut, throwing an arm up and facing away from them. And still, it's too fucking bright.

As fast as it hits, it fades. My retinas burn with a massive blank spot and I fear I'm blind. I feel a hand in mine, and it's pulling me, guiding me. I follow, unseeing.

The hand, Lex's, walks me to a spot. Then, with hands on my hips, I'm positioned to face a specific direction, and my hand is guided to the Staff. I feel a thrum of energy as my hand makes contact. I blink away tears, and the spot suddenly fades, as though wiped away, and I'm able to once again make out details.

I'm standing in front of my father.

Young Talia—no longer glowing—has taken up the spot at the far back of the Staff. The anchor. The thrum under my hand becomes more pronounced.

The shrouded figure throws off their covering, and Chloe, no longer needing to protect herself from the light, steps in front of me and takes hold of the Staff.

Opposite her, Sam takes her position.

At the sharpened end of the Staff, Lex takes hold in front of Sam, and older Talia opposite her, in front of the vampire. Each time another hand is added, I feel the increase in power, initially in my hand, but then all through my body. I'd swear my hair was standing on end, but no one else's is. I've felt this before. I remember orgasms in a field in the middle of nowhere.

In the two or three seconds it takes for all of us to gather, Nyarlathotep, though no longer bathed in light, still reels in pain. The demon has dropped to his haunches, one shovel-blade hand in front of him, supporting him. His body bleeds smoke and ashes as the darkness knits itself back around him.

He's not breathing heavily, he's not gasping for breath. He simply holds that position, and I realize he's gathering his strength back.

Fuck, I think, *we gotta do this fast.*

Chloe's voice is the weight of the damned, the emptiness of deep space, the darkness of the most hateful of souls. **"Nyarlathotep, spawn of Azathoth, brother to the Nameless Mist, brother to Darkness, hear me well."**

She speaks, and her voice thrums through the Staff, amplified by the Talias at each end, and Lex, the Staff wielder.

Nyarlathotep raises his black head, turns his black eyes on her, furrows his black brow.

"Nyarlathotep, you will *destroy* the Books. And then, Nyarlathotep, you will *leave* this realm and *never* return. Hear me and obey."

"Why would I do such a thing?" he says. His voice is thick with sarcasm as he stands to his full height. Lex subtly shifts the end of the Staff to follow him.

"You will *obey*, or you will be *obliterated*."

"I will, or I won't. I do not care much either way."

That catches us a little off guard, not gonna lie. Even the two-hundred-year-old vampire. She says nothing for a moment.

Nyarlathotep fills the silence with a question. "What is so precious about life that you fight to continue to keep it?" He smiles, and I have to look away. It's ghastly. "There are realms upon realms, realms *within* realms, existence beyond life, beyond death, beyond memory."

He leans down. "You have *no* idea."

It's not going to work.

He pins Theo with his eyes. "You believe, *boy*, that all'Gueroth is gone forever?"

No! I think.

He shifts focus to Lex. My Lex. "You believe, *granddaughter*, that Marcus is truly dead?"

Fuck you! I think.

To Chloe. "You believe these *friends* will truly let you roam their ball of mud with no restrictions?"

Bastard! I think.

He rears back then, standing to his full height. "You cling to this fragile speck of time you've been allotted. You have no sense of the size and shape and expanse of everything around you. You can't." He points to our group, clustered around the Staff. "And your little stick and your scribbled pages?" He waves a dismissive hand. "Useless."

He shakes his head, as though he's sad. "You are pathetic creatures."

I fill with rage.

I've been angry before. I've been furious. But never in my life have I felt something like this. A burning in my gut, a throbbing behind my eyes, all my muscles tensed and ready to fight. The Staff pulses under my palm, and It feeds me, heightens my anger, sharpens my vision. I feel the breath sliding in and out of me. I feel the rhythmic thrumming of my heart. I feel every cell of my blood pushing through every artery, vein, and capillary. I feel the tiniest arcs of electricity jumping from neuron to neuron in my brain.

I.

Feel.

Anger.

"You know what?" I say, and release my grip on the Staff. "Fuck you."

Lex sees me step forward, yells "no," and Nyarlathotep smiles his ghastly smile.

I give him back a smile that's just as fucking ghastly.

CHAPTER TWENTY-NINE

I'M NOT SURE if it was the comment about being pathetic, or asking why we fight so hard to stay alive. I think, as I spare a glance at the father I never knew, that it's likely more the second.

Whatever it is, I find I can't stand back and let others fight for my family. I can't let my friends be shit on.

"Hello, Monica," the Outer God says.

"Fuck you," I repeat. "You say we're pathetic creatures on a ball of mud."

He laughs, as though we're engaging in friendly banter. "I do indeed."

"So why do you keep coming back and manipulating us with this so-called useless Book? Why are you so fucking fascinated with creatures that should be beneath your attention?"

I can't read the expression that falls over the Outer God's face, but somehow, I know I just lawyered his black ass.

And then I realize I've pissed him off.

◆ ◆ ◆

NYARLATHOTEP SNARLS, AND I feel my feet leave the floor. I also feel like a million fishhooks have been sunk into my body, not just the skin, but muscles and organs, and I feel everything pulling.

I can only think, *Oh shit*, before the pain.

♦ ♦ ♦

TALIA WATCHED FROM her position opposite Hedges, at the tip of the Staff. She watched as the Outer God's expression turned from hate, to anger, to rage.

But when Monica rose from the ground and began to scream, she knew what was going to happen next. She'd seen it thirty years before, in this bookshop.

Dan.

"Lex!" she screamed.

♦ ♦ ♦

"LEX!" TALIA SCREAMED, and Lex unfroze. She still held the Staff, but her other hand shot out and latched on to Monica's wrist.

What happened next took everyone by surprise.

Chapter Thirty

THERE'S A STRONG grip on my wrist and I know, without looking, it's Hedges, always looking out for me.

At first, it's just the simple sense of touch, of skin on skin, a feeling that she and I have shared many times. It feels like home. It feels like love. But that simple contact is subsumed in a greater wave of sensation. There is a passage of energy, an opening of circuits, and the flow of…what?

It's information. It's knowledge. It's memories and feelings and loving and hating and contentment and hurting. It's fear and it's love.

It's Talia hiding under a tree and finding a new playmate. It's Theo inviting a sad kid named Pete to play poker. It's Rainer stroking the head of April, her baby, with her husband close by. It's Sam in a hotel room, a woman named Jake fighting for both their lives. It's Lex wondering whether she should kiss Monica or not. It's Chloe standing in a doorway in the rain, waiting to be invited in to a birthday party. It's her father feeling his unborn child kicking in his wife's belly.

It's all of them. The minutiae of every one of their lives, flooding in, all at once.

But it's more than that.

Oh god, it's too much.

Still, my mind is hungry for it. I don't sip at it, I gorge myself on the lives of those with me, but also on the tools we brought with us.

The Book. The Books, both the one held by young Talia, and the one Sam controls, thirty years more experienced and three decades more malevolent. And there's the Staff of Solomon, older than the world. Each of the three supernatural tools open themselves to me, not like flowers to the sun, more like uninhibited lovers, eager to share everything, to give everything.

And oh, what they show me. Wonderful things.

Terrible things.

Hellish things.

Things strangely beautiful and beautifully strange. Things I didn't imagine. Things I can't imagine. Things that can't be true, but are. Things that can't exist, but do.

There are more things in heaven and earth, Horatio, than are dreamt of in your philosophy. No shit, Shakespeare.

I take it all. I open my mind and let everything in.

I am filled to the brim with the lives, speared through with the experiences, encompassed by the *worlds* of all my companions and the magical artifacts, shot through with arcane knowledge and experience and abilities. I fear my skull will crack.

And I scream, as much with the pleasure as with the pain.

My scream goes on for centuries. For millennia. And then it goes on longer. It cascades out to the ends of the universe. It finds other universes to echo through. It goes on forever.

♦ ♦ ♦

AND THEN THE maelstrom in my mind ceases. Everything remains, but the flood has stopped.

As I realize I have everything that my friends and family and the dark tools have to offer, I hear muffled thumps and the clattering of wood behind me.

The staff is on the floor, nothing but a useless stick now. The two books, one at the far end of the Staff with young Talia, the other near me, are also on the floor. The one near me has fallen open, but the pages are blank and, as they curl up, as if on fire, but clearly not, I see the entire book is blank.

And I know, they are *books* and *staff* now, not Books and Staff.

The nine people who had held the staff are now prone on the floor.

Dead or unconscious, I can't be sure.

Did I wipe their minds like I wiped the books?

I don't know.

♦ ♦ ♦

I GLANCE AT Nyarlathotep, and he actually appears bewildered by all of this.

I find, however, that I can play this entire event back — I can do that now — and I understand that, for me, I was…what? Incapacitated? Offline? I don't know what the proper term would be…I was out for hours, years, decades. But the sum total of time it took?

.087 seconds.

I don't know how I know that, but I do.

Just as I know it took ten times that long for the staff and books to fall from unconscious hands to the floor. It took slightly longer for the owners of those unconscious hands to fall.

I also know it happened too fast for Nyarlathotep to do anything other than begin to wonder what he just witnessed.

I watch as his eyes widen, and a single massive hand begins its slow rise to meet me. I realize I have time to do one more thing before that reaching hand becomes a problem.

♦ ♦ ♦

DON'T ASK ME how I do it—hell, don't even ask me how I *know* how to do it—but I simultaneously turtle back into my mind while also exploding outward to encompass the entire room.

Despite everything that flooded into me, every second of every life in the room, every thought and action, despite feeling…no, that's not right…despite the absolute certainty that my head would split like rotten fruit and all the madness would leak out only moments earlier—now? Now my capacity has increased in proportion to my hunger.

I will make no mistakes with Nyarlathotep. Because he exists for the chaos that exists in mistakes.

I need more information. I know where I'll get it.

I push my mind out, and acquire more. While I do, I understand that I underestimated the sheer violence of the act. The books explode like firecrackers, one after the other, each one shotgunning their pages through the spine of the book and into the air, to flutter down like leaves in an October forest.

It happens so fast, with each book in succession, that it sounds more like an extended ripping than individual cracks. It again takes less than a second, and I survey the result.

Everything has fallen to the floor. All the fluttering pages and flapping books. Like Talia's and Sam's books, the pages are all blank. I've pulled every single book into myself. Michener. Clarke. Melville. Leonard. Orwell. Sheldon. Asimov. Shakespeare. Bradbury. King. Robeson. Howard. Lovecraft. All of them.

I pulled the meat from the bones of each of their stories, each of their characters, and cracked the bones to suck out the marrow of the meanings and the motivations.

All of the stories, both good and bad. They're all part of me now.

Nyarlathotep's hand has moved only a fraction of the distance it has to cover.

I dive in for one last morsel of knowing.

♦ ♦ ♦

WHEN I'M FINISHED, the Outer God's hand is very close now, the fingers spread wide, the palm eclipsing most of my view. As I pull back into myself, I watch as that hand stops for the merest of moments. Tremble just a bit. Then continue its path toward me.

Nyarlathotep's hand wraps around me, much as it did with my grandfather in another version of this time. I've seen it through the eyes of the elder Talia. His massive fingers tighten on me. He's going to crush me.

I draw on the miasma of knowledge and ability swirling through me, and I refuse him.

His fingers spray open, his thumb unwrapping from the small of my back.

He stares at his hand as though it has betrayed him.

"What *are* you?" he says.

And I think, *That's a good question.*

♦ ♦ ♦

HOLDING NYARLATHOTEP AT bay, I think it over.

What am I?

Am I the Book? The Staff? Am I even me? Or just the information I now hold in my head?

Am I a god? I look at Nyarlathotep a little uncomfortably. *Am I like him? A demon?*

Who am I?

What am I?

As I mull it over, I think of everything I took in. It's stories and it's magic and it's lives. It's a wealth of accumulated and acquired perception and comprehension. It's the commonplace drudgery of everyday life and it's the mind-strangling wonder of all that exists in the planes of the various realities. It's the epic and the mundane and all that runs in between.

But it's more than just me taking it in. It's more than just what I carry in my head.

All of it, all the epic and the mundane, it's not part of what I am, it *is* what I am. It is me. I am it. From my rafters to my foundation. It's in the warp and weft of me.

I've created a new tool of supernatural ability.

Then I wonder, *Should I give it a form? Something to hold and wield?* I should.

Not a book.

Not a staff. Or sword.

Not armour. Or a shield.

Not a crown. Or helmet. Or gauntlet.

A ring? I hear my father say, "How very Tolkien of you, Monica." I do it anyway.

I hold up my hand and splay my fingers. I create a glowing circlet of light around one.

Nyarlathotep stares on, snarling and struggling as I work my magic. I look at my finger, encircled by a ring of light. I twist my hand this way and that.

As I look at the light I've created, my mind darkens.

No.

Every talisman has been stolen, misused, or manipulated.

And then, for whatever reason, I think back to a conversation Lex and I had a million years ago, or thirty years from now, whichever is more accurate. A conversation about possibility.

I remember saying something about how, depending on circumstances, every person's possibilities ebb and flow. How we can choose a certain path, and those possibilities are narrowed. Then, we can zig or zag in a different direction, and the world opens up to us.

I remember realizing I'd taken Duane's possibilities away.

I remember taking my own away, too, drowning them in bottle after bottle. Ignoring their calls from the expression on Lex's face, the sadness in her eyes.

But now, here, in the face of the demon, in the company of my family—because they'd shared too much to ever just be friends now—I'd found new hope.

New possibility.

You just haven't had your chance to shine, yet.

I can be anything now.

Anything.

I flex my mind slightly, and the ring's light burrows back underneath my skin. At the same time, I have another realization. It comes from all those others in my head with me.

While there's still a lot of me—of Monica Holt—in here, there's just as much of everyone else.

I realize that, while Monica Holt still applies, I struggle to put a coherent description together, but Hedges does it for me.

I am he.

You are she.

You are we.

We are all together.

Yes. Monica is not just me anymore. I am we.

Dropping our hand, we face Nyarlathotep. He stands, trembling with rage and frustration, his massive hand spread open and only inches from us.

We regard this fearsome beast, this god spawned of idiot gods, and give him our answer. "We are the talisman. The talisman is all of us. We are power. We are possibility."

Then, unable to resist, I add, "We are *Monica Holt*, motherfucker."

Chapter Thirty-One

NYARLATHOTEP MUST SENSE a slight relaxation on our grip, because the fingers in front of us tighten slightly. Without knowing how we sense it, we feel the Outer God try to once again trap us in a hold while he works to tear us apart, then spray us to atoms. We actually loosen our grip, just a little, to give him hope.

Yeah, we're a bitch like that.

We feel him try to lean into that advantage, to exploit the weakness. His fingers tighten enough that we can feel the frigid cold, can see up close how the light contorts and profanes itself to twist away from him.

Then we rebuff him yet again. And we laugh.

We have a thought then. A complex combination of thoughts from Theo and both Talias and Sam and Rainer.

Yes, we think.

Once again, he constricts his massive black hand, and, this time, we let it wrap around us. We have our reasons.

As soon as it makes contact, we're inside Nyarlathotep's alien mind. And holy shit, words have not been invented for the darkness we find inside him.

◆ ◆ ◆

NYARLATHOTEP REALIZES HE has company in his thinking box. We won't call it a brain because the demon doesn't have anything close to a human physiology. There's stones in his body. There's smoke. There's heat, and there's cold. And there's stuff that we simply block, because we absolutely don't want to know.

We weren't sure Rainer's ability would translate to demon, but hot damn, it do.

And Narly Nyarlathotep knows this. Seems he doesn't like it. As soon as he senses another presence within him, he reacts violently, trying to release his grip.

This time, with my friends and family close, we keep our enemy closer, maintaining the contact.

His struggles increase, to no effect, but then, as Lex says, shit gets real.

In quick succession, the Outer God shifts shape, living up to his God of a Thousand Forms tag. His body melts, turns to smoke, and bends and warps and contorts into new forms, each one worse than the last.

A stereotypical devil, complete with forked tongue, horns, bent-back legs, and pointed tail, flicking and snapping in anger. Only difference is, he's still black instead of devil red.

Then he diminishes in stature, ending up as a tall, swarthy man. Looks like an Egyptian pharaoh.

Then he's a monster with tentacles and bat wings. Then a faceless god with three legs, clawed, elongated hands at the end of misshapen arms, and a gaping mouth. Then he's a sickening mound of writhing tentacles.

Other shapes that defy reality and, even with all our new and combined knowledge, our eyes and mind hurt just looking at it.

So, we don't. We need to check on a couple of things, so instead, maintaining contact with each more disgusting form, we dive in and go excavating.

◆ ◆ ◆

NYARLATHOTEP SCREAMS IN rage at our manhandling of him. He's screaming and bellowing through ever-changing mouths, but also screeching in our head. All along the lines of *How dare you touch me?*

We don't care. We need to step through his garden for a bit, and that's what we do.

There's nothing that truly surprises us. At his base, Nyarlathotep craves madness and chaos. That's the universe he wants to bring into being.

What does surprise us is the realization that he and his kind—the Outer Gods, the Elder Gods, and some other things we will never speak of—they are outside of time. It's a stupid and incredibly inadequate analogy, but if time's a river, then Nyarlathotep is a bird that can soar high above it and see from one end to the other.

Holy shit, we realize, *he can see all that's happened, and knows all that will happen. He knows how it all started, and he knows how it will all end.*

And somehow, despite the orderly progression that he knows will occur, he strives for chaos. Order enrages him.

There's something else, though. Something worse.

Something causing him fear.

Us. This new us that is Monica Holt.

We somehow surprised him.

We dig deeper. Then…

Oh. We see it.

Nyarlathotep knows exactly how this was supposed to go. One time, two different events.

In the first event, he kills Stan Holt, he kills Dan Holt, Talia sends him back to Abbith. Then everything that happened to us…happens.

And then…

The second event is the group of us showing up here as we just did. We do our best to defeat him, but we fail. Nyarlathotep, now free and in our reality, is finally free to push the two Books out to others to sow chaos, and the Staff in another direction to the same end. And Nyarlathotep, the most dangerous agent of chaos, weaves his spell and creates a node of destruction that starts here and ends only when there is nothing left. What happens…happens.

What *doesn't* happen—what has *never* happened, what never *will* happen—is that we prevail. What doesn't happen…is what has now happened.

What he never saw was Monica Audrey Marilyn Danielle Holt stepping forward and becoming a god.

What happens next is unwritten.

It's all possibility.

We happen.

◆ ◆ ◆

"YOU. WILL. RELEASE me."

Yeah, not gonna happen, Narly. He continues to bellow and bitch. Rather loudly, if we're being honest. For us, being inside him, it's easier to just drop our thoughts into his head. He really doesn't like that.

As the singular Monica, we've had bad thoughts before. We've thought things we shouldn't think. Doesn't everyone at one point or another? Whenever the singular Monica did that, the immediate reaction was always to immediately distance ourself from it. *Ohmygod I'm going to hell, stop that!* That sort of thing. Mentally, we'd throw the thought to the ground, stomp on it, then kick dirt over it, and swear to never think of it again.

We've done that. Over the course of our combined lives, we've seen countless others very obviously do the same thing.

With nine people's combined history of thoughts in our head, we know we're not alone. Everyone has their version of it.

But we've never experienced a mind actually *recoiling* from a thought, like a 1950s housewife from a mouse. Nyarlathotep actually somehow abandons each thought we drop on the field of his mind, committing that patch of mind to exile. It's possibly the strangest thing we've ever witnessed, collectively or individually.

Of course, with all of the sarcasm pooled in Theo and Sam and Dan and Lex and Monica, as soon as we experience this, we just lob a barrage of thought bombs at him.

You think you're trapped now? Just wait.

We're not just going after you, Narly. If we could capture that idiot Lord of the Outer Gods father of yours, we damned well would.

We can run down the rest of your family tree, though. All but one. We can't kill you. We know that. But we can make eternity a very bad existence for you, and all that are linked to your particular brand of stink.

We reach out our hand, our fingertips touching to thumb. Ensuring that the Outer God is paying close attention, we flick our hand wide open and, between us and the demon, a small spot appears, so small it's hard to pick out in the room.

But Nyarlathotep sees it all the same.

"What's—" he whines, but the thought is interrupted as the spot grows. We both serve as witness to its birth as it widens. Stretches. A hellish green light pours forth, then a shape, broken and twisted, is birthed through it.

The ruptured, contorted creature that comes through is almost as horrible to look at as some of the forms of Nyarlathotep.

Still, it's precisely the creature we need right now.

"Peter," we say.

Chapter Thirty-Two

ETER WILSON—STINKY Pete to those who don't know him well—has changed…evolved…since he summoned the demon known as both all'Gueroth and Swlabr.

Through Theo's memories, we know the Book destroyed his human form, bent and convoluted him, and made him into something other. His spine had been broken, and his upper body bent backward so his shoulder blades were now over his buttocks, ribs poking out from the skin. His head, we remembered, had sprouted a large horn just off slightly to one side. A head that had housed at least one eye that looked more feline than human. And from his genitals and buttocks had been plant-like tendrils.

Now, the horn had been joined by several more, thrusting out from around Peter's skull, a misshapen crown of rabid cacti.

His legs and arms had withered and atrophied to useless, dangling things that only moved when something brushed against them. What brushed against them were no longer thin tendrils, but thick, pulsing tentacles, mottled pink and green, with shiny black spots here and there. Each one had a strange, irregularly shaped tip that could have been a tooth or a claw. We didn't want to know.

That cat's eye rolled toward us, and the Peter-thing opened his mouth. A thick, triple-forked tongue slid between toothless gums and slathered its lips with a gooey, moist substance, more slime than spit.

"And you would be?" Peter says, apparently unsurprised at his summoning.

"We are Monica Holt," we say. "Friend of Thelonious Clarke."

"Thelonious lives?"

We hope so. "Yes," we say, because it's easier than explaining.

"Mmm," he says. "Indeed he does. I am pleased." We give Peter time and watch as that single eye casts about the entire room, frankly taking in first us, standing in front of him, then the others on the floor. Then his eye rolls the other way, to take in the demon.

"Nyarlathotep?" he says. "You've captured Nyarlathotep, father of all'Gueroth?"

The Outer God once again screeches his outrage, and changes through three different forms, doing what he can to rattle the cage. "We have."

"And now you have summoned me from the formless void," he says, no betrayal of how he felt about the void, or his summoning. "To what end?"

"We believe we can offer you something of a present."

"Indeed?" Peter says. A couple of tendrils make a *carry on* motion that's disgusting. We keep our expressions locked down.

"Back when the book found you, your original plan was to summon and hold all'Gueroth under your command, but the book betrayed you. Correct?"

"The way you say that word…" Peter says.

We raise an eyebrow in question.

"You say *book*," he says. "Not *Book*."

"It has fallen. It is now a part of us."

"I see," he says. "Interesting."

"Yet not relevant to our current predicament."

"Indeed."

"So," we prompt. "The calling…"

"That was the plan, yes," he says. "I was, however, an uninformed fool." Tendrils spread away from his body, the tips then pointing back toward him. "Obviously."

"Be that as it may," we say, "what was done to you, we can't undo. We lack the permissions, the power, the insight."

That great horned head tips in acknowledgement. "Understood."

We point to the struggling, shape-shifting demon. "We can, however, give you Nyarlathotep."

"What would I want with that?" Peter says. "The quarrel I have is with its offspring, all'Gueroth."

"Understood," we say. "We do, however, have other gifts to give you. They will assist with understanding." We regarded him. "May we provide the next gift?"

That cat's eye regards us unblinkingly. "I was promised gifts once before," Peter says. His tentacles point in toward himself. "As you can see, those gifts didn't provide the expected benefits."

"This time will be different." We hold up a hand. Peter angles a tentacle forward, hesitates a moment while that eye regards us, then the unpleasantly cool limb touches our own.

Talia's ability to implant memories is a shockingly useful tool to deliver great gouts of information in a moment. We feel Peter's limb jerk, stiffen, and then, a moment later, fall away, which is fine. We've delivered everything we needed to deliver.

His cat's eye closes for a few seconds as he processes all the information. It would take a while, but—

The eye opens, and he says, "Fascinating." Then, "Thank you."

Obviously he processed it faster than we expected. "That's the first gift," we say.

"There's more?"

"Yes," we say. "You understand now why Nyarlathotep is one of the gifts we offer?"

That cat's eye loses focus as it turns its gaze inward, accessing the new, old memories Peter now possessed. "Ah, Nyarlathotep was the architect of my meeting with the book."

"And the spells you would use," we say, "as well as the ones it kept hidden from you."

"Yesssss," he says, drawing the word out. He understands.

"Knowing that," we say, "we can give you Nyarlathotep, here, as well as all'Gueroth. We can give you his son, Marcus, who's true name is Tokq."

"Marcus will do fine."

We pause then. "However," we say slowly, "there's only one we hold back, one that's off-limits." We point to Lex, then turn back to Peter. "She is ours. She is…" We struggle with the foreign word in our mouth, but it's the right word, the only word. "She is *mine*, as…I…am hers." We swallow thickly, then continue. "She's not like the others."

"Are you sure about that?"

It's a valid question. We consider. We ask ourselves…*all* of ourselves…the question. *Are we blinded by the love we feel for her? Are we overlooking some element, some divergent sign?*

The answer comes back from all of us. And we nod. "Yes," we say. "We're more than sure. We know it. It's an indisputable truth."

It's Peter's turn to consider. To consult the knowledge bases we've placed within his reach. After a time, he nods as well. "Understood," he says. "I accept this caveat. Alexandra Hedges will not be part of my gifts."

We extend both our hands, fingertips to thumbs again. We splay them open again. And, yet again, we create tears in the air of the bookstore. Two of them, this time, one for each hand.

The infinitely small holes stretch and yawn. We cast a glance at Peter, and he winks to let us know he's ready. The first opening births a human-shaped figure.

"Marcus," we say.

"You," he says.

Peter snares him with the wave of a tentacle, and drifts him up to hang suspended by his own grandfather.

The other portal must stretch far wider to let a much larger beast through. Of course, as with the first time, all'Gueroth — though the Theo part of us still thinks of it as Swlabr — releases the small creatures, all clacking claws and gnashing teeth, first. Peter captures them easily, ready for them this time, and holds them, snarling and snapping, in a tight ball. Then he does something surprising. He shoots his tentacles into the portal and drags the big demon out by a massive leg.

"He's seen what was waiting for him on this side," Peter explains. "He wasn't going to come through uncoerced."

We nod our understanding.

And then they are together. Nyarlathotep, all'Gueroth, Tokq.

Lex's voice comes to the fore in our head. "Three bigger assholes you'd never wanna meet." We can't help but agree.

"You will have them for all eternity, Peter," we say. "You can visit every punishment upon them that you wish. You will be their hell."

"I believe I know just the thing to start with," Peter says, smiling. His smile is an awful thing to see. "Nyarlathotep is such a scion of chaos and darkness."

His body tightens, and his tentacles go rigid, draw back, then spring forward, as though each were throwing a fast pitch at the creatures. The only thing thrown was a frightening new reality for the demonic creatures.

They were bathed in a massive ball of light that we had to turn away from and still squint against.

"A prison of light and order," Peter says, obviously proud of himself. The sounds that escape the light can only be described as unholy.

"Music to my ears," Peter says. "Unless there is anything else…?"

We shake our head no.

"Then, one last thing. This is for Theo."

We feel Theo come to the fore. "Peter," we say, and Peter seems to understand this is one he wishes to address.

"You once tried to be kind to me. Though I refused it, you should know I didn't want to, and I'm grateful you extended a hand in friendship. It is a moment of solace I return to constantly."

We can't even imagine the existence this creature has led in the time since the book abandoned him for Theo.

We nod our thanks. Theo extends our hand one last time, and Peter reaches out to touch it briefly. "Thank you, all of you," Peter says.

He pulls back from our hand. "I thank you for all the gifts, and I will take my leave."

We didn't ask where he would go. Truth be told, we didn't want to know.

He gives one last nod and, with a goodbye wave from a tentacle, Peter and the screaming, light-encased demons simply pop out of existence.

The only thing we feel is a slight tug, but and we drop to the ground to physically and mentally hold on to Lex. Peter wasn't trying to take her, it was just her genetic connection to the others that tried to drag her along.

We sit down then, in the dark, suddenly quiet bookstore. Our family is all around us, prone.

We check to ensure they aren't dead, now that we have the time, and, though it could be corrected if they were dead, we are relieved to find they are not.

For a moment though, we simply sit and take in the quiet of the bookstore. We're surrounded by our friends and family, by two useless books that used to be important, and one stick that used to be powerful. The floor is littered with pages that used to hold the thoughts of men and women much smarter than us.

Now, each of these pages, and each of these minds, are blank. They are possibility.

We take a moment, and we let the tears fall for those whose possibilities were erased too soon. The tears come hot and burn their paths down our cheeks. We tip forward, elbows on our knees, and we sob and cry and grieve for all those other could-have-beens.

We cry with the anguish of nine souls who have lost so many. We cry for a very long time. We cry until there's nothing left.

It's hardly a fitting epitaph for those who we have lost, but, for all our power, for all our ability, for all our possibility, it's all we can give.

We can only hope that it's enough.

◆ ◆ ◆

WITH NOTHING ELSE left to give, we stand and take one last look at our bookstore. Our father's bookstore. Our friend's bookstore.

Then we move to each prone body, one after the other, pushing a thought into each of their minds that will gently wake them.

And we're relieved that we can simply push the experiences of the past few minutes that they'd missed into their memories. No explanations required.

When that's completed, we move to the cash desk, sit down in front of it, and lean back. We're tired, but we take one last moment to look around the bookstore. It's a mess, but it's only *things*. We can replace the things.

We did okay.

It's done, we realize. *We did it.*

We wonder what happens next.

"I'VE DECIDED I'M not going back with all of you," Sam says. "I'm going back to 1975. I'm going back to be Talia's babysitter. Her and her sister."

Much of the group, especially Theo and Rainer, don't like that idea, and tell her so. Theo says, "Isn't that going to fuck up time or something?"

Sam, quite rightly, tells us that we've already done so. "What do you think is going to happen now? Dan's not dead. Monica's going to grow up with a father. With Narly out of the way, maybe Marcus has Lex, maybe he doesn't. But one thing's for sure." Sam points at the two books. "They're useless going forward. So, even if Rainer and I meet up with Theo, there's no way I kill the werewolves, because there's no book to do it with."

"Shit," Rainer says. "She's right."

"Which means we probably can't get to the staff as easily," Lex says.

Chloe says, "The staff is destroyed as well."

Lex goes over to it, picks it up. Holds it in both hands. "Yeah, this is kindling now."

"What about your promise?" Chloe says.

"Don't worry about that," we say. "If it isn't fixed with the staff being broken, I'll correct it."

Chloe nods her thanks.

"So, shit's fucked up already," Sam says. "Maybe I can do

a bit of influencing if I start back in '75 to try and fix some shit along the way."

"If everything's messed up, why haven't I disappeared?" Lex says.

"Don't know," Sam says. "Do you?" She stares pointedly at us.

"No idea," we say.

"Then I'm going back."

◆ ◆ ◆

EARLY SPRING 1975

THE BELL RANG above her head as Sam entered The Last Word for, if not the first time, at least the earliest time. A very young Dan Holt sat behind the counter, reading—rather predictably—*Carrie*. He stuffed a piece of paper in the novel to hold his place and said, "Hey."

"Hey yourself," Sam said.

"Can I help you?" he said.

"I'm new in town. Heard this was the hoppin' place to find the best books."

"Sure is," he said. "Might even say it's the last word on the subject."

She cocked a finger gun at him. "Just gonna browse for a bit."

"Cool," he said, and picked up his paperback again.

Ten minutes later, she'd found what she was looking for. She set it on the counter, knowing Dan would see something other than what she saw.

He picked it up, and said, "Whoa! Heavier than I expected." Then he studied the cover. "You like him too?" he said.

She had no clue who he was referring to, but gave an enthusiastic nod. "Yeah, love him."

"Me too," Dan said. She watched his brows furrow. "Never saw this title before, though. Must've just come in."

"Must have," she agreed. He gave her a price, wrote out a receipt, and slipped it in a paper bag for her. "Oh, one more thing?"

"What's that?" he said.

"Any idea if you're hiring?"

"Don't know," Dan said. "Above my pay grade. But I can put in a good word with the old man if you'd like."

"I would," she said. "I'm trustworthy if that helps. Just got two babysitting jobs, watching Talia Davis and Dennis Bussik?"

"The Toad's mom really likes her bingo."

"So I've heard. But yes, if you could talk to your father, I'd appreciate it."

"Cool. He's in tomorrow, all day. Come back then. What's your name?"

"Sam," she said. "Samantha."

"All right. I'll let him know."

"Thanks," she said. As she opened the door to leave, she turned, gave him a smile, and said, "Be zyxting you."

Dan's eyes widened comically.

♦ ♦ ♦

SPRING 1975

ONE THING DONE, Sam thought.

The 1975 version of the Book — still the Book at this point — was in her possession, safe from falling into the wrong hands. She hid It away where no one would get It.

And when it came time, she had a harmless replacement for a certain young girl.

In the meantime, she had to find the Ambrose brothers. Tim and Jeff.

She would be the last person they ever dealt with.

◆ ◆ ◆

SUMMER 1975

"HEY, MIZ D!" Sam said as she came through the front door. Alex scampered unsteadily toward her and Sam set down her bag and scooped the child up. "And aren't you a big bundle of smiles today!" Sam laughed at her gap-toothed grin and boinked her lightly on the nose and Alex giggled, then squirmed to get away, so she put her back down.

"Hold on, kiddo," Sam said. "Got something for ya." She reached into her bag and pulled out a plush Dino the Dinosaur from *The Flintstones*. Alex squealed with delight, grabbed it, mumbled "thangoo" and jammed Dino's head into her mouth, then scuttled off like an ungainly spider.

"Oh, Sam," Diane said, "you shouldn't have. You're gonna spoil them."

"Couldn't resist," Sam said, smiling.

Talia ran to Sam as well, wrapping her in a big hug. "Oh my goodness, Tal! Did you grow another few inches since I last saw you? Holy cow!" Talia beamed. "Got you something too!"

Talia bounced from foot to foot as Sam reached into her bag again, then presented her with a book. "It's *Oh, The Places You'll Go!* by Dr. Seuss."

Talia's eyes grew wide. "I *love* Dr. Seuss!"

"I know you do, but this one's special, kiddo," Sam said. She dropped to her haunches and leaned in, whispering as though offering a secret. "Because I know you're going to go so many places and do so many amazing things."

"You think so?" Talia said.

"I really do," Sam said. She smiled then, seeing the woman that this child would become.

♦ ♦ ♦

LATER

TALIA AND HER younger sister Alex are a handful, but grow up to be good friends, though they live on opposite coasts. Talia bounces from job to job until she finds her calling, becoming a champion for abused children.

Neither Talia nor Alex ever do find out why their dad left, and they never hear from him again.

♦ ♦ ♦

1980

IT TAKES A long time to get him to talk. She's twenty-one, way older than his seventeen, but she looks younger, and she just happens to walk home from her job at The Last Word at the same time he's heading home from school. But, eventually, Sam befriends a lonely boy named Peter Wilson. Never once does she think of him as Stinky Pete.

She knows Peter has a rough home life, and she's always there as someone to talk to, or a shoulder to cry on. When Thelonious Clarke breaks up with Marcia Mayer, it's Sam who introduces the two of them. Marcia's a regular at the bookstore, so it's easy to architect the meeting.

Marcia is good for Peter.

After fifty-four years of marriage, Marcia eventually passes away from a particularly virulent cancer. Peter follows her two days later.

◆ ◆ ◆

1984

DAN HOLT TELLS the group that he only wants to see his wife Lila. But he makes a deal with them.

One month later, he is overjoyed at the birth of his daughter, Monica. His father Stan spoils the girl, as every grandparent should.

Stan's heart takes him when Monica is just four, but she never forgets his love or his kindness.

Lila doesn't suffer at all when the brain aneurysm takes her. Dan knew, to the minute, when it would come, and she is in his arms as she passes away. For eight years, he knew it was coming, but when it does, it still shakes him to his core. Monica has just turned eight.

Lila is buried, and it takes about a week for the well-wishers and casseroles to slow to a trickle. Then Dan and Monica plan for what comes next.

◆ ◆ ◆

1992

SAM GETS TO know Monica Holt after her birth.

There is, however, no Marcus Hedges. There is a Sandra Smythe, but she moved away a few years ago.

Over the years, she's fretted that she wouldn't be able to bring Lex and Monica together.

But then, of course, Monica's mother Lila passed away, and that changed everything.

◆ ◆ ◆

1997

SAM WAITS ON a lonely stretch of gravel road, her heart thumping in her chest. She's waiting for something. Someone.

She gives it an hour longer than she feels she needs to, just in case. But to her relief, no one comes by.

This time around, Raymond Hedges was not able to convince Kayla Young to get into his truck for a ride home.

"Good for you, Kayla," she says.

◆ ◆ ◆

1999

JUST BEFORE THE turn of the century, Sam, now forty but looking like she's going on twenty-five, gets into a conversation with a woman and her child as they wait in line for coffee. Turns out, despite the age difference, Sam and Rainer have a lot in common, and become close friends.

Three years later, when Rainer loses husband in car accident, Sam waits the appropriate time for her to grieve, and eventually introduces her to a slightly older gentleman named Thelonious Clarke, who Sam has known since high school.

◆ ◆ ◆

2000

SAM MEETS A beautiful, shy, tattooed woman named Jake when they happen to be doing their laundry at the same time. Sam mentions that she's seen tattoos like Jake's on a certain website.

By their second coffee together, they're fast friends.

When Jake becomes an ad hoc babysitter to — interestingly — a young girl also named Sam, the two friends talk about the younger Sam's father, Zach. He's equally shy, and it takes some doing, but eventually she convinces Jake to ask Zach out on a date, because she knows he'll never do it. They're very different, but they have fun.

They have a wonderful life together.

♦ ♦ ♦

2011

THE MOON IS low in the sky when our group reappears in the backyard of the house where Hedges and we live. We stand in a circle. Lex, Theo, Rainer, Chloe, Talia, both young and old, and us. There's a gap where Sam should be, and Theo and Rainer stare at it sadly.

"I've got no idea what time it is," Lex says, "but goddamn, I could use a coffee. Anyone else?"

Everyone nods, with the exception of Chloe. "It's nearing sunup," she says. "Monica?"

We grow still for a moment, closing our eyes. Focusing. Then we open them and say, "It's done."

"Then I will leave."

"Wait, Chloe," we say.

Chloe turns, impatient.

We hold our hands extended, fingertips to thumb. We spread them both wide, and, as Chloe takes a suspicious step back, we say "It's okay, Chloe." We say, "You'll like this." We turn to Lex. "You will too."

The first pinhole in the middle of our circle widens, then yawns open.

Then a vampire steps through it.

Lex says, "Rory." The hate drips from her voice. "Monica, what?"

The returned vampire stands, confused, in the middle of our circle. He looks ready to pounce, so we twitch a finger and hold him down.

And then the second pinhole stretches and yawns, and someone else steps through the portal.

Kelly. Lex's lover.

"I can give you both back those you have lost."

Chloe says, "How?"

"I pulled them from their times, just before they died." We step up to Chloe. "Lex is in here," we say, tapping our temple with a finger, "as are you. When Lex did what she did to the Red King, she left a…distinction, is the word, we guess…she left a distinction on him. We were able to tug on that. And because of that distinction, we could track through to the one he…did what he did to. All debts are paid, both events are now victimless crimes, and we are at peace with each other. Your family and mine."

Chloe gives us an unreadable look, but we think we read something in there we've never seen before.

Respect.

"My family and yours." She nods. "And, because of today's events, you and I are also family," she says. "We are at peace," she says. "Thank you, Monica Holt."

She tilts her head to Rory, we release our hold on him and, though he looks confused, he follows his First as they leave, silently fading into the night.

Everyone stands, trying in vain to track their final movements.

"What the hell?" Kelly says.

"Come in for coffee, Kelly," Lex says. "It's a bit of a story." She nods toward the house. "Let's see if we even still own the place or if I'll have to kick my asshole brother out of it."

♦ ♦ ♦

COFFEE IS BREWED and sandwiches are built and consumed. Thankfully, there is no brother needing kicking out. The conversations ebb and flow around the group. Things are questioned, things are explained, things are wondered.

About an hour later, we catch Hedges's eye from across the living room. Lex raises her eyebrows, and we nod. We both know what we're talking about, with no words spoken.

It's time.

We head out to the backyard, just as the sun is clearing the horizon.

◆ ◆ ◆

"YOU GOING TO be okay with this?" Lex says.

"Yes. No. Yes," we say...I say. "I think so."

"You're back to 'I' statements?"

"I still think in terms of we," we say.

"I am he as you are she..."

"Yeah, we're all together," we say. She gives us that Hedges smile that always made us melt. "It's going to be tough, and we're—shit, see? *I'm*—likely going to fuck up, but I imagine I'm going to get some strange looks in the bookstore if I suddenly start talking in the collective we way."

"Makes sense."

We stand quietly for a long time, just looking across the lake, holding each other's hands.

"How am I still here?" Lex says. "And not just me, but the house...all of it?"

I consider how the water doesn't think, but simply moves to be where it's supposed to be.

"I don't know. How have any of the people in our home come to be?" We turn to Lex. "As far as we—dammit—as I'm concerned, I'm looking at it this way...You? Me? We were meant to be together. Don't consider it, don't overthink it, just know that I'm here, and you're where you're supposed to be."

"I doubt any of that would hold up to any sort of scrutiny."

We smile and nod. She's not wrong.

"Anyway, before we start this, babe, I just want to say, I'm glad I'm here. With you. But even more, I'm glad you're back. All of the yous," Lex says.

"Me too," we say. "I'm sorry."

"Me too," Lex says.

We kiss. And it's a good one. A kiss that fulfills the promise to never take them for granted.

When we're done, Lex says, "So, we gonna do this?"

We sigh. "Yes."

One last time, we hold out our hand with fingers pressed to thumb. One last time, we splay our fingers open, as though the digits explode out from the palm. And one last time, a pinhole appears, then widens, stretches, gapes.

And Dan and Monica Holt step through. Our father, and our self.

◆ ◆ ◆

WE GIVE IT a few weeks, then we bring Dan into The Second-Last Word. He's introduced as our…as my nephew, and the young Monica his daughter.

The older customers never fail to remark on how Dan reminds them of my father.

◆ ◆ ◆

THERE COMES A day when Lex and I are sitting in the How You Bean? coffee shop, just across the road from The Second-Last Word. From our table at the window, we can see Dan shelving books, a ten-year-old Monica, the spitting image of her great aunt, helping her father.

As Lex sips her coffee, I say, "Was it worth it? I know it all turned out better, but I can't help feeling there's a cost down the road for all the changes we made."

Lex puts down her cup and considers. Then she says, "Remember the night we came back, when we were all kinds of frayed and still trying to make sense of it?"

How could I not? I nod.

"Don't know if you heard him, but I remember Theo saying something about forty years ago, he was just a dumb kid concerned with, if I recall, 'comics and science fiction and getting laid.' But then he said he'd found out there was a much larger world that none of us had any idea existed, and it was all around him."

"Okay," I say, not sure where Lex is going.

"My point is," Lex says, "we may have fucked up the timeline, we may have created an alternate universe, or this may be the way it was all supposed to work out. Like you said a few weeks back, about me still being here because we belong together. Who knows the reason?"

We both shake our heads. Neither of us know, that's for sure.

"But what I know is, like Theo said, we were all blissfully unaware of this reality until we each stepped in it. But now we all know it's all around us." She looks out the window to the street, but she's not looking at anything specific.

"So, who's to say things like this don't happen all the time? Who's to say that Kennedy wasn't a two-term president that someone went back and changed? That 9/11 wasn't supposed to happen, but did?"

"Whoa," I say.

"Exactly, right?" Lex says, turning back and lightly slapping both palms on the table. "Or that Theo and Rainer, or

Talia and you and I weren't supposed to meet, or whatever, but through the machinations of all of this, we got thrown together?"

"That's…some heavy shit."

"It is," Lex says. "But it doesn't have to be." Lex reaches out and grabs my hand. "I think we take each day for what it is. A gift. We just make sure we surround ourselves with good people who love and protect us, and take each new thing as it comes."

We stare across the street. Dan has gone from view, but the young Monica sits in the window, flipping through a book.

Over there, she's a young girl, full of possibilities.

And here, I'm one of her possibilities, powerful enough to ensure that that young girl across the road grows up to find her own.

Just like I did.

Author's Note

AND…THAT'S IT. The end of the road.

It's been one hell of a twenty-five year journey from the initial, first germ of an idea to me typing these words in the last third of 2021.

♦ ♦ ♦

WHEN I INITIALLY came up with the ideas for *Out For Blood* (originally called *No Hope*) and *Blood Loss*, there was no thought of connecting them, no ideas of a series of stories sharing characters or elements. None of that.

As I talked about in the *Bad Blood* Author Notes, the first novel, *Out For Blood*, had gotten an offer to publish that was delayed, and the idea was floated of writing something shorter, maybe in the same world as the novel. This begat, of course, *Bad Blood*. I guess I could trace back the germ of the idea of writing a connected story back to that.

Along the path of writing *Blood Loss*, I came up with the ending which, if you've read it, obviously ties back to the previous novel. So, by time I'd finished that, I now had three interconnected stories, all with the Book as a player in some form.

At that point, I figured, hell, I might as well keep going, see where this ride takes me.

Problem was, I had no idea where it was going. I only know I'm a fan of closing things off, giving them an ending. And for me, that initially was—to misquote *West Side Story*—to work out the answer to "How do you solve a problem like Theo?" I mean, initially, he was kind of stuck with that damn Book, right?

Well, then I fixed that.

And created more issues.

I had more ideas, I wrote more stuff. I found I wanted to know how Talia was doing, so I brought her back.

Which was the next germ. If I could bring Talia back, could I bring anyone else back?

And, if so, how? Why?

I didn't know.

♦ ♦ ♦

FOR THE LONGEST time, I thought the last story was going to be more science fiction than anything.

I had an idea to go back to Roswell, and have someone on the run, shielding the alien survivors from being captured by…well, someone. Details have grown hazy.

I do know there was a weird fracturing of time in the story somewhere—have I mentioned how much I love a good time travel story?—and I remember the crux of the piece was, the aliens had this strange material that was incredibly thin, and it could be folded, but would spring back to original shape with no creases. I think I read something about it somewhere in one of the Roswell conspiracies. Anyway, I was going to have the aliens come across Theo and the Book, and they were going wrap up the Book in their cosmic tinfoil and take it away, where it would never be heard from again.

Honestly, it sounded *much* better in my head.

But the more I thought about it, and from the two legitimate attempts I did at trying to write it, it simply wouldn't come together. There were fun pieces in that aborted start, but overall, it didn't work.

I had to find another way.

◆ ◆ ◆

I'M A READER. A huge reader. Always have been. And, there was a point way back in the seventies when I discovered a bookstore downtown that had the coolest selection of books. It was called Good Books and Magazines, and I loved the place. Haunted the place. It wasn't big, but it had, hands-down, the best selection of science fiction and horror novels I've ever seen. I went in looking for comics and, instead, this magical store introduced me to the pleasures of Robert E. Howard, Graham Masterton, Larry Niven, Frederik Pohl, and a bunch of others that, almost fifty years later, still sit on my bookshelf and call to me.

There was always this guy, probably midtwenties, sitting behind the cash, always smoking, always reading. His long hair was usually pulled back into a loose ponytail. The type my mother would have called a "hippie" and my stepfather would have dismissed as a "long-haired asshole." But the cool thing was—from my yet-to-be-jaded point of view—he always had an encouraging comment about whatever book I was buying. He talked to me, a twelve-year-old kid, like I was an adult. An equal.

And, on top of that, the store had the *coolest* bookmark ever. It wasn't your typical one or one-and-a-half inch by six-inch standard fare. Oh hell, no. It was a good three inches wide. A bookmark you could never lose.

It had this weird, hazy image of someone with their arms out, elbows level with shoulders, and hands covering the lower half of their face. Male or female? Who knows? It was in stark black and white, no shades of grey. It looked like it was supposed to *mean* something.

The reason I'm telling you all this is, because, about five years ago, looking through my old paperbacks, I found that damn bookmark. And I've been using it ever since. Nothing but fond memories.

And, with that, there came a day when I was sitting in my living room, and I'd just pulled out that forty-odd year old bookmark from the book I was reading. For whatever reason, I took a harder look at the bookmark, and I felt that weird, writerish portion of my brain kick over and start chugging on…something.

I stared at the bookmark, just letting my mind go wherever it felt like. And the thought that it kept coming back to was the phone number prominently displayed at the bottom. My mind started asking the questions it asks when it's in writerish mode.

What if I called that phone number? What if the long-haired guy who used to sit behind the cash counter, reading and smoking, actually answered it as, "Good Books and Magazines. How can I help you?"

Then I thought, *What if one of my characters did that, and got hold of a long-dead relative?*

I'm not exaggerating when I tell you that my next thought was to make that character Monica, and from there, within about a minute, I had her father's full backstory, and what would need to happen toward the end of the novel to bring back a bunch of the significant characters from the previous novels. It would mean having to make significant edits to the previous novel, *Blood Relations*, because I had her owning a completely different business, and her parents were alive.

Sometimes, it really sucks to be a character of mine.

Okay, let's be real: very *often* it sucks to be a character of mine. There's a writers' saying that goes something like, *When you're writing your characters, chase them up a tree, then throw rocks at them.* Basically, make them suffer and have to work for their successes.

But me? I throw them out into the mid-day desert with no water, run them down until they can't move or think, then start lobbing grenades at them.

Anyway, I decided to make Monica's upbringing much more dreadful than originally envisioned, and now, I had a story.

A final story. Because the other thing that came incredibly quickly was the ending, with all the returned characters from all the previous books. My own *Avengers: Infinity War/Endgame*, if you will. In fact, once those movies came out, I kept calling this one "my Avengers Endgame novel."

The biggest issue I had was I simply could not wrap my head around getting the novel just before it, *Blood Relations*, done.

I'm not the fastest writer, by any stretch of the imagination. I think my record for pounding out a novel-length manuscript is a couple of years. Why? Because I get a solid chunk of it done, then something stops me, then I sit on it for months, then get frustrated with myself and get back on the horse. I often have to rely on my unconscious thought processes to chug along at whatever snail's pace they set and just wait for them to solve the problem. I think I mentioned something about this during the writing of *Out For Blood*, too.

Stupid unconscious thought processes!

So, that happened with *Blood Relations*. And it wasn't until the last of the three lockdowns (so far) occurred that I got back to it and completed it.

But this one? The one you now hold in your hands? I don't know if it was because I'd been sitting on it for so long, or if it was just because I'd gotten into the habit of daily writing due to COVID-19 lockdowns and such, but this one was done in just about one hundred days.

Personally, if I have to put it down to anything, I put it down to the fact that I've been living with Talia and Theo and Rainer and Sam and Chloe and Lex and Monica for so long that it was less like writing and more like the bunch of them saying, "You wanna write a novel with all of us in it? Stand back, Elliott, and hold our beers."

♦ ♦ ♦

ONE LAST LITTLE note.

Speaking of characters who take over and push their story on the so-called author, turns out Monica had one last surprise for me.

This novel's a touch shorter than the other ones, and I was wondering if there was something that needed to be added. When I wrote the rest of these Author's Notes, I'd figured there was nothing left in the tank.

Back when I taught creative writing, there was a few questions that came up in class after class, but one of the more popular ones was, "How do you know when it's done?" There's a quote out there in a few different forms, and attributed to many different people, but I'll go with the quote from poet and philosopher, Paul Valéry, who said, "In the eyes of those who anxiously seek perfection, a work is never truly completed...but abandoned." I firmly believe that to be true.

I went to bed last night (as I write this) with the vague feeling that I'd abandoned this one perhaps a bit too soon. And, with that thought on my mind, I fell asleep wondering, *Is there something I left out?*

The unconscious thought processes must have liked that thought. I woke up with a very vague idea to go back to the time between Monica's mother passing away, and her eventual adoption by the Muracks.

I will say, I did not have any idea where that idea was going to lead, and, for the first time in my writing life, what I wrote left me shaken and with tears in my eyes.

That was an unsettling thing, to have that happen.

But Monica had spoken. She needed that last bit out.

◆ ◆ ◆

AND NOW, IT'S done.

Gotta be honest here, I'm actually truly bummed. I'm grieving the fact that these guys won't be taking up the same amount of space in my head going forward. I won't hear their banter. I won't be pleasantly surprised when they push my brain off to the side and take over writing their own stories.

I'm actually grieving them.

Anyway, if I've done my job, and you've come with me on this full journey, first of all, thank you, but more importantly, I hope you may be grieving them a bit too. I hope all these characters in my head take up a bit of space in your head for a while, too.

They've been good friends to me, and they've gotten me through some tough times.

I'll miss them.

About the Author

TOBIN ELLIOTT HAS written for most of his life. After some unfortunate incidents with walls and permanent markers, he switched to safer things like pens and paper, and later, typewriters and then computers. Though science fiction was his first love, horror has always had a powerful hold on him, even back before he wore big-boy pants. He likes to have the shit scared out of him, and he likes scaring the shit out of others. Somehow, it always comes down to shit with Tobin.

Tobin spent his formative teenage years in a small town about four hours northeast of Toronto. Those experiences, and the magic and wonder of that place, never left him, though he left the town through no fault of his own. He currently lives within a three-hour drive of the place, and occasionally gets back to top up on his sense of wonder and nostalgia.

Based on that town and surrounding areas, Tobin has written several novels in his Aphotic World series.

Along with those writings, Tobin has been fortunate enough to have had three horror novellas published, as well as seven stories in various anthologies. He has been a board member of both the Writers' Community of Simcoe County (WCSC) and the Writers' Community of Durham Region (WCDR), and, for five years, was an annual participant in the Muskoka Novel Marathon, a 72-hour writing marathon to raise money for adult literacy programs.

Finally, he also taught creative writing for two different continuous learning programs. Tobin writes ugly stories about bad people doing horrible things, and it was his pleasure to show other people how to do the same thing for almost twenty years.

If you're interested in more ramblings by Tobin, well, he's not much into social media. He sees it as a blight on humanity of almost Bookian proportions. And yet, still, he's on there.

Facebook: The Horror Guy (/tobinelliott.horrorguy)

Twitter: @TheHorrorGuy91

Instagram: @tobinelliott.horrorguy

♦ ♦ ♦

I HOPE THAT this book captured your imagination, and I hope that this series will turn you into a loyal reader.

Because loyal readers are an author's secret weapon. They can influence other readers…how?

Through reviews.

If you loved this book, and yes, even if you hated it, please also consider leaving a review on the site where you purchased it, and/or Goodreads, or anywhere else. You can also drop me a line at TheHorrorGuy91@gmail.com.

As a reader, you have an immense power to influence others.

Please, use that power.